THE COYOTE WAY

VANISHED, BOOK THREE

B. B. GRIFFITH

Griffith Publishing
Denver

Publication Information

The Coyote Way (Vanished, #3)

Copyright © 2020 by Griffith Publishing LLC

Ebook ISBN: 978-0-9963726-3-3

Paperback ISBN: 978-0-9963726-4-0

Written by B. B. Griffith

Cover design by Damonza

❀ Created with Vellum

"Coyote is always out there waiting, and Coyote is always hungry."

- Navajo Proverb

THE WALKER

There is a room at Green Mesa Psychiatric Hospital in Los Alamos, New Mexico, called the Serenity Room. Attendants deliver medicine in soft whispers, waking dozing patients only when they must. Some patients read, some mutter, some simply sit by the huge bay window that faces the chunky orange cliffs of the Pajarito Plateau. The Serenity Room is a place set outside of the day-to-day, where the driving white noise the world makes as it turns can't be heard. Where the sick can live out the remainder of their troubled lives undisturbed.

Then I walk in.

I do my job alone—nobody can see me or hear me or touch me—but over the past six years that I've walked the soul map, snipping frayed threads and sending the dead through the veil and on their way, I've noticed that some people do seem to sense me. For instance, babies don't much like it when I'm near. They start fussing pretty bad. Everyone in the living world can pass right through me, but once a blind guy in Rome walked around me. I stood there blinking like a sheep while he went on his way. A deaf woman at a call I answered in Reno, Nevada, pricked her ear my way when I was talking to myself. I swear that sometimes the very old can track me with their milky eyes, although I'm not sure they know what they're looking at. Stuff like that. But by far the most perceptive are the insane.

The two men who were muttering to each other in the corner a second ago? Now they're crying. The woman who was putting together a puzzle, one that she's been working on diligently for nearly a year? Now she's dismantling it piece by piece. The young man who's been reading the same book over and over again for months? Now he's ripping the pages out and letting them flutter to the floor. It's because of me. Because of what I am. I make them uncomfortable when I'm nearby. They're already half in and half out of the world they live in. They fight every day to cling to whatever frayed strings of sanity they have left, and I'm the type of guy whose job it is to cut threads.

The staff can't figure out why this happens every so often, and they never will. They can only curse under their breaths and scamper around trying to keep these delicate people from falling apart like dried flowers in a sudden wind. One of these dried flowers, perhaps the most delicate of all, is my mother.

You heard that right. Death has a mom.

Mom sits in a decorative wheelchair with a plump pillow at her back, staring blankly out of the bay window at the soft pink New Mexico sunset. When she left us, not long after Ana died, she cut her long black hair short and spiky. It's grown out again now, down past her shoulders, and it's as white as snow. She neglects it, but her attendants don't. It's pulled back and banded behind her head with a beaded leather thong. One of the handful of things she kept from her life before. Something Ana made in school. She wears a clean and neat dressing gown of blue and gold, one of several that the staff rotate throughout the week.

She's not sickly looking, or gaunt. Her skin still has that Navajo cinnamon coloring, even if it's a bit ruddy at the cheeks. In a lot of ways, she looks just like the woman she was back when we all lived in one half of a little duplex on Chaco rez, about an hour north of Albuquerque. The same woman who bundled Ana and me up for the walk to school, who packed our lunches and washed our clothes. Who helped Gam cook dinner and kept Dad's drinking at bay. Who tanned my hide when I chipped a tooth racing around the campers out at the Arroyo at dusk, Joey and I weaving in and out, slapping the corrugated metal of each with the flat of our hands and tearing off before we got something chucked at us, laughing like hell. Our twenty-first-century, dirt-poor version of counting coup.

On the outside she looks just like she did back then, just older. Inside, she's a mess. Many of the patients around her fuss and fidget and mewl as I walk toward her. She takes no notice. Just stares forward until her eyes water and she's forced to blink.

I come here a lot in between calls, but not because I feel I owe it to Mom. I know that she's well taken care of at Green Mesa, which is just about the cushiest extended-stay psychiatric hospital in the Southwest. They have cucumber water *and* lemon water *and* lime water in the front lobby. Water trickles into little ponds, and fountains burble everywhere. The only people who work harder than the doctors around here are the groundskeepers. The place costs a fortune, but the Navajo Nation is footing Mom's entire bill. Medical costs, room and board, extra expenses, the whole thing. The Council took pity on her after she lost everyone. With the Navajo, you take your mother's clan. The Dejooli branch of our clan is going to end with her. It sucks, but in a twisted way it's kind of fitting. Dejooli is Navajo for *up in the air*. I always took it to mean *gone*.

So Mom hasn't paid a dime since the day she got here, almost six years ago now. Good thing too. Mom's broke. But worse than that, she no longer has the wherewithal to pay anything anyway. I don't even think she knows where she is anymore. The day Ana disappeared, Mom started to fade. She backed away from Chaco, and eventually from the Navajo Way altogether. I found Ana, eventually, right as I died. Turns out she was the one who came for me, to take me away, just like I'm the one who will one day come for you. Except I rang a special bell, took her job, and set her free. Mom was already cracked, but when she saw that happen, it broke her.

I take a seat next to her, away from the rest of the patients, who start to settle now that I've settled myself and it turns out I'm not coming for them. I'm barely taller than her, and only slightly thicker. Danny Ninepoint, my old partner back at the Navajo Nation Police Department, used to say that I have tricky muscles, which was his way of saying I look like a wuss but somehow could still hold up my end of a fight. I still wear an NNPD uniform, but it's all black now. It looks out of place, here. I think there's some sort of rule against the color black at Green Mesa.

"Hi, Mom," I say, knowing full well she won't answer. She continues to stare out of the window. Her right finger twitches a little. I cross my arms and watch as a murder of crows spans the horizon, flying away. It's midsummer. Not crow season in this part of the country. But lately the crows have been gathering anyway. Which is never a good sign.

When Mom first came to Green Mesa she didn't need a wheelchair. She was in a state of shock from losing her family, but she was functional. She even showed signs of getting better. She made a few friends, spoke to each of the attendants and doctors by name, had a few lunch dates at the fancy buffet, but then, just about a year after her arrival, she started going downhill. Stopped smiling, then stopped talking. She eventually stopped eating on her own, and then stopped walking. The doctors are at a loss, but I'm not.

Right around the time she started to withdraw, a turquoise knife nearly ripped a hole in the fabric between our worlds. Caroline, Owen, Grant, and I managed to shore it up, but not before something came through. I think she felt it. As whatever *it* is grows in strength, she is weakening.

It is some form of chaos. That's all I know. Since it broke through into the land of the living, it's disappeared, but I think it has some sort of connection with sick people like her. Broken minds are attuned to it. My mother more than most. She's had more exposure to my line of work than your average mental patient. Hell, both of her children ended up as Walkers. She was there when the bell rang and I started my watch. She shares my blood. So you see, I have an ulterior motive here. These visits aren't just one-sided social calls. Mom is a canary in a coal mine.

I look over at her again. Her pointer finger is twitching still, more like scratching now. I try to put my hand over it, to calm it. I pass right through her. Her eyes water, and she blinks free a rivulet of tears. It rolls down her cheek. I try to brush it, but my finger cannot touch her.

"I know, Mom. I can feel it too. Whatever's been simmering for the past five years is about to come to a boil. The chaos thing, the Dark Walker, it's making its move, but I can't find it. Chaco can't find it. Nobody can find it."

I watch the crows wheel and float in the distance like a flock of starlings, which is entirely unlike them. The sun is setting with this feeling of pressure, like it's trying to jam itself into a horizon that's already full up and ready to spill. I think about the river of souls. Five years' worth of souls following a path down the chaos side of the river, swarming around an empty pearl. We stitched up the walls between worlds, but the balance of the river is off. The thing that anchors the chaos end of things is walking free as you please in the world of the living, has been for years now, and it's eluded all of us.

When I turn back to Mom, she's looking right at me. I nearly jump up from my seat. Her finger is still. Her eyes are focused. The canary senses something coming from the deeps of the mine.

"Go home, Ben," she whispers in Navajo.

I reach for her again, my hands shaking. These are the first words she's spoken in years, and the first Navajo words I can ever remember her voluntarily speaking. I reach out as if I could grab them, maybe keep them in my pocket. She still looks at me.

"Go home," she says again. She uses the old Navajo word *Bikeyah*, which means *homeland*. The place of my people. Then she turns slowly to the window again, where the crows have disappeared into the gloaming.

"Mom?" I ask. "Mom, can you hear me?" I repeat myself again in Navajo. Nothing. Her face is blank once more. But my canary has spoken, and moments later I get a tug from the soul map. I stand and swirl it open then turn back to her. My mind races. These things are connected. I raise my hand in a farewell she's blind to, then I step through.

I walk the rope of intertwined souls, looking for the break that calls me, looking for the dimming of a life that needs to be set free. I see it, like a flickering bulb in a sea of warm light. I step up to it, swirl the map open once more, and by this time I have a pretty good hunch about where I'm going to step out. It's the *why* that I can't figure.

The day is coming to a close, but the desert is still hot under foot. It creaks a little, like a massive settling house, with the roof open to a sky that goes on forever. It smells like baked clay and untouched wind. It smells like home.

I'm back on the rez.

2

CAROLINE ADAMS

I'm about the last girl on earth you'd pick as having a little black book. Seriously. You could count on one hand the number of guys I've hooked up with, and you wouldn't need your thumb. To be fair, I'm not exactly hitting the scene these days. I hang out in an RV with two people most of the time, and one of them is a fourteen-year-old kid with a bird for a best friend. The other is Owen Bennet. If what I carried actually *was* a little black book, his name would be the only entry on any of the pages for the past five years, which would make it less of a "little black book" and more of a "penmanship exercise," but like I said, what I carry isn't a little black book.

Sure, it *looks* like one. It's small, thin, and bound in black leather (or at least what I really hope is black leather), but it's also a key. A clue. A map. Some sort of Rosetta stone that can help explain what came through to our world when the barriers broke down all those years ago. The cover says *The Book of the Dark Walker*. Ben is called the Walker too. What I'm really hoping is that somewhere inside I'll find a little bit about Ben Dejooli, about how his world works, maybe even how I can reach him. I don't tell Owen about this last part, of course, but I don't have to. He knows. And it makes me feel like a bad person.

"Does that make me a bad person?" I ask James Parsons, heretofore Agent Parsons and now of AJ's Villa, a four-star bed-and-breakfast on the West Sound of Orcas Island in upstate Washington. It's a bit of a bear to get here, if you're not traveling by crow. That's exactly why James and Allen chose it.

"Well, it doesn't make you a *great* person," James says. He's setting the breakfast table. It looks like they have two couples staying with them.

"It's not my fault I'm the type of girl who needs closure. Ben and I shared something that changed me, but he died before I could figure it out," I say, flopping down on one of their puffy living-room chairs that face the bay.

"Did you just blame a guy for dying of cancer?" James asks. He adjusts the alignment of a fork.

I put my head in my hands. "God. Maybe I really am a bad person."

"Don't listen to him, Caroline," Allen chirps from the kitchen. I hear the sizzling of eggs and bacon and the clunk of the oven door opening and closing. "He's just grumpy. It's completely normal to take five years to figure out where your heart lies."

I hear the *glugluglug* of coffee being poured. Allen Douglas comes around the corner with two mugs. He uses neutral cover-up to mask the light-pink scarring that Chaco left on his face back when Allen was trying to kill all of us. He's gained weight since then too. Happy weight. He holds one cup out to me.

"I can't tell if you're being serious or not." I take a sip. The mug is a ceramic pineapple. The decor here is a little too tropical for my tastes. The San Juan Islands always struck me as more *hot toddy* while AJ's is clearly channeling *mai tai*. But their coffee is outstanding, and Allen is a heck of a cook, and the view ain't bad, either. I watch the sunrise over the choppy waters of the sound, always hoping to see an actual orca. I haven't seen one yet, but I do see lots of crows. Even way out here. I phase over here sometimes when living in an RV day after day with Owen and Grant starts to grate on me. Don't get me wrong, I love the guys, but Owen is too bright to be as bored as he is, and Grant is. . . well, Grant is fourteen.

"I *am* being serious," Allen says, sitting down for a moment then getting right back up when something dings in the kitchen. "Just look at the two of us. This took five years," he says over his shoulder.

"That doesn't count. You were in a fugue state," I say.

"I'm just saying," he calls back.

"Have you at least gotten rid of that disgusting book?" James asks, turning to look at me. I reach involuntarily to my jacket pocket. He notices.

"Caroline Adams," James says, in a remarkable imitation of my mother. "What did I tell you about bringing that thing into our house?"

"It's not gonna hurt you. It doesn't *do* anything. That's the problem."

"You mean besides push you and Owen apart? When it's not brainwashing people?" He lowers his voice and glances toward the kitchen. These two hate the book, with good reason. They were following it when they broke through beyond the veil, but whatever they saw in it has been wiped away, along with their memories. Allen in particular is terrified of it. He has the scars as souvenirs.

"I can't just throw it away," I whisper. "It's says it's the

Book of the Dark Walker. What if it helps us catch that thing that came through?"

"It's blank inside, Caroline. Has been for five years," James whispers. "Whatever we were reading, it's gone."

"What if it comes back?"

"If you ask me, I think you're less interested in finding whatever came though and more interested in seeing if it'll tell you how to find a certain Walker in particular. One named Ben Dejooli."

I can't claim otherwise, so I hide behind a big sip of coffee. I dream sometimes that it's a two-way journal. That I write things in it and they go to the other side and Ben can read them, and that Ben can write things in it that I can read. Things about that last kiss we shared before he died. Or the time our fingertips touched through the thin place. Chaco says the agents followed it like a map when they were beyond the veil. A map can lead to a lot of things. Maybe even to Ben.

"Are you two whispering?" Allen asks, bringing out steaming bread in a covered basket in one hand and a plate of food in the other. James turns back to the place settings. I prolong my sip of coffee.

"This is about that awful book, isn't it?" Allen asks primly, setting the bread basket down with a bit more force than necessary. "We already told you we can't read it. I don't even remember carrying it. It's blank to us too, and God willing it will stay that way forever."

"I'm sorry Allen. I just. . ."

"Can't let it go. I know. But be careful. That's how it starts." Allen pats my shoulder kindly. "Now eat. Before the guests come down and we have to explain you away. You look thin."

"I'm definitely not thin. You should see Owen. *That* is

thin." But I take a hefty bite anyway as Allen refills my coffee.

"Maybe it's those crow totems," James says, sitting down next to me. "Watch out with them. You need to get outside. Less thin place. More sunshine."

"We know what we're doing with the totems now," I say, but now that he mentions it, I do look paler. I was never a tan girl to begin with, but these days I have that milquetoast, sat-in-front-of-the-TV-all-day look. I think it's less from the phasing, though, and more from the fact that we've been spinning our wheels for a while now, going from place to place, always stuck in transition. I wear a lot of loose, func-tional travel clothes, and my hair is in an endless string of ponytails. I look rootless. I *am* rootless, and it shows.

"Don't listen to him," Allen says again. "You look beauti-ful. He's just grumpy."

3

OWEN BENNET

You would be absolutely flabbergasted if you saw how many wires and circuits are in a large RV. Ours is technically called a motor coach, but let's not glamorize things: it's a single-wide on wheels. Still, looking at this fuse box, you'd think I was driving the space shuttle *Endeavor* around the country. I've never really had a good look at the guts of it before. Aside from the handful of times Caroline's tried to dry her hair while Grant's played his videogames and a breaker got tripped, I've really had no cause to go rooting around down here. But then I decided to do my little project.

Caroline thinks I'm losing it. Like this is my Bridge to Nowhere and I'll be chipping away at it until I die because I've got nothing better to do. Fine. Let her think that. While she's off obsessing over that book I'm here trying to plan a future. Grant is indifferent, but he's indifferent to most things lately, except the color black. I do catch him occasionally watching me tinker, wearing this look like he's watching a squirrel bobbing around on one of those trick bird feeders.

After ten years in medical school, another ten years

working the hospital floor, and another five traveling the country carrying the crow totems and the bell—tools that are essentially the nails that keep the tapestry of the living world hanging straight—it's amazing how much you *don't* know. Like how to wire a trailer hitch for a 240-volt electrical system, for instance.

I'm lying on my back on the floor at the rear of the RV, which we affectionately call the boat, the top half of my gangly frame stuffed awkwardly under the aft paneling, one hand holding a green wire. I've got a penlight in my mouth. I'm about to make a risky soldering decision when I hear Grant from up front.

"He's back," he says.

I freeze. I mumble around the penlight, "Seriously?"

"Seriously."

I sigh, scoot out front underneath the paneling like a dog scooting along the carpet, then sit up. Grant is looking at me with one earbud still in, the other dangling down his front. He gestures out the big side window with his head.

"What is with this guy?" I ask. It's rhetorical, of course, but these days Grant isn't one to skip an opportunity to fire off a droll answer.

"I think you know. I think we all know. If it's not this guy, it's the weird lady back in Pagosa, or that hick in the Pawnee Buttes, or those drunk college kids in Mendocino. They've all got the same thing."

I button my shirt up and straighten my rolled cuffs. "The itch. Yeah, I get it. Thank you, Grant."

Grant nods. That was sarcasm, but that seems to roll right off Grant these days as well. He's only capable of giving it, hasn't quite figured out how to take it.

"Stay behind me, out of sight," I say, moving toward the door. Grant gets up anyway and follows me, but he does stay back. *The itch* is a term I came up with, one of very few new diagnoses I do these days.

If Caroline were here, she could use her second sight to see what is bothering him, figure out exactly what to say, exactly what buttons to push to make the guy go away. She could see the script written in his "smoke," wafting off him in waves. If Chaco were here, he might be able to scare him off by virtue of being an enormous crow perched on top of the RV, but he's off too, looking for the thing that came through. So as it stands, it's just me. The only thing I can sense wafting off this guy is booze.

"Can I help you?" I ask, stepping down from the RV and closing the door behind me. He wears a tattered red T-shirt under oil-stained coveralls. His work boots are frayed at the steel toe. The guy looks like a mechanic, but then again, that's sort of the de facto dress code at this RV park. For all I know he could be the mayor.

"Whatcha buildin'?" he asks. His eyes flit to the trailer addition but always settle back to me and then behind me, to the right, where Grant watches behind the curtains. He's got the itch all right.

Most people are completely normal around the bell. Most wouldn't even know Grant carries the thing. But every now and then somebody gets the itch. These people, they come in all shapes and sizes, some mean, some just curious. Mostly mean, these days. It's been getting worse and worse ever since that thing broke through. They're troubled people, drawn to the world beyond ours. Drawn to the bell that could get them there. They end up in front of the RV without knowing why. They're the reason Grant, Caroline, and I have to pack up and head out every couple of months. They're the reason we can't ever establish ourselves anywhere.

"Just a trailer hitch. Now, I think you should move on, sir," I say.

"Uh-huh." The man nods without seeming to hear me. He takes a step forward.

"Stay back," I say. "I'm warning you." I'm not really sure what I'll do. I was not a fighter before I met Caroline. I've been in a fair amount of scrapes since, but every time I'm confronted with another one I feel like a mathlete trying to talk down the captain of the football team. I wish I'd kept the soldering iron. I could at least threaten to solder the man.

"I just want to check it out," he says. I don't think he means the trailer hitch. He steps forward again, and this time I take no chances. I step into him and try to push him back, but he hangs on to me. I'm taller than him, but he's bigger than me. He could bowl me over if he wanted to, but instead he just flails behind me, like I'm a stuck turnstile. He's got a one-track mind, this one. This is as focused as I've ever seen an Itch, and I'm dreading what I'll have to do to subdue the guy, when the door to the RV opens and Grant steps out. He has a gun.

"Get the fuck away from us," Grant growls. He levels the gun at the man. I don't know a thing about handguns, only that I hate them. This one looks as heavy and gray and dully evil as the rest of them. Grant is decked from head to toe in black, and with his shaved head he looks like that crazy type of fourteen. Child-soldier fourteen. I'm so shocked that I put my hands up right along with the Itch. Grant furrows his brow at me.

"I didn't mean nothin'," the Itch says. He blinks. His eyes seem to have cleared a bit. I can see that he's not quite sure how he got here, only that he needs to get out. He backs away for several paces then turns tail and scampers. I'm still holding my hands up.

"You have a gun?"

"Put your hands down, Owen."

"You have a *gun*?"

"Come on. That dude'll be back. They always are."

I step up and into the RV, close the door, and lock it behind us. Grant looks sheepish now, much more like the young boy from Midland that I know.

"Grant, this is not acceptable. Does Caroline know about this? What does Chaco think?"

"It's fake. See?" He points to a plastic ring around the muzzle. "Stop freaking out." He tosses it on the couch. I lean against the wall, less relieved than I thought I'd be. Grant sounds disappointed that it's fake. "I traded some kid at the edge of the park a bunch of games for it. And good thing, huh?" He looks up at me pointedly.

"I could have de-escalated the situation," I say.

"Uh-huh."

"And now we have to get out of here, of course. So there goes that."

"Good. This place sucks anyway. It smells like dog food." He flops down on the couch himself, which is something he does when he's frustrated. He learned it from Caroline.

"And stop cussing. You never cussed before. Don't start now. It's classless."

"I had to get my point across to the Itch," he says, rubbing at his head. I see a flash there, at his wrist. A bead bracelet. I have one of my own, a gift from a Navajo girl I treated back at the Chaco Health Clinic. I'm not naive enough to think he wants to be like me, though. The only thing Grant likes more than the color black is Joey Flatwood.

He worships the man. Grant collects crow feathers wherever we go, swapping out for the best ones. I want to tell him that if he plans on weaving them into his hair like Joey, he'd better start growing it out, but no doubt that would blow up in my face too. I decide to leave well enough alone.

I step into the cockpit and fire up the boat to warm up the engine. "Batten down the hatches," I say. Grant gets up and starts to pack the RV away while I do a perimeter sweep, picking up a few loose odds and ends. I text Caroline *on the run*, which is our code for a quick getaway. I'll text her again when we fill up the tank outside of town so she can phase back to us. I survey the camp one more time. We've been here for three months, but I'm not sad to go. It does smell like dog food.

4

THE WALKER

There's no room for coincidences in the Navajo Way. No such thing. So all I can do is nod when I step out of the soul map and find that the tug takes me to Chaco Canyon. In a lot of ways, the whole reason I'm here is because of this canyon and what came from it.

Chaco Navajo Reservation is named for Chaco Canyon, which is this big jagged scoop in the earth in northwest New Mexico. The wash from the canyon created the Arroyo to the north, which edges up to the main camp of Chaco rez, and which is where all this began for me all those years ago when I started digging for more info on an Arroyo man everyone called the gambler. The old-timers and hard-line Navajo that ring the Arroyo in their tents and car camps like to say that they are the Chaco Wash themselves: they are the stones that rumbled down from the canyon over the years in the great rains. They are the pure deposits that were unearthed and the strongest that remain.

The old Chaco River chopped the canyon up into a bunch of jagged mesas to either side of the banks. They look sort of like teeth from far away, and they harbor a lot of old Pueblo and Navajo ruins in their ridges and flats. I'm standing in the shadow of the west mesa, I'd say about forty miles from the rez as the crow flies, and I'm looking at a dead Navajo man.

The soul map tells me this man is Bidzill Halkini. I knew Bidzill Halkini. He was a sheep farmer. An eccentric guy that we occasionally drove out to check on when I was with the NNPD. He wore a New York Yankees baseball cap all the time and wanted everyone to call him Bill instead of Bidzill. Every rookie at one point or another had to make the drive to check on Bilagaana Bill, as we called him. *Bilagaana* is a sorta loaded word we Navajo use for white people. It's not bad, exactly. But it's not good either. With Bidzill Halkini it was a joke because he was about as Navajo as they come—I mean, he was a sheep farmer, after all, and he lived more or less alone for most of the year in what was basically a lean-to out here near the west mesa. Just him, his animals, and the Navajo Way. But he had the Yankees cap and wanted to be called Bill, so there you go.

And now, here he is. But something about him doesn't sit right with me.

The Bilagaana Bill I knew was a desert-hardened, savvy Navajo. Not the type of guy to end up in the middle of Chaco Canyon, miles from anything, without so much as a stitch of supplies. Where are his sheep? Where is his sheep switch? Where is his Yankees hat? And most of all, where the hell is his soul?

I perch my hands on my hips and furrow my brow. I feel this strange, creeping dread that's timed perfectly with the slow wash of the setting sun as it coats the canyon in front of us, cutting a dividing line between the open canyon and our dark corner. I don't know as much as I'd like about how death works, even after all my time walking the map, but I do know that when things in my profession don't line up, it's very bad news. For everyone. And it usually starts like this. With little glitches in the system.

I drop in as the soul pops out, so it should be here somewhere close by. I scan the canyon. Nothing. I turn around and trace the edges of the west mesa where the fading sunlight is strongest. Nothing. I look up in the sky. Nothing. Which is another strange thing. The New Mexico desert is hard country. When something dies in it, something that could provide food for the creatures that live out here, it doesn't take long for the animal kingdom to realize it. Starting with the birds. But there are no birds in sight. No flies, either. No bugs of any kind. It's as if everything is avoiding this man.

"Hey!" I yell. "Bill! Come out! I wanna talk with you!"

Nothing. Not even an echo. This is a strange place even for a wanderer like Bilagaana Bill to end up, and without even a water bottle to his name. His car camp is at least five miles north. Time to do a little rewind, see exactly how he got here.

One of the best perks of walking the soul map is that if I want to see the story behind a death, I can track back the soul thread. Basically just rewind the life of the recently departed. I do this more than you'd think. More than I need to, that's for sure. The last moments of people's lives give me a lot to ponder. A bit ghoulish, I know, especially coming from a Navajo, where we're taught to stay the hell away from death, but I don't exactly have a lot of entertainment options here. You binge-watch TV shows. I do this. So sue me.

I swipe backward on the map, watch the dead man carefully. Swipe backward some more. Keep watching. The guy is still face down on the desert floor. The wind rustles his

hair and kicks some dust up against his cheek, but that's
about it. For hours he's like this. Which makes the lack of
carrion feeders all the more suspicious. Then it's sunrise
past, and all of a sudden I see a coyote. A mangy, feral-
looking thing. Maybe even rabid. I take the thread back a bit
and watch it approach. It senses the dead man and raises its
hackles, but it keeps moving forward, almost like it can't
help it. Once it's even with the body, it lunges at the dead
man's mouth like it was shocked in the haunch, rips around
a bit, then takes off down the canyon. I follow it for a few
steps, but it's hauling ass and I'm not getting any closer to
settling this soul, so I turn around.

I trace the rest of Bilagaana Bill's soul back, and as far as
I can tell, here's how he died: He got up from his lean-to,
neglected everything he owned, from his water to his gear
all the way to his hat, then he walked out into the desert in
complete silence for five miles, where he laid down right
here and died. And then nothing came out.

Now I'm starting to freak out. We've got a body with
nothing to tie it to the world beyond. I let out a big breath.
Take another one in. And then yell as loud as I can for my
bird friend.

"Chaco! Chaco, I need some help here!"

I wait. Wait some more. I start to get a little sweaty
thinking about how I'm gonna deal with this on my own,
and just when I suck in a breath to yell again, I hear the telltale *snap* of Chaco breaking through the plane. There he is,
just a thin black line in the sky, until the line whips back on
itself and sprouts wings and tail feathers and a sharp-
beaked head. He spots me and dives right for my face,
hoping I'll flinch. I don't flinch anymore. He pulls up and
catches himself on my shoulder.

"Walker," he begins, already annoyed, "I got a lot on my

plate these days. If this is another one of your sob stories, I'm gonna peck your face off."

Chaco doesn't understand how I can get wrapped up in my work sometimes. I admit I tend to get sentimental. Especially when I use rewind. But this ain't no sob story. Not yet.

Instead I just point at the body. "What the hell is that?"

"You're the expert and everything, but it looks to me like a dead guy."

"I know that, thank you. He's Bilagaana Bill. But where's his soul?"

"Billa-what?"

"His soul never left him," I say, holding out my hands, staring at the space between them as if it holds the answers.

Chaco twitches his head like he's shaking off water. "That's ridiculous. Of course it did. You just missed it."

"I didn't miss anything. Could the map be wrong somehow?"

"The map has never been wrong. *Never.* And it's been around *forever.* Walkers, on the other hand, have been known to fuck up a fair amount. No offense."

I crouch down again, and Chaco walks up my shoulder to perch on my head. Both of us peer down at the body. "I ran his thread back all the way. He walked out here and died, but nothing came out of him."

Chaco hops off my head and flutters down toward Bill but then flares his wings out at the last second. "Whoa, whoa," he says, skittering to rest on the dirt beside him. "He doesn't smell right."

"Well, he is dead."

"There's a right dead smell and a wrong dead smell. This is a wrong dead smell. And probably why none of my kind are anywhere near this thing." Chaco scans the sky above him with little ticks of his head.

"I thought that was strange too. Although there was one coyote. . ." My eyes trace the path the coyote took when it bolted. I feel like I'm missing something vital here.

Chaco looks up at me and tucks his wings in to make his back streamline straight, almost like he's pointing at me. "You're sure that you ran this thing back?"

I nod.

"And you're *sure* that you looked all around this place for his soul?"

I nod again.

"You'd better be really sure, Walker. This isn't *where the hell did I put my car keys?* stuff. This is *you're telling me up is down and down is up* stuff."

"I'm sure. And you know as well as I that for the past five years, up has seemed a little down and the other way around."

"Maybe the veil took it without you. Maybe your department is getting downsized, as they say. Maybe this is your cosmic pink slip and they got a robot to do your job."

"Ha ha. I gotta cut 'em loose first, asshole. There are rules. You know that."

"Yeah, yeah. So what are we gonna do?"

"Maybe we should call Caroline in," I say, trying to seem nonchalant. "See what her sight shows her. Maybe she picks something up that we can't see."

Chaco is quiet, and I pretend to be looking the body over again in the silence until it drags out too long. When I glance at him, he's staring right at me. "What? It's just a thought," I say.

"Uh-huh."

"Am I wrong? She's very perceptive."

"She's also deep in the trenches of some *matters of the*

heart that seem to continuously feature you, despite the fact that you both know you're dead."

"I can't help that." I'm glad that I don't have the blood to blush.

"You could by leaving her alone," Chaco says, taking slow bird-steps around the body until he's on my side again. He looks askew at Bilagaana Bill and puffs up his breast in a sigh. "But you're right. We gotta get this straightened out. And the crew is on the move again anyway. Maybe they can swing by here."

"I'll be here," I say. "And Bill ain't going nowhere."

Chaco gives me one last look that says *watch yourself*, and I know he's meaning around the body, but also with Caroline. But Chaco isn't my bird, and I don't work for him either. We're just two poor saps trying to keep the balance between worlds, and I'll take any excuse I can to see Caroline. He's up, up, and gone, and then it's just me and Bill and the rez. All of us waiting.

5

GRANT ROMER

We pick up Caroline at a 7-11 outside of Pueblo, Colorado. She phases into the parking lot behind the boat, where I'm sitting watching the gauge at the gas pump tick over again and again. She blinks into reality mid-stride. She's getting really good at it. Both of them are. I remember when I first met them, they couldn't hold on to the thin place for more than a few minutes at a time, and if they walked in the thin place, there was no tellin' where they'd end up. It ain't that way no more. Sorry. It *isn't* that way *anymore*. I'm working on that. How I talk. I'm tired of people thinking I'm some dumb hick from Nowhere, Texas, especially when that place isn't my home anymore.

"Itch?" she asks, glancing toward the store where Owen is stocking up.

"Yep," I say, fingering my bracelet. Joey Flatwood gave it to me when we crossed paths a few years ago. He's always off somewhere with something to do, someplace to be. We're always off somewhere too, but the difference is we never seem to know where we're going.

"That was quick," Caroline says. "What, two weeks?"

"Three." But Caroline was only there for two of them. The rest of the time she was chasing after what might or might not be inside that book. She's quiet until I look up at her and find her watching me.

"Shit," I mutter. She's reading me again. "I thought you said you weren't going to do that."

"Watch your language, buddy. And I said I'd *try* not to read you. I didn't say how hard I'd try. And I'm already well aware of how you and Owen feel about the book."

The gas pump finally snaps off. Caroline and I look at the total, and we both clear our throats. Owen isn't gonna like that. He's been more and more concerned about cash lately, which I think means we have less and less of it.

"It's Owen who doesn't like that book. I don't care about it." Which is true. If it could help us find what came through, or figure out what the Dark Walker of the title is, we'd know by now. Personally, I think it ain't much more than a creepy doorstop. Although I do think it's a convenient way for Caroline to get away from us and call it "research." Or maybe just get away from me. Because I have a tendency to be a bit of a drag on people who end up taking care of me. Even before I got the bell and became the Keeper and started attracting all sorts of weirdness that makes us pick up shop every few weeks, I was a problem. Pap had to come out of retirement to provide for me after Mom and Dad died. I always muddy the waters wherever I am.

Joey doesn't need anybody. He can fend for himself. I can't, yet. But I will be able to one day. Sooner rather than later. Caroline is looking at me still. I don't know how much of this she can read in my smoke. Not all of it, but enough. My look is a challenge to her, to tell me otherwise if she understands me. She looks away.

Owen comes around the corner with two baggies full of drinks and gas-station food. He passes each of us a scratch ticket. This is his gas-stop ritual. He calls it our only chance at retirement, and I think he's only half joking.

"Welcome back," he says to Caroline, letting his words linger for just a second. He gives her a delayed hug. I can't take the awkwardness, so I push around them and walk up into the boat. "How are the agents?" Owen asks her, both of them stepping up after me.

"Oh, fine. Not a lot of help, as usual. They hate the book more than you do, but it's good to see them anyway." Caroline settles in the co-captain's chair up front. She kicks her shoes off and tucks her feet underneath her, rummaging around for her sunglasses. The August sunshine cuts right through the enormous front window. You get a full-body blast when you sit up front, which is why I never do.

"I don't hate it. I just don't trust it," Owen says.

"It's a book, Owen. Not a car salesman."

"I don't like how much of your time it takes up," Owen begins, before stopping himself. "But you already know that, and you know that I've said everything I'm gonna say about that thing. Did you know Grant has a gun?" he asks, completely throwing me under the bus just because he can't talk straight with her.

"Fake gun," I say quickly as Caroline turns to me. Owen does this stuff sometimes when he gets annoyed. Throws out hand grenades to see if Caroline has already picked up on their smoke. "It's an air gun, Caroline. No big deal. Jesus. And it's how we got away from the Itch too."

"So that's what you two were fighting about," Caroline says.

"We weren't *fighting*," Owen says, starting the boat up with a rolling roar of the engine. "Guys don't *fight* like that. I was just letting Grant know that I don't like guns. Of any kind." His pale skin blushes bright red. He was always pale, but he's gotten paler. It's a side effect of being good with the crow totem. Well worth it, I'd say. I'd love to have that freedom. To go across the country in a few steps, see some friends, be back whenever I wanted. The bell is sort of the opposite of that. It hangs around my neck and keeps me here. It's heavy. It pulls other people toward me, in fact.

Caroline sets her hand over Owen's for a moment, tries to get him to look at her, but he's flustered. He doesn't shake it off, exactly, but he gently moves his hand to the steering wheel, and hers falls away. I take notice of these things. I've been tryin' to figure the two of them out for years, and I'm still guessing. I think I have it figured out, then one of them stops talking to the other, or Caroline blinks out for a couple days, and it's just me and Owen and an awkward elephant in the boat.

One time, about a year ago, I walked in on them having sex. In the boat there's not a lot of privacy. They have the back bedroom, and I have a couch bed that pops out of the side and can fold up for some extra space. For whatever reason, the door to the back bedroom was open, and I came home early from walking to get dinner at the burger place that was across from the Alamo Placita RV park where we were camped at the time, and there they were. Owen was on top of Caroline, his skinny white back to me. Thankfully his butt was covered by the sheets, but it was definitely moving. Caroline practically threw him off of her when she heard the outside door open, and then they scrambled to cover up, but I saw basically everything. All that evening Caroline was too embarrassed even to talk to me, and Owen talked too much: explaining everything at once in birds-and-bees style like I was still ten years old.

I know what sex is. I know how it works. And it's not like I was scarred or anything. It's not like I walked in on my parents. Owen and Caroline aren't my parents, despite what they sometimes think. They're more like my older friends. So it wasn't gross, just awkward. The next day during home-school Owen still hadn't come off it. He was babbling and stammering and trying to explain penises and vaginas using terms like *genitalia* and *ejaculate* and *menses*. I sat there and nodded, but all I was thinking about is how it'd be nice to have someone to do that stuff with. Or even to hang out with, without the sex.

There's been no repeat of anything resembling that little run-in since, though. At least not that I've seen, and I've been a bit more on the lookout for it. If anything, it seems like they were the ones that got the most awkward about everything. Now there's that extra little half-beat pause before they hug, or when they decide to hold hands. Like they're thinking too hard about it.

Day in and day out I have to see this stuff, and then they wonder why I want to just put on my headphones or zone out with video games or go off by myself to see what other kids are doing. Then I end up trading games for an air gun and suddenly they get pissed? Thank God for Chaco. Having him around reminds me that the world is a lot bigger than the boat, which makes me happy but also makes me a little sad since so far I haven't been able to experience any of it. Oh, I *see* a lot of it all right. It's rolling by underneath the wheels right now. But I can't *touch* any of it.

"Bird incoming," I say, and Owen looks back at me from the rearview mirror and nods. I get up, pop open and slide back the large side window, and Owen slows the boat a bit. I hold out my arm and watch the wind flutter the loose tie straps of the bracelet Joey gave me. Don't worry, I double knotted it and made Joey promise that if I somehow lost it he'd make me another one. But I don't lose things. Ever. I'm the Keeper, after all.

Chaco isn't there and then suddenly he is, pumping his huge black wings and flattening his arrowed head until he's level with the window and on pace, then he reaches out and snatches my arm. It doesn't hurt. He's pretty good at it by now. I carefully pull him inside the boat, and he walks up my arm to perch on my shoulder. He used to be able to perch on my head in the boat, but I got taller, and he's not exactly a small bird.

"On the move again, eh?" he says, moving down to rest on my knee as I sit back on the couch. Only the Walker and I can hear Chaco. His voice is like a thought in my head. I answer him the same way, without ever opening my mouth. He's what he calls a thinning. Some creatures are closer to the thin world and the land of the dead than others. Cats, bats, some dogs, supposedly elephants and sloths too, according to Chaco. And crows, of course. Chaco represents all of them. He's their presence across the planes. It's his job to protect the Keeper. Me. He's been around in one form or another since the dawn of time, but if you heard his voice, you'd think he sounds like a twenty-something beach bum.

"It was the fat mechanic guy," I say. "He came back." I talk aloud this time to let Caroline and Owen know. And to gloat, a little. I'd warned them about that guy a week ago when he was hanging around the cigarette shop across from our parking spot for hours every day. Owen was too busy working on his trailer, and Caroline was too busy with her book.

Owen looks back at me through the mirror and rolls his eyes. "Hey, Chaco. Where to now? Any thoughts?"

"It doesn't matter where we go," I say. "We'll last two or

three weeks, if we're lucky, and then we'll run away from there too." I eye Chaco's feathers. They're huge. They'd be great for my collection, but Chaco knows what I'm thinking and squares up to me with a *don't even think about it* look.

"We're not *running away*, Grant," Owen says. "We're making a tactical move. For the good of the bell. Tell him, Caroline."

Caroline looks up from her magazine and blinks. "Hm? Oh. Tactical, yes. Although. . ."

Owen stares at her for a little longer than is safe when you're piloting a ten-ton vehicle. "Although what?"

"I was just thinking about Ben's grandmother, you know. The last Keeper. She stayed in one place for decades."

"Yeah, the rez. In the middle of nowhere. And that was before that thing came through," Owen says.

"Well, maybe we should go to the rez," I say softly. I finger my bead bracelet. I think of my crow feathers. Two of the strongest men I know came from the rez. Maybe if I go there, I can figure out how to hack it like they did. Like they do. Chaco titters and fluffs and watches me carefully.

"I don't think you know what you're saying, Grant," Owen says. "Chaco rez is not like some teepee camp where the Navajo ride war horses and hunt buffalo." He shakes his head, almost laughing. "And it's not exactly an easy place for a white kid to grow up. Tell him, Caroline."

Caroline is looking out of the side window at the crows on the horizon, the slow passing of the plains, and the even slower passing of the sheet-flat clouds in the distance.

"Go ahead, Caroline," Owen says again.

"I dunno," she says, shrugging.

"What? Are you serious? You were the one who wanted to leave that place five years ago. Remember?"

"I can leave whenever I want, now. I can go anywhere.

And I can come back. This is about finding a place for Grant to stick," Caroline says, with an edge to her voice. "Might as well give it a shot. Worst case scenario, we're out of there in a couple weeks."

"Chaco," Owen says, turning briefly to look at him properly before facing forward again. "Can you talk some sense into these two? Neither the rez nor the surrounding areas are what I would call a great place for an outsider to grow up. Right? Heck, even Albuquerque is questionable depending on who you ask."

Chaco hops up to the couch and settles there in a plop of black. "Funny you all should say this," he says. "Because I was just with the Walker. And we were just in the Chaco canyon, where we found something."

Now he doesn't want to look at me. I narrow my eyes.

"What kind of something?" I ask.

"Something I was hoping you could check out. Some*one*, actually. And maybe *identify* is a better word."

"What are you two talking about?" Owen asks. "What's he saying?"

I contemplate repeating Chaco word for word, but Owen is already jittery about the move and Caroline can and often does change her mind from second to second. I gotta jump on it.

"Chaco wants our help checking something out in Chaco canyon."

"Well," Owen says acidly, "isn't that convenient. Right on the rez. How about that."

"Yeah," I say. "How 'bout that."

6

CAROLINE ADAMS

The dead guy in the desert doesn't bother me so much. I've seen a lot of death, unfortunately. When you work on an oncology floor for as long as I did at ABQ General, it's hard to avoid. It comes to you. Walks your halls. Sometimes seems to perch at the corner of every bed, waiting patiently. You never get used to death, not exactly, but you do eventually get so saturated with it that you become a little blind to it. And that was before I knew it was essentially Ben waiting there. Ben perched on the bed. I wonder, if I had known then what I know now, would it have been any easier working that floor?

Probably not. Cancer sucks. Always has. Always will.

This body looks like it's a set piece. It seems to have drifted down to earth from the sky in the middle of a wide canyon, like a piece of paper carried by the wind, and I'm having a hard time focusing on it because all I want to do is stare at the place where I know Ben is standing. Right now. I know Ben is standing there because Chaco is looking there, speaking with him, then relaying all this to Grant, who interprets for us.

Back at ABQ General we used to have this service called the IP: the Interpreter Phone. We'd get a lot of Navajo and Mexicans coming in and had only a handful of people on staff who could effectively speak Spanish and basically nobody who spoke conversational Navajo. Big problem, right? But fear not! IP was there for us. We'd dial a special number on our shift phones that would patch us through to Spanish and Navajo interpreters, hand the phone to the patients, then get the scoop ourselves.

Chaco is sorta like an interpreter phone with wings. And Grant is like the nurse doing the relay, like I was, standing there getting the scoop, telling it to the room. Ben is the lifesaver on the other end that you can't see. The one tapped in to another world. I have to stop myself from staring into his space. I can feel Owen watching me. Owen's smoke is a strange color these days. When we started on this trip, all those years ago, it was this beautiful aquiline blue, like his eyes. It's changed since then. Not in a bad way, not exactly, but different. It's tinged with a weary color of earthen brown. There's a lot wrapped up in that color. A bit of jealousy, a bit of regret, a bit of sadness, but mostly that unique weariness that comes with Owen's kind of determination to do what's right by us. It's the color of a man growing older. I know that sounds bad, but it's not. Not entirely. In a way, it's just as natural as the blue was, but it's still a little sad.

"The Walker says he just found the guy here," Grant says. He's trying to play it cool, but I can see he's enamored. Ben, like Joey, is a rock star to him. I don't think he's blinked since we got here. "Just like this," he says, pointing at the dead man. "No trace of a soul."

Chaco chirrups then caws. "The Walker wants to know if you can see anything," Grant says, looking to me.

I kneel closer to the body. Look all around it. I cup my

hands over his heart, touch his forehead. I stand and turn back to Grant and Chaco, both watching me intently. My eyes flick over to the empty space that is Ben. "I can't see anything," I say, and the sad weight that comes out with the words makes Owen shift uncomfortably behind me. He knows I'm not just talking about the body, I'm talking about Ben too. "But that's not surprising," I add, standing from my crouch then slapping my hands together and rubbing them on my jeans. "When a person dies, their smoke goes with them. This man's soul has gone somewhere."

"You're sure?" Grant asks.

I nod, thinking of Oren Dejooli, Ben's father. When I came across his body in Ben's backyard, after Danny Ninepoint went on his killing spree, his body was just as empty as this man's in front of me. "I can't say where it went, but it went somewhere."

Grant slumps a little. Chaco mimics him on top of his head. "Well that's just great," Grant says. "What good are we if we can't help out when the Walker needs us?"

"Hey," I say sharply. "Take it easy. I can't make smoke where there's no smoke. I don't know what to tell you."

Grant moves over to the body and kicks a rock near its hip so that it clatters against the canyon wall. I can tell Chaco is trying to talk to him. Grant has been getting more and more pissy lately. I always thought boys were supposed to be the easy ones to navigate through puberty. Although I know I'm not exactly the best navigator. Sometimes I feel like I'm still going through puberty myself.

"Did Ben trace back the string?" Owen asks, startling me. I'd forgotten he was there for a moment.

"He did," Grant says. "The guy acted weird. Basically just came out here and gave up."

"That's it?" Owen asks. "Nothing else?"

Grant listens. "Well, there was this coyote." Chaco flutters to the ground near an incoming stream of paw prints. He follows them over to the body, but then he looks lost. There's some back-and-forth, and Grant looks confused.

"The tracks are gone," Grant says. "They go up to the body, but then they disappear. The Walker says he saw the coyote take off down the canyon. There should be tracks."

All of us move in closer to the body, which by now should at least be putrefying a little bit. It's sundown on the second day. We should be seeing some swelling of the gut or staining of the face, but instead it looks eerily fresh.

"No tracks? Then what the heck is that thing?" Owen asks, pointing at the canyon floor just beyond Grant. We all turn to look, and there, sure enough, is a paw print. A single paw print leading away from the body, down the canyon.

"Chaco says that wasn't here before," Grant says quietly. I can almost feel Ben rushing over to it along with us. Almost.

I can't quite believe what I'm seeing. The paw print looks like it's sitting a hair above the sand, and it seems to glow slightly in the shadow of the mesa. Grant slowly drags the toe of his sneaker across the outer edge. The movement cuts a rivulet through the desert floor, but the track remains whole. Chaco hops over and peers closely at it, then he looks around, no doubt thinking what all of us are thinking. Where are the rest of the tracks?

Grant takes a tentative step past the paw print, farther into the Canyon shadow. The first track fades as he passes it, but a second is illuminated. Chaco hops behind as Grant walks. Each print is illuminated, then fades as he passes. The blurred edges of each print remind me of the tracks the chaos souls made as they smeared their way across the desert back in Texas. My stomach does a little roll.

"It's the bell," Grant says, pulling it out and grasping its chain in his hand. "They light up when it's near." He waves it over the sand, and the prints illuminate, then fade. Chaco squawks, and Grant listens, then turns to us.

"This guy had a run-in with something bad," Grant says.

"Our monster?" Owen asks. There is wary hope in his smoke, that maybe we've found a trail worth following after all, but he knows as well as I do that this stuff never comes easily. Our new jobs make our old jobs look positively orderly. Night shift at ABQ General was a game of croquet compared to watching over the bell and the Keeper. But I still get my hopes up. Why can't something break our way for once? You know, just fall our way without a fight? Without the world teetering on its edge first? It happens to other people all the time. Open, closed. Why not us?

"The coyote took off into the canyon," Grant says, twenty feet away now, following the prints. The tracks cut to the canyon wall, much harder to see in the light. If you weren't looking for them, you would miss them. They trace the edge, until they jump up on a rock, then to another a bit higher. Grant follows the tracks as far as he can, peering closely at the rock face, until he hits an old gravel slide. The tracks race up it, but Grant can't get far. Nobody could. I'd guess it's at a forty-five-degree angle. "Looks like he went up and out."

"What's up there?" I ask, my voice wavering.

"There's the canyon visitor's center a few miles that way," Owen says, pointing.

Chaco caws once. "That's not where it's going," Grant says.

"No, I don't think so either. Another few miles past that you start to hit the rez proper."

Chaco caws again.

"That's where it's going," Grant says, nodding.

We all crane our necks to look up the canyon, as if we could see out and beyond the lip. After a minute, Grant speaks again.

"The Walker says it just looked like a damn coyote. Nothing more."

Owen shakes his head. He looks over to where I think Ben is standing, but only briefly. As if even the empty space is too much for him. When he speaks, his voice sounds defeated already, although I don't think it has anything to do with our monster. "If there's ever a place where a coyote isn't just a coyote," he says, "it's right here."

7

THE WALKER

I know I'm not supposed to play favorites in my job, but you'd better believe I'm nicer to some souls than I am to others. A lot of assholes die every day. With the assholes, I play into the Death stereotype a little more. Ham it up a bit. I try to make it easy on the good people. Help explain things when I can. Sit with them or pray with them or chat with them for a bit, whatever they want to do, until the veil comes.

I'm especially partial to Navajos. Surprise, surprise.

When Caroline, Owen, and Grant leave Chaco Canyon to go call in the body, I stick around. It's just the two of us. Both of us dead, and in a way, neither of us able to move on. It's kind of depressing to realize how much I have in common with this stiff out here in the desert. I'm still not sure what was going through Bilagaana Bill's mind when he walked out here. I don't know what the coyote was, or why it came to him, but I do know that this man was someone, once. He lived on the fringes, but he had a place on the map. There's one less Navajo walking the Way right now, and that hits me hard. So I sing for him.

I sing an old song Gam used to sing to me. It's not a mourning song, or a song about good-byes or anything like that. I don't know any of those. It's actually just a song Gam always sang to Ana and me when we were young to get us up for school. It's about the sunrise, and it's the only song I know by heart. Whenever I'm called to Navajo deaths, I sing this song with the soul as we wait for the veil. It seems to help. Even with the younger generation, who sometimes don't give a shit about the chants or songs or even the Navajo Way, really. Until they're dead. Funny how once they're dead they start to care real quick.

As I sing I get to thinking. I've been singing this song a lot recently. A whole lot of people die every day, and I'm there for every one of them. When you walk the soul map, you have to be a lot of places at once. That's what happens when you clip well over a hundred thousand souls a day: they start to blend together. But this song takes me back to all the Navajo I've been seeing out, and it seems to me like I've been working overtime in this neck of the woods lately. A lot of singing. And I don't like it.

My song done, I swirl open the map and step through. It's time to do some digging and find out where Bill's soul went. I take a few steps and walk out onto my old street at Chaco rez. Here seems as good a place as any to orient myself to the rez once again.

My family used to live in one half of a split duplex on a quiet road about a quarter mile north of the police station. We were pretty broke, all things considered, but the place was always clean and neat. Comfy in its simplicity. Because of Gam. Her mind was as ordered as the rugs she wove, and she was the Keeper of more than just the bell in her time. She kept the house too. Especially after Mom left. Danny

Ninepoint ruined all that. He turned our home from something beautiful into something stained.

My people wrap death and dying up in all sorts of superstitions. One of them is ghost sickness. We think death is literally contagious. Even the young generation, the kids who say they're scared of nothing and think more about their cell phones than the Navajo Way, even they won't stick around a place like this. It's been over five years since Gam and Dad died here, and nobody on the rez will touch the place, not even to tear it down.

Joey and I used to laugh at the old-timers who seemed scared of death. These were supposed to be the champions of the Navajo Way. Men and women who walked in balance, who were so even keeled that if the entire rez was on fire they'd nod and smoke and sweat and say to themselves, "Well, the world can't hold everything." But then when someone dies they won't mention their names because they're too afraid that person's *chindi*, its restless spirit, might come back to haunt them. Might touch them and give them ghost sickness and then they'd die too. The Arroyo crew'll tell you don't even look too long at the dead. Don't even stand too long where they died.

Crazy, right? Stupid superstitious nonsense, right?

I thought so too. Up until I saw a restless spirit wandering the desert five years ago, his soul cut by the turquoise knife we destroyed. I thought so too, right up until I jumped into a river of restless spirits, and I touched them, and I felt like their chaos was catching. Up until restless spirits tried to kill my friends. If Gam saw those things and how they acted, she'd be calling them *chindi*.

I don't laugh at the old-timers anymore. They claim the world can't hold everything. I know it can't. It's my job to keep it balanced. Which is why I'm not especially surprised to find a coyote waiting for me, standing in the shadow of my front porch, looking right at home in the gloom.

The coyote's paws rest on piled leaves, its tail swishing through little fragments of broken glass. It's the same brown and burned-orange color as the faded graffiti that streaks across the door.

If you ask a Navajo about Coyote, the Coyote of our legends, you'll get all sorts of answers. Some will tell you he's funny, some'll say he's tricky. Everyone will agree he's trouble. Coyotes are bad omens. Old-timers say if a coyote crosses your path, turn back. Forget your journey. So I'd take notice even if the damn thing wasn't staring right at me.

I can't see its tracks without the bell around, but I'd bet my best hat that if I had the bell in my hand, this old house would be lit up with glowing paw prints. This is our dark visitor. And it's waiting for me. It's expecting me.

"What did you do to Bilagaana Bill," I ask. I don't know why I expect it to answer. I talk to things all the time in my job. People, rocks, clouds. I've never expected an answer until now.

I don't get one. The coyote looks like it's chewing on something that's giving it trouble. In the low light it looks blurry about the face. Like it's shaking its head really fast. Then it freezes and stares at me again. Then it shoots off into the street at a dead sprint. It moves so fast I can't even react. I watch it stop on a dime in the intersection, oblivious to traffic, like a rabid dog. A car swerves and honks, missing it by an inch. It shakes its head in a blur again. Waits. It turns to stare at me with unblinking eyes the color of gold coated in oil. Then it yips at me a bunch of times in succession, and the sound gives me shivers. It sounds like a thing laughing as it's dying.

I follow it. I get to the end of my block, and it's already

moved a hundred feet farther down the street, almost to the service route that leads to the main drag and the NNPD station. It's really twitching now, and not just like it needs to be put down either. It seems like it's double exposed. It keeps gnawing at itself, then something seems to grip its attention and its head snaps up. Down the street there's a couple walking toward the main drag. A boy and a girl, maybe in their twenties. They're facing away from us and don't notice the coyote. It prowls toward them.

"Hey! What the fuck do you think you're doing?"

It prowls a second step, looking back at me like a mischievous two-year-old holding a glass of red juice over white carpet.

"Don't you take another step. Leave them alone. I don't know what you want, but I'm the one you gotta deal with out here."

It doesn't take another step—

It flat out takes off. It sprints after the couple in dead silence, flying over the hard packed dirt in bounds that seem way too long for its legs. Its big ears are flattened to its head. Its tail jets out like in a streamer behind it. All I can do is yell after it as it leaps to collide with the girl and nails her square in the small of the back with the crown of its head, sending her sprawling to the ground. In a blink it's at her face, snapping and chewing. Its growl is high pitched and whiny, like a power drill.

The man she's with kicks at it. He's calling her name over and over again. It sounds like Polly or Molly. I can't quite tell through his panic. He lands one, then two solid kicks right to the torso of the coyote. The third connects just as I get there and finally pops the coyote away. It scrabbles in the dirt, flailing like a dog running in its dreams, then it flips itself up.

"You little bastard," I growl. I have my hands out like a grappler and reach for it, but my fingers pass right through, which surprises me. This thing and I had a clear connection. But now that I'm close to it, I think maybe I was seeing things. The coyote looks as surprised as the couple, and it's in a good deal of pain too, from the kicking, that it doesn't seem to understand. "What did you do that for?" I ask, pointing at the girl. She's on her back, her hands up in front of her, while her partner strokes her face and calls for help on his phone. Blood from her wounds trickles into her mouth, and she coughs it up right into the man's face.

The coyote is wide eyed, startled. It's trying to slink away. Run from all this. If it ever saw me, it doesn't anymore. It looks like it woke up in the wrong county with a malt-liquor hangover. It takes a few tentative steps before it limps its way off without looking back.

My gut tells me to leave it. I turn to the girl. I hold my hands out, as if I could touch them. Help them. As if I could even offer words of support. I still sometimes forget that I can do none of these things, even after all these years. They wouldn't want the kind of help I can give. It's a bit more permanent than a coyote bite.

The girl is bit up on the left cheek where it looks like the coyote tried to get at her mouth, but other than that she's not terribly hurt. Nothing a few stitches and a bunch of rabies shots can't fix. Already I see a group of people jogging her way down from the service route. I hear a siren. I turn to the guy, wishing I could pat him on the back. Buy him a beer. But he's gone. His bright-red shoes are beating down the opposite side of the street toward the oncoming group. He's hightailing it. Then he cuts across the street at the last second and nearly plows into them, two women and

another man wearing the black polo shirts of Manuelitas—
the tamale shop a few blocks away.

I look down at his girlfriend. She moans, unaware. Red
Shoes hugs one of the women like he knows her, which is
lucky. Then he gets real close to her, which starts a shoving
match with one of the men. Maybe not so lucky, after all. Of
all the times to pick a fight, right?

Red Shoes gets knocked to the ground and has his hands
up in protest. I can't hear what he says, but it's enough to
mollify the man, who points toward us. Red Shoes gets up,
shakes himself off, and starts running back our way. The
man follows, along with one of the two women. The third
woman, the one Red Shoes hugged, stands stock-still. The
other three don't seem to notice that she's not following
them my way. That instead she's staring right at me.

I take a few steps toward her. Her eyes definitely follow
me. The group rushes right through me on their way to the
girl on the ground. I notice that Red Shoes seems a bit
disoriented. He looks behind him like he's trying to figure
out how he ever left her side. He looks an awful lot like the
coyote did after it got up. I start walking toward the
Manuelitas girl, and soon I'm close enough to notice that
her face is a little twitchy, her cheeks a bit stretched as if her
skin is colored just a touch outside the lines of her face.

"Don't move," I say, but it doesn't come out too strong.
I've got goose bumps running up my neck that make me
want to jump around in the hot desert sun for about an
hour. I take another step forward, she takes one back. I take
another step, she does the same. Her eyes light up with
manic glee. She smiles so hard I think it's gonna break her
face. Then she winks at me. Before I can react she takes off
at a dead sprint down the street away from me, her strides
longer than they should be. She covers more ground than

she should, just like Red Shoes did. Just like the coyote did. Before I can get even fifty feet after her, she's turned the corner in front of the police station onto the main drag.

I turn the corner barely a minute later. I find her, but already I know that whatever possessed her is gone. She's leaning against the chipped stucco of the Navajo Gas building barely twenty feet away. Her hands are on her hips. She's taking big gulps of air and trying to figure out how she got there. I'm right in front of her, but she doesn't see me. I spin around, scanning the crowd. An awful lot of people are out here today. A lot of trucks. Flatbeds loading and unloading things. A van of tourists crawls by, not knowing where to park or where to turn off to get to Old Town. A lot of movement. I don't see anybody else looking at me, but I can feel the thing. I can feel it here, and I can see evidence of it everywhere. Two men start arguing in front of Manuelitas. Just a disagreement, or something more? What about the young guy perched at the mouth of the alley half a block down, weaving and drinking from a bag? Is he looking at me, or just drunk? A souped-up sport truck peels around the corner, north toward Wapati Casino. Just some kid trying to swagger a bit? Or maybe the Manuelitas girl got up in his face seconds before? The street seems chaotic—it's everywhere you look, once you start looking. And I think I know why.

Gam used to walk everywhere back when I was young. She'd sometimes take me with her on easy little hikes around the piñon hills not far from the house. They're more like lumps than hills, actually. I'd race around the lumps and cut between the yuccas, thinking I was following animals when I was only tracing the path the water made when the rains washed everything out every year in late summer. I'd never stray too far from Gam, who walked in her slow way, her bony hands clasped behind her back, but I can remember one time when I was running around and she yelled at me to stop. Gam never yelled. She got plenty angry sometimes, but she wasn't a yeller. So you better believe when I heard her yell my name I stopped in my tracks.

I waited as she walked up to me in her own time and then looked down at the path I'd been following. She pointed down at a little furrow there where it looked like someone had run a stick along the dirt. My little shoe print cut a waffle in the dust right next to it.

"You know what this is?" Gam asked, speaking in Navajo.

I shook my head.

"Snake. That's a snake track," she said, tracing it all the way back into a hole on the nearest hill with one sharp finger. "And you just stepped over it."

I stared up at Gam, trying to divine if she was joking with me or scolding me. With her it was sometimes hard to tell. With most old-timers it still is.

"Scuff it out," she said, scraping her leather boots on the dirt to show me. When I asked why, she said, "Because if you don't, the snake will follow you home."

I started scuffing that dirt like my life depended on it. And every time I crossed a snake's path after that I scuffed the track out. All my life. Maybe after I died I got lazy. Maybe I got cocky. Because I crossed something's path beyond the veil, on the shores of the river, and I forgot to scuff out my tracks.

And maybe it's being back here, surrounded by everything I used to be, thinking about Gam and all the other old-timers and their little sayings and wards and superstitions, but if you ask me, I think I got a pretty good idea whose path I crossed.

A coyote can be a lot of things.

If Joey and I got caught raising hell around the rez or goofing off at school and Gam really wanted to scare some sense into us, she didn't talk about snakes. She talked about shape-shifters. Things that could take the form of coyotes, if they wanted. Things that could move faster than people. Things that snuck up on you and took you down, then moved on to sow more evil before you even knew what hit you.

There's one thing that the Navajo hate talking about even more than the names of the dead, and that's witchcraft.

Gam spoke of these witches in low, cautious quiet, telling me how they'd get me if I didn't stop screwing around. I was terrified of them as a kid. As a teenager, I stopped being afraid because I convinced myself that Gam was just telling me stories to keep me in line, to get me to finish my chores or do my homework. That she didn't actually believe them herself.

I was wrong.

Gam called these creatures by their Navajo word: *at'latai.* Kids these days use the English slang: skinwalkers.

I think I crossed paths with a creature of chaos beyond the veil, and I think it followed me home. It's wearing the lore of my people like a disguise. Preying on the Navajo like a skinwalker would. Taking on the most dangerous form of Coyote. The trickster. The witch.

8

GRANT ROMER

We'd intended to go all the way up to Chaco City proper, but Owen got lost on the Navajo roads, and we ended up swinging too far southwest. We have no phone service, and since Owen shorted the dash GPS doing all his trailer-hitch tinkering, we drive for over an hour through the flats with our asses in the air, Caroline trying to politely tell Owen he's completely lost and Owen trying to politely take her advice without turning the boat into oncoming traffic.

Then we start seeing crows. A lot of crows.

We end up pulling in to a rez town called Crownrock, on account of all the crows we see flying overhead, and also so Owen can get out of the boat before he busts a button on his collared shirt.

The dinged-up Navajo Nation sign off Highway 371 says the population of Crownrock is three thousand. At first glance I think that may be generous. I notice the population number is written on an interchangeable metal plate. I'd say it's due to be knocked down a peg. Still, I'm excited. I can't tell if it's the bell stirring itself on my chest or my heartbeat shaking it, but I haven't felt this excited about a new place since we left Texas.

The crows are flocking here for some reason, and wherever crows flock, something is out of whack. They line the side of the street and watch us pass like a crowd at a parade. They hop out of the way of people and cars a little slower than they ought to. They perch twenty and thirty deep on the overhead wires, and bunches of them swarm here and there, worrying at scraps of trash in the gutters and road kill on the shoulders.

The thing about crows is, they're not bad, but they're not good either. They're just crows. They've got their own agenda. Chaco will be the first to tell you. Most of the time it's in line with ours. Sometimes they just want to sit back and watch the carnage and wait to clean up. But wherever there are a bunch of them, something's up.

The whole town isn't much more than a mile across. We spot a KOA-style campground a little ways in where we can plug in and dump out the boat, and all of us get out to stretch our legs and wait for Chaco, who's gone ahead to get the lay of things. I can see him soaring above. The crows here are like ribbons of smoke in a wildfire, but he's impossible to miss. I want to start checking things out immediately, but I can see both Owen and Caroline are exhausted.

Wandering around a new town like zombies won't do any of us any good. They pack it in, and I busy myself in the main room, listening to music, playing video games, messing with my feathers, until eventually I nod off too.

Owen wakes me up on his way outside. I'm shocked at how late it is, already mid-morning. I must have been more exhausted than I thought.

"I remember this place," Owen says, stretching his back. He starts doing old-man calisthenics right there in the middle of the parking lot, and for the first time in a while I thank God I don't know anybody here. "Crownrock. Yeah. We did some off-site work here for the CHC back in the day. House calls and all that. Mostly smiling and shaking hands. Checking insulin pumps and blood pressure levels. Making the Tribal Council look good. Pretty quiet town."

"Well, something's going on," Caroline says. "This place feels. . . troubled." She walks out to the street and carefully watches the people walking by. She shakes her head. They look fine to me, a little twitchy maybe, but that's about it. Then again, I can't see feelings like she can.

What I can see is tracks. Faint paw prints everywhere I step, fading in and out of view.

"Uh, guys," I say, pointing. Owen and Caroline say nothing. They just stare. A definite path of those weird paw prints runs down the main street.

"Looks like our coyote beat us here," Owen said. "Damn backcountry roads. Would it kill them to put up a few more road signs?"

"I'm sure the Tribal Council is all over that. Top of the list," Caroline mutters, kneeling down to get a better look at the crisscrossing tracks in front of me. "But I don't think it matters how fast we got here. These things are layered all over one another. The coyote has been all around here for some time."

"Looks like a bunch of coyotes to me," I say as Chaco floats down our way in big, looping pinwheels. He lands with a series of hops and surveys the tracks, ticking his head along them like a typewriter.

"This thing has been all over the rez," he says to me. "The Walker is up north, in Chaco City. He ran into the bastard itself yesterday."

"What?" I yelp, causing heads to turn. "Did he catch it?"

Chaco shakes his head.

Owen clears his throat. "I'm guessing this has to do with Ben," he says, and there's this tiny sigh in his voice.

Caroline watches Chaco and me intently as Chaco relates the story. I can't quite believe it myself, and I'm sure I sound as confused as I feel when I tell it to Owen and Caroline.

"It's a shape-shifter. Jumps from body to body, leaving hell in its wake. He says it's a lot like something the Navajo call a skinwalker. Fast, strong. Can be anywhere, or anyone."

Owen grimaces. "Skinwalker, huh? I think I liked it better when we called it just your garden-variety Dark Walker. Or the *thing*."

"It looks to me like it prefers the coyote," Caroline says, following close behind me, eyeing the prints. If the bell could light up the whole street, it would look like a coyote run.

"So what's it want?" Owen asks.

"This thing came from the black pearl," Chaco says to me. "Its job is chaos. That's what it's doing. Problem is, chaos takes many forms. This bad boy tricked the agents into breaking it out of the pearl. It fought its way through the veil. I have a hard time believing it's just here to start street fights and make everyone nervous, or even to kill someone like Bilagaana Bill. It wants more."

"Something big," I say, translating. "It wants a big meltdown."

"And there's another thing," Chaco says, perching on my shoulder. "It could be anywhere in the world. It's clearly fast as hell, and it can disguise itself as anyone. But it's here. Right here. On the rez."

"It's personal," I say, turning back to Owen and Caroline. "It wants chaos, and it wants us to be in the middle of it. All of us. The Walker too. It brought us all here because it knows you have history here. The Walker is from here." I didn't add that it was essentially my idea to get us out here. There's no way this coyote could have known that, right? About how I'd always wanted to see where Joey and Ben came from myself? About my feathers? I fiddle with my bead bracelet. Does it know about that too? It's been here for five years. What if it was watching us the whole time?

"So it's leading us into a trap?" Caroline asks.

Chaco nods. "Smells like it to me, but what can ya do?" he says to me. "When you don't know the game, you gotta get played a bit until you can figure it out." Chaco spreads his wings and lifts off in three slow blasts. "I can see better from up high. Coming in here, it looked like a lot of people headed thataway for some reason, down the street."

"A lot of the coyote tracks go that way too," I say, stepping forward, studying the ground. Owen and Caroline get that I mean to follow, but I look back at them anyway and wait for them to decide. Sometimes I think they like to think they're still in charge of what happens here. Owen particularly.

Owen puffs out his cheeks and lets out a breath, shrugging. "By all means the smart thing to do here is follow the coyote's exact steps into whatever trap it's setting. Sounds completely rational to me. A lot healthier than a candy trail into the oven, that's for sure. In terms of sugar intake."

Caroline lets out a snort, and I turn around before he can see me smile. I know he's kidding. His sense of humor is drier than the desert sometimes. But I bet Ben and Joey ain't laughing at a time like this. Chaco ain't either. Sorry. *Isn't.* Chaco *isn't* laughing.

"All right, then. It's settled," I say.

We start following the tracks.

9

OWEN BENNET

W hen CHC would have us do courtesy calls across the rez, we'd sometimes come here to Crownrock. You can count on both hands the number of towns across Chaco rez that have more than a thousand people in them, and we made it a point to visit each at least once a year. Memories come back to me as we walk the street. There's a great hole-in-the-wall Mexican food joint somewhere here. It doesn't have a name, just "Mexican Food," but it does the best Christmas-style enchiladas you'll ever have. Half green chili, half red. One hundred percent glorious indigestion. The volunteer crew would stop there whenever we passed through, usually me, another resident, and a nurse looking to help out a community we had no idea how to approach. We were full of righteous medical science then. There to make a difference. We were looking for *Heart of Darkness* experiences. To get deep in it. We were convinced we were the real deal, and everyone else was just a tourist.

You wouldn't know that looking at me now, walking down the center of Crownrock like I'm lost in Manhattan.

All I'm missing is the oversized map and the sandals with black socks. The man I was would watch me now with narrowed eyes. At least until I was able to explain to younger me about Caroline. About how she still looks to me every now and then like I know what I'm doing, like we're back on the hospital floor and not out here navigating the rest of life together. About the way we sometimes find ourselves holding hands without meaning to. I think the man I was might start to understand. I didn't know Caroline back then. That was years before she came to ABQ General. But I had a place in my heart waiting for her.

Young Me might ask about Grant too. *Your kid?*

Not exactly, I'd say. Definitely not if you go by what he says. And as for Caroline, she's not in that place with me. Might never be. When we have sex it's more like the kind of sex you have because you're stranded on an island with someone. You have your pride and your principles in one hand, and in the other you hold some small part of a beautiful woman's heart. All that she's willing to give right now. At first you're stalwart. You insist you'll wait for true, fully reciprocal love to seal the deal. Then the days turn to months and the months turn to years and you're still on the island, and all of your principles start to seem foolish. Eventually you take whatever piece of her she's willing to give you.

I hope it's worth it, Young Me would say. *What would Dad say? What would Grandfather say?*

I think about it every day, I'd reply. They'd tell me to weigh what was lost when I forwent my cause here to be with her. And I do think about it every day. And it's still worth it in moments like this one, when she nudges me softly with her shoulder as we walk side by side, following

Grant as he scampers after the tracks. It doesn't seem like a lot, man. I know. But it is. You'll understand one day.

"Everyone is going over there," Grant says, pointing at a big square building one block off the main street. It's built of whitewashed concrete inset with thin windows at regular intervals. It looks like a prison, but it's actually a school. Crownrock High School. We used to hold community health meetings there and give our little talks about heart health and weight management. We had to give out free pizza to get people to come. Which is sort of counterintuitive, if you think about it.

We pass row upon row of trucks in the parking lot, most of them battered F-150s, which we used to call the Chaco state car. We fall in with a steady line of Navajo walking toward the open double doors of what looks like a big gymnasium. It has a large stenciled eagle on one wall and Home of the Eagles written in thick black lettering underneath. We always did our presentations in the classrooms. We never got this much attention. This looks like some sort of town forum. Grant stares up at the eagle until I have to pull him along. I'm more interested in the three NNPD squad cars parked front and center near the entrance.

Inside, the hallways are scuffed and narrow, the lockers are dented, and the paint on the walls is chipped and cracked. The school has that stale basement smell that seems to permeate all high schools. Above a leaking water fountain the wall is peppered with signs for the upcoming Enchanted Desert Homecoming Dance along with several flyers that read, "If you live in a shelter, a car-park, abandoned building, or train station *you may qualify for certain benefits under the federal McKinney-Vento act.*"

The doors to the gymnasium are propped open, and on each hangs a big, colorful poster advertising the upcoming

Native Market of Santa Fe. It occurs to me that this might be a community gathering in preparation for the market. It's a pretty big deal. I went a couple of times back when I lived in Albuquerque. Hundreds of Indian artists with works of all kinds, from beaded dolls and woven coasters all the way up to sand-cast silver and turquoise jewelry that can run you in the thousands. It's also a bit of a zoo. Santa Fe tourism cranked up to eleven.

At a glance I'd say the gym has about two hundred people in it already, and more are filing in with us. Someone is already talking at the front of the room, and it takes me a second to recognize that it's Sani Yokana, the NNPD chief of police. Back at ABQ General we'd see a fair number of Navajo with criminal records. The guys that were repeat offenders in our neck of the woods were often repeat offenders in Sani Yokana's as well, so I had some dealings with him. I remembered him as a stout, powerful-looking man with a wide head, like a stone mountain with long gray hair. I'm shocked to see how much older he looks. His bulk seems deflated. His long hair is grayer and receding a bit at the temples, but he still has that flinty gleam in his eye that hints of the kind of mettle that's kept him in his position for all these years. He's addressing the crowd, and the tension is palpable. His tone is flat, professional, and deliberate.

"You know me, many of you personally. I'm telling it to you straight, and I'm telling you what I know. That's why I'm here today, because there are a lot of rumors out there already, and people are getting concerned. First, the facts. We have three separate incidents here where we've found unmarked bodies, two men and one woman, all three Navajo. One in the Escavada Wash, another south of Nageezi, and now this third in Chaco Canyon. Without going further into it, suffice it to say we think all three are connected."

The crowd murmurs, hushed and low. I notice teenagers here too, standing with their parents. Most likely Crownrock students. This is definitely a neighborhood affair.

"Now it's important to note that all three were discovered in remote locations. Not within the cities or even the settlements. We've doubled the officers on each shift, and they're out patrolling Crownrock and the other towns right now, nonstop. This is a time to remain vigilant, not a time to panic. Normally we'd keep all this in the department, but recently everyone seems to be on edge and talking anyway, so we're going around to head off rumors and calm some fears."

"Is it a serial killer? One of our people?" someone shouts from the crowd.

Yokana flinches as if the thought physically twinges him. I'm sure he, and any number of the other old-timers here, think the idea of a Navajo killing another Navajo is basically tantamount to treason.

"What did I just say about not panicking? About rumors?" Yokana says. "*Serial killer* is about as loaded a word as my job's got. I wouldn't use that, no."

If the NNPD found three bodies in quick succession, and they are in fact connected with Biligaana Bill, then they don't need to worry about the killer being Navajo. The killer isn't from this world at all. The way that Caroline squeezes my hand, like she's on a rollercoaster ride about to drop, I know she wants to tell Yokana as much, just like me. Grant is pointedly not looking at us, as if he might give us away if he did. All of us want to say it. None of us can. At best they'd think we're insane. At worst they'd think we're involved. I called in an anonymous tip from just outside the canyon, and Chaco says he brushed our prints from the scene, but that wouldn't matter if we start talking like we know what happened to Biligaana Bill.

"Three dead," Caroline whispers to me, her lips brushing my ear, confusing my body. "Busy couple of nights for Ben."

"Is the market still on?" comes another shout from the crowd.

"Yes. I want to be absolutely clear here," Yokana says, holding up his hands. "The Native Market is on as planned. Our department is teaming up with the Santa Fe PD to boost security there and help keep an eye on our people. If you've participated in the Native Market, we urge you to do so again. It's important that the Diné are represented."

The faces I see are flat and unreadable in that uniquely Navajo way, but I see determination in the way heads nod. I think it would take a lot to shut down the Native Market, or even to postpone it. The market is a serious source of revenue and publicity for the rez, and not just for the Navajo either. Hundreds of tribes gather in Santa Fe. One of my first years at ABQ General I helped coordinate a medical tent for the market thinking I'd be helping out the rez. I spent seven straight hours giving water to fat white people who had too many margaritas and forgot they were at eight thousand feet. 150,000 people came that year. That's a lot of water for a lot of sunburned tourists. I was sort of put off the whole experience for a while. I'd planned to go back and drink and shop on my own, maybe buy some art I definitely didn't need, but then I met Caroline.

More people are shouting out questions now, but Yokana preempts them by saying he's said his piece but will stick around for a while to speak with whomever wants to chat with him. I wish I had his dogged calm. A lot of it comes from his heritage, but a lot of it is learned. I need to work on that. I used to have it, but I think it's left me. On the drive over here yesterday I was about ready to chuck myself out of the driver's-side window listening to everyone's thoughts on how to find our way back to the 387. We've got a coyote prowling the countryside that can change shapes, for crying out loud—the fact that I made a wrong turn or two means nothing in the long run, but we're still at each other's throats. This whole rez is on edge. It's infectious.

Most of the crowd disperses. A few of the latecomers stick around to speak with Yokana in person. He addresses each of them in turn, quickly but warmly, shaking hands and patting backs. I turn to corral Grant so we can get back to the boat and talk this over, but he's disappeared again. He does this more often, now. You'd think we have bars on the boat the way he scampers away whenever we park it somewhere and open the door.

"Did you see where Grant went?" I ask Caroline. She's looking carefully at every single person in the room. Testing for smoke like a drug dog at the airport. It's important, I know, but so is Grant. He's our first charge, after all. I think Caroline senses my annoyance, because she focuses on me again.

"He's around here somewhere," she says, scanning the room for his smoke. She senses something, peers around a crowd of Navajo speaking to each other quietly in their rhythmic way, as if every word was already written and they were just reading it out loud to one another. I walk around them and stop. Grant is in the far corner of the gym, with the other kids, talking to a Navajo girl. A girl his age. And he's *smiling*. I mean, he looks like he doesn't know what to do with his hands, but he's smiling.

"Dr. Bennet, I thought that was you." Yokana steps over

my way after disengaging himself. "I wasn't sure we'd ever see you again our way," he says. He grasps my hand warmly, and although I know he doesn't intend it, Yokana's words hit me with a wave of guilt, as surely as if Young Me were standing in the corner, watching, shaking his head in disappointment.

"Are you in town for the market?" Yokana asks.

You were a tourist after all.

"No," I say. "We're... we're back for a while."

Yokana looks pleasantly surprised, and I feel a bit better. Young Me shuts up at least.

"We?" he asks.

"I'm with Caroline Adams. I'm not sure if you remember her. She worked the CHC too. And that one—" I point to where Grant has now thankfully put his hands in his pockets while he's talking to the girl, instead of holding them out like claws. "He's with us too. Checking out the school and all."

Yokana nods. Thankfully doesn't delve. I've always loved that about the Navajo. I disappear for five years and show up with a fourteen-year-old kid, and all I get is a placid nod.

"Crownrock High is a good place. Open enrollment. They'll take him if he's interested. It's not very diverse, but that's the rez for you. And you've never had a problem with that."

It takes me several seconds to realize he thinks Grant wants to attend Crownrock High School. I look over at him again, surrounded by kids his age for once. Yokana is right. There's only one other white kid that I can see. He's watching Grant carefully.

"Dr. Bennet," Yokana says, quietly drawing my attention again. "If you're here for a time, I was wondering if you might do me a favor." Suddenly he looks tired. As if he's spent all his energy keeping his face together for the crowd, and now that they've mostly dispersed he's drooping.

"Sure," I say. "Name it."

"We have three bodies at the CHC morgue that nobody can make heads or tails of, in terms of cause of death," he says softly. "Maybe you could take a look at them."

"Me? I'm not sure what I could do."

"As strange as it might sound, I'm not all that surprised to see you here, Dr. Bennet. These cases, they give me the same type of feeling that I got with Dejooli and Ninepoint. Before they disappeared. Back when you were nearly killed. And if we don't get it settled soon, it's gonna attract the attention of Gallup, just like last time. Or something worse than Gallup. Maybe you'll see something the morgue missed. You and Ms. Adams are quite. . . perceptive."

I can't tell how much he knows or believes about what happened the last time we were all at Chaco rez and the agents hit the hospital. Certainly not the whole of it, but maybe little parts. By Gallup he means the FBI. They've got a station there. Parsons and Douglas couldn't be traced back to the FBI, but Yokana didn't see what we saw. He was convinced they were federal operatives of some sort, and he doesn't want their kind of trouble again. The way he says *or something worse* makes me wonder if he doesn't sense a bit of what's at work here now. He's an old-school Navajo, after all. And a cop. That's a double whammy.

"Sure. I'll check it out." I give him my phone number and tell him to call me to arrange a time. He nods again, takes a deep breath, and puts his face back on.

"Now if you'll excuse me, I have two other towns to visit on this little tour, and then I've got to go try and make sure a hundred thousand tourists get what they pay for at the

Native Market, and nothing more. Good seeing you, Dr. Bennet."

He turns and makes his slow way to the exit, stopping here and there to say good-bye to everyone who greeted him.

A hundred thousand people. That's a lot of bodies that could harbor our coyote shape-shifter. That's a lot of potential for chaos that I don't think it would pass up. My stomach sours, and I turn to Caroline. She's watching people, but she catches my gaze, shakes her head. No skinwalker here. But still, I feel like it wanted us here. We followed its tracks here, after all. Maybe it wanted us to hear about the trouble it's already causing. Maybe it wants us to think about what it could do if it had a real crowd to whip into a frenzy. Say, a crowd of over a hundred thousand people at the Native Market.

When we finally get Grant's attention and take our leave, the afternoon has settled over Crownrock like a heavy blanket, and pinning it down along the edges are rows and rows of silent black crows.

10

CAROLINE ADAMS

I t's three in the morning, and I'm making a list for us in case one of us gets snagged by the coyote and turns into a skinwalker, so we'll know. I have two columns next to each of our names. The first is for the tell, the hint that we need to pick up on in order to realize that we're no longer ourselves. The second column is tips for how to take us down, if it comes to that.

First, Grant. I was going to say watch out if he drops his accent, but he's been doing that already. When we finally had to pull him away from the gaggle of kids he'd found at Crownrock High he was speaking slowly, carefully, making sure all the drawl was gone. He sounded like a politician. Devoid of accent. I suppose if he comes out dressed in any sort of color, or maybe if he were to ask either Owen or me how our day was, that would be major red- flag material. Very out of the ordinary.

How to take him down? Give him a hug. It paralyzes him. He hangs there like a sheet drying on the line.

Next, Owen. I'd know things were amiss if he wore his shirt two buttons down or untucked. Other than that, I suppose if I caught him dismantling his Trailer to Nowhere after nearly killing himself running an electrical line to it, I'd know he was a skinwalker. Or if his smoke ever stopped reaching for mine. If that ever happened, I'm not sure what I'd do. I'd be too shocked to even try to take him down.

As for me, it's easy. If I ever get a good night's sleep, you need to take me out back and shoot me because I am not in my right mind and am most likely a skinwalker. Worry and insomnia are the normal for me. I worry about Owen, about Grant, about how my new family can fit with Ben. All of it. Sometimes when Grant is quiet or moody I ask him what he's thinking about and he says *nothing*. What the heck is that? How can you think of *nothing*? What's that even like? Is that like what a cow thinks of? What I wouldn't give to just go into cow mode when I'm up yet again in the middle of the night. It gets so bad sometimes that I even miss Big Hill's moonshine. The stuff tasted like socks, but even a thimble of it would put me out for the count. I'd wake up feeling like poo, but sometimes it was worth it. Come to think of it, that's how you can take me out if I'm a skinwalker. A shot of moonshine. Either that or take away my magazines. Or you could make me cold. I hate being cold. I'd just complain a lot and then be really easy to shoot.

I'm actually listing all this, by the way. Writing it all down in my journal under the thin blue light of my bedside lamp. Owen is sleeping softly next to me, one long arm wrapped under his pillow, the other tucked in to his chest. He doesn't fit this bed. His feet hang over by a few inches, which would drive me nuts, but he's never complained. He doesn't complain about anything. Ever. Even when I can see it on him, in his smoke, that the Ben situation makes him feel like a fool. He's outrageously in love with me. Every fiber of him. All he wants is the same in kind from me. And I do love him. Just not with every fiber. Some fibers are wrapped up elsewhere, and he knows it, and it makes him feel like a chump.

Owen thinks I'm obsessing over this book because it offers me a link to Ben's world, and I want that connection because I want Ben. But it's not like that. At least not completely. I'm not some love-struck tween. I know how long five years is. I know the life I chose. More and more I just want those fibers back. I want to close that chapter. And to do that I need to see Ben again. I need to speak with him. But Owen wouldn't understand that, even if I found the guts to tell him, and the words came out the way I wanted them to.

What Owen does understand is that we need to figure out a way to stop these murders and corral this coyote. And for that, we need the book.

I think.

The truth is, I have no idea what's in the book, and I'm no closer to figuring it out than I was when the agents gave it to me five years ago. It might be a detailed history of the coyote we seek, or step-by-step instructions to cross between the lands of the living and the dead like the coyote did, or maybe it's a book of its favorite Crock-Pot recipes. Nobody knows. Not Chaco, not Ben, not Joey Flatwood or Big Hill. I've used microscopes and magnifying glasses. I've used blacklight and firelight and UV light. I put out an APB to the Circle for ideas and got a bunch of shrugs. The general consensus was don't worry about it unless it starts causing trouble.

Now people are dying. We don't have the luxury of blank pages anymore. If there's any way the book can help us, I need to figure it out right now. So that's what I'm gonna do.

I slowly sit up, my legs hanging off the bed. I ease open

the flip lock on my built-in nightstand, I pull the book out from under the makeup and lotion and even a few condoms that I set on top of it to discourage Grant, or anyone else, from browsing. Not that it matters. Grant couldn't care less about the book. He's got a big bird that serves as his connection to the other side, if he wants it, but he'd rather listen to his music and play video games. He's got other things on his mind. Most likely that Navajo girl he was gawking at over at the school. Basically all the condoms do is serve to remind me that I'm not having enough sex with Owen, or that I'm having too much sex with Owen for the wrong reasons. Did you know it's possible to have too much sex and not enough at the same time? Neither did I! Then Ben and Owen happened.

I shove those thoughts out of my mind and flip through the book. Blank as always, but the pages have felt a little different ever since we crossed over to the rez. They feel heavier, like before we came they were your standard-issue paperback, and now they're that fancy pressed paper chock-full of weird fibers that costs a fortune at the stationery store. I think it's reacting to the coyote, being close to the thing, surrounded by its tracks that seem to stain the very air and refuse to go away.

Which got me thinking about the agents. They've got a few marks of their own that don't seem to wash off, and I'm not just talking about the special mark Allen's brunches have left on my heart. Or even the scars on his face, although they aren't going anywhere. I'm talking about the searing marks they have on their palms, where they held the knife that ripped a hole through the veil. They hide them well. I mean, how many times do you look at someone's palms, after all, but they're there, and when you see it, you see it. The knife had some serious firepower behind it. And when they held it, they could also read the book. Maybe it's a coincidence, maybe not, but it's all I've got to go on.

Now, since the knife is gone forever and we're immensely better off for it, I need to use the next best thing: my totem. The knife was made of the same vein of turquoise as the totems. In the past, I've only held the book while phasing in and out of the thin space. Once or twice I gave it a glance while traveling but saw nothing. This time, I'm betting things might be different if I stick out the cold burn of the place and really hunker down with my crow totem and refuse to quit.

I look over at Owen as I slide my totem pouch from its spot underneath my pillow. He doesn't stir. He breathes softly, his lips barely parted. I loosen the pull on the worn leather bag, the first gift Owen ever gave me, and one that matches his own. I take a deep breath and tighten my grip on the book with one hand then reach inside the bag with the other.

The world snaps into a windblown sepia color around me where all that I see are faint outlines and shapes of the living world, like a rough-draft artist's sketch. Owen's own totem glows warmly beneath his pillow. In the next room I can see Grant sleeping splayed out like a ragdoll, the covers on the daybed askew, but the bell around his neck glints and shimmers with a drowsy power. It's asleep now too, but it's always waiting.

The pain is already starting, but I've gotten used to it by now. Living people like you and me aren't supposed to hang out in this in-between space, neither fully dead nor fully alive. It's unnatural, and our bodies rebel from it after a while. The stinging cold used to take my breath away instantly, but I'm not such a lightweight anymore. I've got the body to prove it too. The agents were right, my skin has this super-attractive midwinter coloring that seems to stick around no matter how many hours I lay out on the roof of the boat under the summer sun. Owen calls it Arctic chic.

I flip open the book one handed and leaf through a couple of the pages. They're still heavy, but in the thin place they glisten too. As if they're running with invisible ink. I put the book right up to my face, as if I'm an old lady with a dinner menu. I think I see something, but it looks more like those little floaties you have at the corner of your eye, the little strings of pearls that flit away from you when you look right at them. I flip through another few pages with my thumb, staring, and then another few. I'm starting to get a headache. I pull myself away from the book, muttering all sorts of swear words. I massage my temple with the hand that holds the crow, but the headache isn't going away. The stinging burn of the thin place is strong. Stronger than it should be. It comes at me in a wave, like the stinging pinch of getting a shot at the doctor—at first you don't feel it at all, then the pain comes, then it comes hard and you try not to embarrass yourself by crying as a grown woman. I drop my crow.

I snap back to the bedroom. The crow lands on the book with a thump that makes Owen shift around for a second before settling again. The boat feels wonderfully warm. I realize that I'm trembling. I look at the clock on my night-stand. It tells me nearly thirty minutes have passed. That can't be right. I was in the thin place for two, three minutes tops. Maybe Owen shorted out the clocks or something doing his "improvements." I light up my phone, and the time checks out.

I was in the thin place for half an hour. I've never been in it for that long. What happened? It's as though I was in some sort of trance. The book bewitched me. But I was so *close.* I could see something! I could see the place where letters would be, if they weren't. . . not there. Sort of like in the old days when you used to use correction fluid to cover mistakes but unless you really coated your paper with the stuff, a hint of the word shone through. I was getting hints!

I lay my hand flat and hold it out in front of me. I watch it shake, then tremble, then shimmy, then twitch. Then nothing. When it's as calm as a lake, I grab my totem again.

11

OWEN BENNET

I'm back at ABQ General on the ninth floor, and I'm late for my shift. I slept in, forgot to set my alarm, doesn't matter how. All that matters is that I've left all my patients on the line. I had a full schedule, twenty-minute visits through to lunch, half an hour for lunch and charting, then a full afternoon of twenty-minute visits. I've let them all down—they'll have to be rescheduled too, so I've let down my staff as well. The other oncologists, my nurses, Caroline in particular. I'm running around the floor, going door to door to try and catch up, papers flying everywhere, my lab coat fluttering behind me, but I can't find anyone I'm supposed to see. All the patients look the same: faceless lumps in hospital gowns staring silently at me as I run. All I can hear is this strange tapping noise, like a man with a cane following me. Or maybe the clicking claws of a coyote.

I sprint around the *U* shape of the floor, trying to match my appointments with the charts on beds and on exam-room doors, but everyone is staring at me in faceless silence. There's only this tapping, and it's getting louder. I spin all around trying to find the source of the sound. My heart feels like it's in my throat. I have no idea how I can save these people if I can't see them, if I don't know who they are. The tapping burrows into my skull—

I shoot up from bed. My head is pounding, and my chest heaves with great big breaths of air. The tapping continues, rattling everything, and it takes me a moment to understand that it's Chaco at the window. He looks like he's trying to break in. Just then Grant bursts into the bedroom, his hair sleep-crazy and his boxer shorts crooked. The bell on its chain bounces off his bony sternum.

"Where's Caroline?" he asks.

Before I can answer that she's obviously right here next to me, he's already at her side of the bed, flipping the covers back. And her side's empty.

"Where did she go, Owen?" he asks again, his voice cracking in panic.

I haven't worked moisture into my mouth quite yet, but my eyes are focusing, and the first thing I see is her bedside drawer open and the book gone.

"She took that damn book somewhere," I say. "Maybe back to the agents?" Chaco is still slamming his head against the window again and again. He lets out a raucous trio of caws. "What's his problem?"

"He says she's not gone. She's here. She's stuck phasing or something."

"Stuck?" I ask as Grant swipes at the place where Caroline should be, and finally everything clicks into place. I reach under my pillow, tear at the tie to my pouch, and grab my totem. The cold sting of the thin place slams over me, and suddenly I see her. She's right there, sitting on the bed. Grant is swiping right through her. I call her name, but she doesn't answer. My words sound as though I'm screaming through a windstorm. I carefully pivot myself around the bed, taking care not to walk in this place, or else I might find myself a mile away in the blink of an eye. She's upright, and her eyes are open—staring, actually—and they glisten with an icy film. She's shivering uncontrollably, the black book tremoring in her hand. She has her crow pressed to the page like it's a penlight.

"Caroline! Let go!"

She hears me, but none of my panic registers. She looks up at me slowly, like a sloth, and the white in her eyes slips a little as she recognizes me.

"I can almost read it, Owen," she says. "I get whispers. It's beautiful and it's awful and I. . ." Tears well in her eyes and freeze to pearled drops on her cheeks. "I can't look away." She slowly reverts her gaze to the book.

"Help me," she whispers.

I fall upon her hand, tearing at her crow while holding my own in place, but her grip is locked. Frozen. It's as cold as a butcher's block. She lets out a frightened sigh that's oddly sexual, as if it's both pain and pleasure in one, and I see that with both our crows on the book, the page is darkening in waves of a script, like a scrolling computer code full of characters new and ancient. The effect is like when your brain shifts to finally comprehend those 3-D pictures, only this picture is the equivalent of the Sistine Chapel if it were painted above the devil's own throne. It paralyzes me, but the characters only click for a minute, then they scramble. The sight of them drills into my eyes like windblown sand. The pain is immense, but I don't care. I'm only thinking about how to get Caroline out of here.

If she won't let go of her crow, maybe she'll let go of the book. I wind up and slap the black book with a flat-palmed forehand and it goes spinning from her, vanishing from the thin place back into the living world, where it falls to the floor like lead. Caroline crumples, and I seize the opportunity, punching her crow from her grip. She blinks back, and I follow in the next instant.

Caroline falls forward and off the bed like a badly positioned mannequin. Grant catches her head before it bounces off the floor. Chaco is frozen, staring through the window at her, not even blinking. I whip our blanket off the bed and wrap it around her, trying to warm her hands in mine, pressing my cheek against her forehead. She feels like she's just been dredged from the bottom of a lake. At first she's still, her eyes on the book, her blue lips trying to form words that won't come, and this is when I'm so scared I think I'm going to vomit. I'm going to vomit from fear. It's a new sensation for me, the thought of such horrible outcomes, such terrifying potentialities, striking me in the stomach with the force of rotten meat. I think I'm going to have to grab the trash can, but then she starts to shiver. Trembling at first, but then she starts shaking so badly the blanket slips off her. I battle my nausea down. Shivering is good. Shivering means her body is still with it enough to fight, to contract to keep her warm. If she can fight she can live.

I take off my shirt and bear hug her. Grant unhooks the window so Chaco can hop in and float down inside, then Grant steps between Caroline and the book and sits down. Something about Grant—and the bell—being between her and the black book finally snaps her out of her trance. She blinks and looks up at him, and this time the tears are able to roll down her cheek instead of freezing there.

"What did you do?" Grant asks, his eyes wide, confused. Almost like he's angry at her. "Why did you do that? You could have been killed." I see in his eyes that he's grappling with the same fear as I am. Likely he feels about ready to vomit too.

"It. . . it was like staring into. . . the darkest part. . . of the sky. . ." she stammers. "The sky between stars. It. . . sucked me in. . ."

Chaco walks over to the book and nudges it open with his beak, tittering to himself. The cover thuds to the ground, and moments later Chaco squawks loudly and hop-flies backward, settling in a crouch on Grant's head. Grant turns around and goes to the book. He picks it up, unafraid. He holds it out to us, open to the first page. The one Caroline was looking at. The one both of our crows illuminated in the thin place. I flinch, expecting to see the flowing of those horrible words, but the page is white again, except for three words scrawled as if by a dripping pen quill across the top.

It reads: The Coyote Way.

12
THE WALKER

In between work calls I walk the streets of Chaco looking for our coyote. I jump around to the different rez towns and off-map settlements at random: Matagorda, Ponca City, Wheeling, Las Cruces. I drop in on Crownrock a fair amount too. I don't feel like so much of a stalker now that I actually have an excuse to check in on Caroline. But I spend most of my time in Chaco City, my old stomping grounds. I used to walk all over these streets as a kid, both the pretty paved main streets and the beaten dirt outskirts. I know the people and the feel, so it's easy for me to see how much the coyote has changed things. I got called to two other deaths not long after Bilagaana Bill, same scenario. Unmarked bodies without souls. The coyote ramped up its game real quick. The way things have escalated feels chaotic, which would be in keeping with the thing, but part of me also feels like it cased this place for years. Maybe waiting for us.

When I was a rookie at the NNPD, back before I got partnered with Ninepoint, I had to use my own truck for calls. We only had so many cruisers, and they went out based on seniority, so I puttered around the rez in a beater Toyota that Mom left me because I think she was embarrassed to be seen in it in Santa Fe. It had a couple hundred thousand miles on it and desert dust caked into the paint job. The AC had all the power of a panting dog, and the whole time I drove it I kept thinking how I wanted a new one. Soon enough the universe started rubbing it in, because I was seeing new trucks everywhere. That's what it's like now with the coyote's trail. I haven't seen anyone outright staring at me, but now that I'm looking for it, I can see evidence of the thing everywhere. I can feel it in that plucking sensation you get when you know someone's staring at your back, but when you turn around nobody's there.

This used to be a tight neighborhood, but now people don't talk to each other on the streets. No *ya-at-eeh*s. No tipping of the hat. When people do run into each other it's prickly. People seem rubbed raw. Hungover without being drunk first.

If you didn't know better, you'd think that the upcoming Santa Fe Native Market was the reason. People are working on their booths in the streets and alleys. Loading trailers and packing up artwork. Some are painting signs and assembling costumes. Especially on the main drag, where the more established pottery and rug places are located to catch tourists. The market runs all weekend, but the first day is the big day and the big party night. Most of these people can't afford a hotel in Santa Fe during the winter dead season, much less during the market, so they'll be driving in and out all weekend. Two hours each way. Usually everyone does it happily. The market's where they make a good chunk of cash for the year. But nothing about them looks happy now.

I see people muttering to themselves, shielding their work from others, closing the blinds of shops and galleries, rushing boxes to and from trucks, locking the doors each time. You'd think the market is a big competition with one winner instead of a huge celebration.

Now, I'm not crazy about the Native Market, but I know how important it is to a lot of people on the rez. There's a lot of shuckin' and jivin' going on there, true. You see a lot of stunning pottery and silver and whatnot, but sometimes it's right next to mass-produced corn-husk dolls and beaded jewelry that you'll swear came from China. And I won't deny that pretty much everyone selling there is hoping the white people with the twelve-dollar frozen margaritas take out their wallets, but the market is more than that. It shines a spotlight on a group of people that the rest of the country seems to constantly want to forget. It's supposed to be an opportunity to bring together a bunch of tribes and peoples, always has been, so I know all this shade everyone is throwing is coming from something else. From the coyote.

I feel the pressure pop of Chaco coming into my plane. I don't break stride as he flares his wings out over me and settles on my shoulder, just like the old times, back before he had a Keeper to look after. His weight feels good. Substantial. I live in a world where sometimes I wonder if I have any weight at all, or if I'll float away one day like the souls I bring to the veil. Chaco seems to understand this in that silent way he has of reading me. He fluffs up and plunks down harder.

"How is she?" I ask.

"She's fine. Still drinking a lot of hot coffee."

I knew she'd recover fast. Caroline has techniques of pulling others out of tailspins, knitting together broken hearts and frayed souls. I have no doubt she used them on herself. Any other person who spent that long in the thin space with that book would be dead or insane. Except maybe Joey. But he's a little crazy already. Always has been. After I heard what happened to her I stepped over to see her for myself, but it's too hard to watch her in pain when there's nothing I can do. After the fourth time I tried to touch her hair and my hand slid right through her, I got up and left. I told Chaco not to tell anyone I was ever there.

"Nothing more from the book?" I ask.

Chaco shakes his head and sighs, puffing out his chest feathers. "It still just says *The Coyote Way*, and we're still drawing a blank. Caroline wants to take it to the Circle, maybe someone has some idea. I don't know, maybe it's some dark self-help mantra. You know? Like a twelve-step program to achieving your inner chaotic potential?"

"I don't think so, bird."

"Oh yeah? And I suppose you got a better idea?"

"I might," I say, which surprises him. "What, you think I just walk around all day in between calls, taking in the beautiful views of backwater Chaco?"

"No, you spend a lot of time staring at Caroline too."

"Shut up. Here, follow me for a second."

Before he can reply I swirl open the soul map and step through. He shoots in behind me. It's a quick trip, just a skip away on the map, the souls shooting by us like stars in warp. I hold up my hand to stop us and swipe my way out again. Chaco blinks onto the scene a heartbeat later. He flops onto my shoulder again and looks around us, the sunset reflecting off his eyes like red marbles in a bucket of black.

"The desert? So what? I've been seeing a lot of desert lately. Been hoping for less desert, actually. More beach."

"The Arroyo is behind us, about a quarter mile back, where a lot of old-timers and hard liners live, alongside your run-of-the-mill bootleggers and meth cooks." I start to walk up a low rise, and when I crest it we see a broken string of rounded huts in the distance. The sunlight cuts just over their tops, where you can see a black opening in the ruddy brown mud ceiling of each. Three of them are close to us, but none of the three are standing the way they should. They're slumped, half exposed, their wooden bones bleached by the sunlight.

"The hogans?" Chaco asks.

I shield my eyes from the last of the sun.

"I've been thinking a lot about Gam. About the old-timers back down the way. About how Joey and I used to laugh at all the things they used to tell us. The old ways and the old warnings and all that. None of that seems so funny now."

I know Chaco thinks a lot about Gam too. She was his last Keeper, and no matter how much he loves Grant, he was with her for decades. He watches the hogans quietly. He looks tired. He has to keep tabs on Grant on top of all this coyote business. Gam was an eighty-year-old woman at the end. Grant offers entirely new challenges, of the exhausting teenaged variety.

"What happened to them?" Chaco asks, his head bobbing along with my steps as I walk toward them.

"There used to be six here that I knew of. They were pristine. Status symbols for their clans. They used to meet here from time to time. Perform ceremonies and cleanses. Or just sweat it out. But then the elders kept dying and the younger kids stopped caring so much."

"That sucks," Chaco says.

"It happens. Every generation thinks the old ways are forgotten, lost on the young shits running around in their lifted trucks blaring their rap music. But it ain't the end of the world. The Navajo seem to go through cycles. Tipping too far off the path, then eventually coming back to what's in our blood. We can never stray far from the Way for long. It's a balance. Or at least it was until the coyote came to town."

We pass all three run-down hogans. Hollow, brittle shells of themselves. Even the smoke stains are barely visible.

"I gotta tell you, Walker, I don't see what you're seeing here. This place looks forgotten to me."

"Not totally," I say. "Not yet."

We pass around the third hogan, and we're faced with about a thousand feet of desert, clumped and pitted by shadows that looked bigger than they are, the sunset playing tricks on us. At the edge of the sunlight, just now plunged into darkness, stands a complete hogan, smaller than even the broken ones we'd passed, but tended and whole. As we approach it, I point out the smoke hole up top, patched and trimmed. I point out the eastward-facing door, the mud fresh. I pass my hand through the mantel above it and can almost feel the pollen there. We walk in, and I can almost smell the traces of pinon smoke. I know Chaco can, because his beak noses this way and that. The fire pit is brushed clean, and its rocks are placed neatly in a circle. The dirt floor looks swept.

"This one is still used," Chaco says.

"This is my clan's hogan. Gam brought me here once, when I first found out I had cancer all those years ago. She sang over me. Performed a Way chant that I thought was for healing. But now I'm not so sure. I think she knew I was going to die."

I point at the swept floor beyond the fire. "Two old men sandpainted the Holy People right there, but there was a fifth figure in addition to the four. A dark figure with turquoise eyes. I saw Ana during the chant. Up until about a week ago I still thought she was a vision. Now I think maybe I really saw her. I think the chant called her and opened my eyes for a short time. Maybe Gam wanted me to see what was in store for me so it'd be easier for me to take it when the time came."

"A Way chant," Chaco said softly.

"That's right. We have a bunch of them. The Blessingway and the Evilway are the most famous, but there are a ton more. Enemyway, Nightway, Shootingway. There was even a Ravenway and a Dogway a long time ago, and more that are lost to time. Each calls the Holy Family's attention in a different way, for a different reason. Brings them to the song."

"The Coyote Way," Chaco says, amazed. "It's a song. A Navajo chant."

"Why not? And think about this: the coyote is untouchable right now. It's a skinwalker. It can be anyone and anywhere. But what if we could bring it right here? Right to this hogan. What if we could call it?"

"We could trap it," Chaco says excitedly.

"Why not?" I say again.

Chaco and I stare at the cold fire pit in silence. It's the logistics of the thing that are tricky. If there ever was a Coyoteway chant, it's an ancient memory now. The instructions might be in the black book, but is it worth risking Caroline's life for them? And even if we did know what to do, what to say, it takes talent and preparation to sing. Gam brought Ana to me, but she was an accomplished Singer with decades of experience under her belt and a full Singer's pouch. And what if we actually catch the damn thing? What then? We got a lot on our plate, and time is running out.

Still, I can't help but smile a little. Maybe we caught a break. And what's more, maybe we can catch another. Somebody is keeping this hogan clean. If we can find them, maybe they can help us before this becomes coyote country once and for all.

13

GRANT ROMER

I'm talking to Chaco on the way to school. That's right. I'm going to school. And not school where Owen is the math teacher and the science teacher and the history teacher and whatever other teacher, either, with Caroline showing up every now and then to tell me I should read more literature and do some art. Like she reads much more than her magazines anyway. No, this is a real school, with real kids, and real lockers, and real desks, and a real football team.

Chaco ain't so keen on the idea. Sorry. He *isn't* so *happy* with the idea. Texans get *keen*. Other people get *happy*. He sort of slow-floats above me, riding thermals, but we still talk. Every now and then he passes behind a slew of other crows floating the thermals too as they careen to get out of his way.

"Something is wrong with this place," he says. "I can feel it."

"Something is wrong with every place," I say, muttering some of the words, thinking the rest. I've been doing a lot of talking out loud to Chaco when I don't need to. Now that I'm around other kids, I need to keep him on the downlow.

"You know what I mean, bro." And he's right. I do. I can see paw prints all around Crownpoint High if I look close enough. The town itself is pretty bad, but this place is bad in particular. It's a good thing nobody else notices what I see. They might not leave their houses. Which would suck because I want to meet them. That girl in particular. I didn't catch her last name, but I sure remember her first name. Kai. It sounds good. It sounds like how she looks. I don't speak any Navajo yet, but if I was to guess, I'd say a *Kai* is that little tiny smile she has on the corner of her mouth. Or maybe a *Kai* is when you wink your eye without winking your eye, like she can.

"Well, you watch my back, right? I mean, if something is going on here, one of us needs to figure out what."

"I can't always be there for you. I do my best, but you're growing up, man. You're in all sorts of different situations now, and it's all I can do just to keep up."

"Maybe I don't always need you lookin' after me," I say, and the way Chaco suddenly gets distant, in the sky and in my mind, makes me immediately regret it. After an awkward silence Chaco chimes in again.

"The things that are coming after you aren't always as easy to spot as the agents. Snakes don't always look like snakes, Grant."

"I'll be careful, man. Why can't you be happy for me? I'm finally off the boat."

And with those words hanging in the air, I walk under the eagle painted above the doors of Crownrock High for my first day of school.

· · ·

THEY PAIR me with a white kid to show me around the place, which I'm sure they think will make me more comfortable or something, but it isn't exactly what I was looking for. His name is Mick, and he's as pale and scrawny as I am. He wears these baggy gangster clothes, big printed T-shirts that go down past his butt, and baggy b-ball shorts with huge work boots, and they sort of swallow him up. We talked for a minute or two at the town meeting in the gym. I meet him in the hall outside of the front office after I hand in my enrollment papers.

"It's you," he says. "I wondered if I'd see you again. Thought maybe you'd be scared off the place."

"Scared off?" I ask, trying not to sound nervous. "Why?"

"Well, you saw. At the meeting. There aren't a lot of white kids here. Matter of fact, I think you're number ten or so in the whole school now."

"I don't mind."

"Not yet you don't. But you just walked through the doors."

I don't know what to say to that, so I just shrug.

"C'mon," he says. "Your locker is over here."

We walk down the halls and everything is quiet. Mick is quiet. I can feel Chaco nearby, but if I can't see him I have trouble talking to him, so even he's quiet. I can see everyone already in class as I pass the doors.

"It's first period right now. Which I hate, so thanks for getting me out of it."

I can't tell if Mick is being friendly or not. I think maybe he is. He looks at the ground a lot, almost like he's following some invisible tracks of his own. I think he's just one of those people who doesn't like looking straight at you. "You'll start at second period." He snatches my schedule from my hand. "Which looks like Geometry for you. Good luck with that shit. Room 108, right over there, after the bell rings."

We walk past a row of small lockers, some of them hanging open. A few have little hearts and hand-drawn signs on them with things like Go 18! Beat Sargaso!

"What's Sargaso?" I ask.

"High school in Santa Fe. We always play them in football the Thursday before the market. It's a big stupid deal. Why do you wear all black?"

He asks this like it's right in line with football and big stupid deals.

"Just like it is all. Doesn't stain."

Mick doesn't laugh. He does nod, though, like it was good advice or something. I think my sense of humor is getting a little dusty. More Navajo, hopefully.

"Here's yours," he says, popping his fist on the farthest locker in the line. "Upperclassmen get all the good ones," he says, reading my mind. "Your code is in your folder. Put your shit in there, we still got a few minutes to walk."

Mick shows me the cafeteria. "There's where you get the food, there's where you eat it. Can you eat lunch?"

"You mean like do I have lunch?"

"Can you pay for it. You got money?"

"A little," I say. Owen gave me twenty for lunch, even after I told him I wanted to walk solo.

"A'ight, well, if you got money trouble, they help you out. There's programs and stuff." He shoves his hands in his pockets. "But if you do got money, keep that shit to yourself."

We walk again without talking much. Just the sounds of Mick's boots squeaking against the tracked floor. He points out the art-and-music hall, where I see the wooden framing of a booth.

"It's the Crownpoint booth for the market." He sneers. "I

gotta help paint it 'cause I got busted skipping first period last week. If you wanna check it out after class, I could use the company."

He vaguely gestures out a big window in the rear toward the sports fields. I see one half of a dusty baseball diamond and take his word on a football field just out of sight. All in all the place is old, pretty small, and well worn. Discolored paths snake along the concrete floor where kids have walked for years. But I don't mind. I'm used to old places. Pap's house was old before he bought it. I'm used to small places too. I live in a car—a big car, but still a car. As for well worn, well, I got no problem with that. The bell I wear around my neck might be the most well-worn thing on this planet.

Mick looks at his watch. A big, plastic, cheap-looking thing. "Shit," he says. "Time's up."

The bell rings. The period switches over, and a couple hundred kids go from in the classrooms to in the halls in a blink. I try to keep my eye out for anything weird, or for anyone eyeing me funny, sensing the bell, but all I see is kids. Tons of them. More than I've seen in my life. And all of them look at me as they pass: I'm the new kid. One of a handful of white kids in the whole place. Of course they're gonna look at me. But still I feel as hot as I've ever felt in my life. And that's before I spot Kai.

She's walking out of a classroom, talking with two other girls at her side, and putting a notebook away into a woven bag at her hip. She's wearing a Lobos Football T-shirt and very short pink shorts. The way the shirt falls, it almost looks like she's not wearing shorts at all. She laughs at something one of her friends says, then she looks up, and then she sees me staring like a cow. I know I should look away, pretend I was just scanning the hall, but I can't. She recognizes me. She looks surprised, but not in a bad way.

She opens her mouth a little, then she's surrounded by a group of older guys who come laughing down the hallway, and soon all of them go off in the same direction.

When I turn back to Mick, he's already looking at me with a smirk on his face. His mouth twitches a little, like he wants to say something, but he just shakes his head. The hallway is already clearing out. The passing period is winding down.

"Remember, you're in Room 108. Good luck, lover boy."

14

CAROLINE ADAMS

I'm freezing. I mean, I know I get cold. I always have. I'm the type of girl to blow dry my feet for ten minutes after I do my hair, just because I can. In the winter, if it were socially acceptable for me to walk around in one of those huge Carhartt monkey suits the rig workers have, I would do it. I'd sleep in it too. But it's August, in the desert, and I'm way too cold for August in the desert.

The book almost killed me. The thought of how close I came to having my life sucked out of me in the thin place makes me a bit dizzy. So now I'm cold and dizzy. It's been a few days since that night, and I'm still not right. I came close to slipping away forever. Really, really close. I try not to tip Owen and Grant off about just how close, but I think they know. It might have something to do with the fact that I reheat my steaming-hot tea in the microwave every thirty seconds. Or that I'm drinking cup after cup of steaming-hot tea in the first place, in the co-captain's chair, under the blazing windshield.

Anybody else wouldn't have made it back. I don't want to toot my own horn here, but it's the truth. I had to coax my own smoke back to life, which is tough, because I can't exactly see it on myself. All I know is I felt it guttering, like a little spark at the bottom of a pile of straw, only the pile is on the desert plains and a big wind is trying to scatter it far and wide. I had to put my hands around it, breathe on it, whisper to it, just like I did with the agents when they first tumbled out of the break in the river, when they were half dead too.

I focused on thoughts that would warm me. Not things like tropical islands and Carhartt monkey suits, which would warm my body, but things that would warm my soul. Things like remembering Grant when he stood like a little superhero, holding the bell out in front of us to protect us in the Texas desert. Things like Ben. Everything I can remember about Ben, actually. But the problem is, I'm remembering less and less about Ben. I have a bunch of core memories that I go back to all the time. Playing cards with him when he was getting chemo, holding him in the dry grass of his backyard when he got sick, kissing him for the first and last time before he left me. These are all important to me, but I've been bringing them out of their special memory box and shining them up too much, and I think I've forgotten other stuff. I had a lot more Ben material once. I know I did. Every moment I spent with him was special in some way, but all I have now are the superstars, and the more I bring them out, the less shiny and the more bronzed they get. The rest seem to have faded altogether. That, more than anything, reminds me of all the years that have gone by.

The Ben memories helped, but they didn't bring me back. They're more the type of thing I talk to James and Allen about over a cup of French press up at Friday Harbor. They're great "last thoughts," the kind of things you run up the flagpole right as you're checking out, and I thought I was checking out, until a stupid memory popped into my head. It was of Owen, frazzled and red faced and damp about the ironed neck of his button-down, trying to make a twenty-point U-turn in the boat when we were lost on some Navajo road west of Chaco Canyon, and even though I couldn't laugh with my frozen mouth I ended up laughing with my soul. And just like that, the icy-iron grip of the thin place and the creeping insanity of the book were snapped. I'd live. What can I say? I guess I have a soft spot for frazzled men.

Speaking of frazzled, Owen has been in a constant state of mild frazzlement for days now, ever since he slapped that book away and pulled me back. He grasps my fingers like straws whenever he sees me, as if they were thermometers that could measure my core temperature. He does this without talking sometimes, just reaches over and grasps my fingers, and, yes, they're cold. I tell him that they're always cold, which is true, but I can tell he doesn't buy it. His smoke is so gentle. It's this softly resting blue, like a cloud plunked over a mountain, afraid to leave. Which is why he's really not happy about what we're about to do.

"Are you sure they're all gonna show up? I mean, if it's just you and me, we're really underprepared for this. Criminally underprepared," Owen says. He's pacing the main room of the boat, his head cocked at forty-five degrees so it doesn't bump the ceiling.

"Chaco got word out. Everyone will be there," I say, trying to grab him as he passes, but he's lost in his analytical world again. The one that measures outcomes and risk and determines best practice. The oncologist's world.

"You *just* stopped shivering in your sleep, Caroline."

"We don't have any more time. You've seen this place. It's falling apart. And Grant is in the middle of it. Ben thinks this could be the key to trapping this thing. If there's a chance we can get any more info out of the book, we have to take it." I check the dash clock on the boat. It's almost time.

Owen mutters to himself, still pacing. I hear the words *Grant wouldn't even let me walk him halfway* and *goddamn book*, but I know he's in with me. He's pulling his totem pouch from inside his shirt. He chose to wear it there because his neckties used to cover up the bulge. He doesn't wear ties anymore, but he still keeps it there. He has racks and racks of ties in the closet that he hasn't touched in years, but he still keeps them too.

"Are you ready?" I ask gently.

"No."

"Owen."

"Fine."

I count down from ten. I have the book in one hand, flipped open to the Coyote Way page. At one, I grab my totem. Owen phases right along with me, his hand grasped around my fingers.

The bite is immediate and twice as painful as I've ever felt it, so soon.

"Don't look at it!" Owen screams. He brushes my cheek with the hand that holds his totem and nudges my line of sight toward him. "Not yet!"

We're alone. Each second that ticks by makes us more alone. I think maybe I was wrong and Owen was right. Maybe this was another stupid decision in a long line of stupid decisions with this stupid book. And if you peg this book as stupid, and me as stupid for getting it, then the whole house of my life starts to look like a stupid deck of cards.

I shake my head. That's just the melancholy of this place talking. I can't let it win. But there's no denying that we're here alone and I'm holding on to a mental time bomb with the hand that doesn't hold my totem. I stare into Owen's eyes, as muted and sepia-blown as they are, and he stares into mine, both of us willing each other not even to glance at the book. Another interminable number of seconds ticks by. I want to leave. I want to blink back. I dip my gaze, but Owen squeezes my fingers. I look up at him again.

Then there's a weird sucking sensation, like when you're bobbing in the ocean and caught in the retreat of a wave that pulls your legs out from under you. Another hand falls on my shoulder, bracing me. I turn to find Joey Flatwood watching me with calm eyes, his long black hair spread out behind him like a ribbon, splintering into fragmented strands of gray that blend into the thin place. He says nothing, only clamps his hand onto my shoulder and nods.

I feel another pull, a big one this time. All three of us bob like bottles in the waves as the refrigerator form of Big Hill pops into sight, mid-lumber. He settles next to Owen and clamps one hand on his shoulder. He's washed in gray, a charcoal painting of a man, but I can see one of his constant kerchiefs around his neck. He looks like the world's hugest train robber.

"Hold on now, hear?" he bellows. "They comin'!"

More distortions around us. I feel like my body is floating on the crest of where two seas meet. The first, the thin place, is freezing. The second, the Circle, is warmer, and with each wave that hits me the gripping cold lessens. I close my eyes and let the current take me, confident that Owen's grip, and Joey's, will keep me from floating away. When I open my eyes again I see our chain has become a circle at least twenty strong. Most I recognize from when we fought with them in the desert. I see the old Aborigine and the staid gentleman with his cane. I see the soldier next to the businesswoman. I see the tribeswoman and the monk, and several I've never seen before—a young girl and a man hunched and bent at the back, and three tall women who look like triplets—all of them swathed in gray, smudged and blurred, but standing determined. Outside of Joey Flatwood, I don't know any of their names. I don't even know Big Hill's real name. But I don't have to know who they are to know that we're a sisterhood and a brotherhood. It's like a family reunion. We all have our separate battles, but when the time comes to do our part, we pick up right where we left off, mid-conversation even.

With all of us here, the chain unbroken, the bite of the thin place is bearable, but I know we can't sit on our duffs. The book is already responding, just as I'd hoped it would. My theory is simple. If Owen's totem combined with mine made a few words appear, maybe a whole mess of totems would make a whole mess of words appear. Two totems brought a little stick to the fight. I want to bring a big stick. Looking around me now in the wind-tunnel scream of the thin place, it's pretty clear I brought a big damn stick. I brought a log.

I step into the middle of the Circle members, and their chain wraps around me. They eye the book warily, flinching away from it already. Glancing at it in snatches like you would a solar eclipse. It's time to play cheer captain.

"Bring it in!" I yell. The Circle closes in, totems out. Their collective turquoise burn is blinding. Even if I wanted to look at the book, I couldn't. Instead I close my eyes and feel as each member plunks an edge of their totem onto the page. I feel like those scientists who watch bomb blasts from behind lead walls with mega goggles over their eyes. Even the backs of my eyes are bright. After the last plunk the book gets noticeably heavier. I can feel the words forming, their ink soaking in, the pages saturating.

Owen squeezes my hand, and if I could see him I know he'd be grimacing. Despite all of our power, the thin place is fighting back. The bite is getting stronger. There's no beating it back for long. But that's fine, because I think we have what we need.

"I think we did it!" I yell. I have this absurd urge to break it up like a cheer captain again. *Circle on three! One, two, three, CIRCLE!* But instead I just drop the book. It blinks out of the thin place and falls to the floor of the boat. The Circle members blink out, each stepping back to where they came from. Joey gives me a thumping pat on the back first and then blinks away himself. Owen and I are the last to go.

This time I don't collapse. Neither does Owen. He looks for my eyes. I nod to reassure him, then both of us stare at the book, open, on the floor. The page still says The Coyote Way, but now there's more. Much more.

15

GRANT ROMER

Chaco ain't happy with me right now. He's hanging over me all the time, chiming in when I'm trying to talk to people, chirping off opinions here and there about classes and teachers and kids I'm trying to be friends with.

"They needed you there, Grant," he says. He's sitting on top of this huge window well outside of the art department. I hear his voice in my mind. The other ten kids painting the front face of this booth are oblivious to our conversation.

"They're fine," I say, hoping he gets the tone of my thoughts. "They had Joey, they had twenty Circle members. They got what they needed."

Chaco shakes his head. I can tell by his shadow. He nearly blots out all the light coming in from the window. After class that first day, when my head was still sort of spinning, Mick came up to me and reminded me about his work duty on the booth. I told him I wasn't much of a painter, but then he said that Kai was on the market crew too. So here I am.

I'm trying not to get red and blue paint on my black

jeans and sort of succeeding. I'm dabbing at a glob that landed on my T-shirt with my thumb, trying to ignore Chaco, when someone says, "You should just take it off." I look up with my thumb still pressed to my gut, and I see Kai.

"Seriously, the way you paint, you oughta just take your shirt off. It's not staying clean."

My mouth suddenly seems too dry to form words, but I do manage to put my thumb down. She smells like paint and sawdust in a way that makes me think strangely of my grandpa, of the way he used to smell coming out of the shop. But his was on top of a glass of whisky, and hers is on top of this flower smell that's either on her skin or in her hair and that I have a crazy urge just to huff. She cocks her head, waiting for me to talk. I work spit into my mouth.

"How do you paint, then?" I ask. I absolutely am not about to take my shirt off. I'm a hundred and twenty pounds soaking wet, and she'd be blinded by how white I am. She grabs my hand and steps in to direct me, and I have to tell myself to close my mouth.

"You slide, see? Up and down. Slide it. Don't slap it." She slides my hand a few more times, letting the brush flip over itself, up and down the corner post of the booth. I'm stumbling around saying *thank you* when my words die in my mouth. Three older guys have come into the room and are standing a few paces back. They're all Navajo, and they're watching me like I'm taking a leak on their car door. Kai sees my look and seems to know instantly what's up, even without turning around. Her face falls. No more wink. No more hint of a grin. She plucks her hand from mine. Goes over to her side of the booth. Acts like they aren't there. But the whole room is silent. The older guys let her go, but they're still looking at me. I recognize them from the first day. They were the swaggering crew that swallowed Kai up in the hallway.

I almost apologize to them, but at the last second I wonder what Joey would do. He damn sure wouldn't apologize for no reason. So I return their gaze, paintbrush in hand, blue droplets trailing up my sleeve.

The lead kid, the one in front, isn't a big guy. He's my height, maybe ten pounds heavier, but he's cut. He wears a sleeveless T-shirt from some local diner that I don't know, cut open at the sides near to his ribs. He wears b-ball shorts and tan work boots too, just like Mick, but somehow I doubt this kid is following Mick's cue. More like the other way around. The two guys behind him are big, thick boys with creased necks and pudgy foreheads and open mouths. I notice Mick in the back with the stencils and spray-paint. He meets my eyes for one second then shakes his head and gets back to spraying. I look out the window and see Chaco's shadow standing stock-still.

The front kid says something, and for a second I think maybe I'm messed up in the head because it's coming out in gibberish. My second thought is that I've found our skin-walker. This guy is why the crows are perched two- and three-deep on the roof and cars, this is why the place has all those coyote tracks. This guy. Right here.

Then my head clears, and I recognize that he's speaking Navajo and he ain't even talking to me. He's talking to Kai while he's looking at me. I can't understand a word of it, obviously, but I catch a few other kids grinning, looking away. I know it ain't good. I catch one phrase in English: Indian lover. That one gets Kai's attention too, and she snaps something back at him. I've talked with Owen enough about these things to know that if you call a white man an Indian lover he's at best a tourist and a fanboy. At worst he's a pervert. Someone here to taint the blood.

"Whoa, whoa man," I say, holding up my hands in a way I hope doesn't look too wussy. "I'm just here to paint. No big deal."

"Just here to paint." He has no accent at all. He shakes his head like I can't read the writing on the wall, but forget the writing, I don't even see any wall. "You make sure it stays that way," he says.

Before I can dig myself into anything deeper, he nods at a few of the boys in the back by Mick, and a bunch of them head off into the corner where they speak in low Navajo. They look shady, but they've apparently forgotten all about me, so I'm OK with that. I spend another minute or so half-heartedly trying to paint the cross post before the lead kid calls Kai away from her friends. She chances an unreadable glance my way out of the corner of her eye as she goes over to him. I see Chaco's shadow tip its head; he's trying to listen as hard as I am, but it's no use. They argue a bit, not much on her part, before he leads all of them out.

After another minute the air cools enough that people start to get back to work, and the low hum of conversation returns. I'm not sure what the heck just happened. I feel sweaty and red and like I'm breathing too loudly. Mick scares me half to death when he taps on my back. I didn't hear him take a step my way.

"See what I'm telling you, man?" he says under his breath, dipping a brush into my bucket to paint along with me. "If you're trying to find a place here, I'm just gonna tell you, it's not with them."

"Is that her boyfriend or something?" I try to keep my stroke even, keep it from shaking with the adrenaline I feel coursing through me. I've never run into anything like that before. Heck, before I stepped foot into Crownrock High I hadn't really had more than a passing confrontation with anybody my age, ever. Not since the boys in Midland would chase me on their bikes. And even then it was mostly them hollering at me and me pedaling for my life, hoping they got bored before I got tired.

"Her boyfriend? No. Worse. That's Hosteen Bodrey. Everyone calls him Hos. He's her big brother." Mick scratches at his neck and looks away. "Don't take it personal man, it's called the Native Market, after all."

"Meaning what?"

"Meaning I'm only doing this 'cause I got caught ditching and they made me. It's the Native Market. It's for Native Americans. They don't want us doing it no more than we want to be here doing it. Sorry you had to learn that the hard way."

I'm not so sure. Kai didn't look like she didn't want me here. Looking around the room now I see a lot of eyes watching me with distant expressions, but they're not angry, not mean, just distant. Quiet. Even as they work in their own groups on other parts of the booth, they seem quiet. Mick sees what I see and murmurs while he whaps his paint-brush clean.

"Like I said. Don't take it personal. It makes me want to burn the place down sometimes too. And I've been here for a year now."

He stands up and tosses his brush down. His post looks more cat scratched than painted. "That's good enough. You guys got the rest, right?" he asks the group. "For your big show?" A couple of the nearest kids look up at him and roll their eyes. They aren't unfriendly, though. Mick may be as much of an outsider as me, but he's an accepted outsider.

His section leader ticks her head toward the door and tells him to get gone if he wants to leave.

"Adios, then," he says. "C'mon, Grant, I got something I want to show you."

But I'm not feeling like leaving yet. Taking off right now feels a bit too much like running scared, which isn't something Joey or Ben would do. I may be the new white kid, and I may have no family save the two who took me on and one bird, and them more on account of what hangs around my neck than on account of me. But I'm still Pap's grandson. I'm still here walking through more hell than these kids have seen in all their lifetimes, Navajo or not. I don't feel like leaving just yet. I feel like painting my goddamn post, the right way, sliding, not slapping.

"You go on ahead," I say.

Mick cocks his eye at me. He looks around. He holds out his hands and spins a little, shrugging. "Fine by me," he says, his voice quiet and flat. He shakes his head as he leaves.

"That guy is trouble," I mutter to Chaco, dipping my brush again.

"Which one?" Chaco asks. He fluffs and settles in the shadows, and I realize he's been about ready to break through the glass this whole time. "They all seem like trouble. Everything here seems like trouble." I can sense him staring at me through the wall. As if I'm the one to blame.

"So it's my fault I decided to take the front lines of this mess?" I ask, starting to slap and stopping myself. I take a deep breath.

"That's the problem. Do you know what they might do to you if they knew what you have around your neck? What anyone might do to you? What if they smoosh your head into the floor and notice the tracks running up and down the halls here? Ever thought of that?"

"I'm not some stupid kid riding his bike in the dark anymore. I know what I'm about. Did you at least catch anything Hos and his crew said?"

Chaco is silent, and I think I've gone too far. In the quiet seconds, while I'm standing alone doing someone else's work, nobody taking notice, I wonder what it might be like without Chaco. Without Owen or Caroline, without any of them. I was basically alone before them. Pap and I were together, but we were both alone. I hacked it then, and I was just a kid. What could I do now, just me and the bell? But then Chaco chimes into my thoughts.

"After he got done telling her not to touch you, he and his boys said something about the market. Something about being ready for it." Chaco's voice is quiet. I wonder, not for the first time, how much of my thoughts he can read. If he hears more than I let on. But this only pisses me off more.

"Yeah, that's what this stupid booth is for," I say.

"I don't think he was talking about the school art booth, bro," Chaco says, his voice full of snark. "He wanted Kai to come with his crew, to get ready for something. She didn't want to. I think he's got some other plan, but I couldn't make anything else out. Sorry, your highness. Is that enough for you? Can I have my shiny bauble now like a good crow?"

"Shut up, Chaco." That's the first time I've ever said it to him and meant it. And I expect him to snap something back at me, but he doesn't. He shuts up. He hops up and takes flight, and I expect him to leave me. Go somewhere to blow off steam or maybe just check out altogether for a bit like Caroline does with the agents sometimes. But not Chaco. I still feel him near, just higher up, trying to get a better view of what I've thrown myself into.

16

OWEN BENNET

I'm lying on my back on the floor inside the trailer hitch. It's the only part of the thing I've managed to finish completely, but no need for applause. It's just a ten-by-six-foot slab of carpet. And it's the thin stuff too. The stuff you find on the floor of elevators. You can glue it down without much work. I managed to wire a 240 line, but now I've got nothing to hook to it. The walls are bare, the ceiling is bare. It's dark, but that's because I closed the back. It's also outrageously hot, but I feel like I need the heat. Like it might give me some sort of clarity. The Navajo sweat it out. I figure I ought to give it a try. Of course, I'm drinking a glass of bourbon as well, which isn't part of the Navajo ritual. I'm dribbling it into my mouth a half sip at a time and swirling it around my teeth.

I don't really know what purpose I thought this trailer would serve. When I started it, all I wanted was to be doing *something*. I guess serving as a place to swish bourbon around my teeth in the dark is as good as anything. Sort of like a hick sensory-deprivation chamber. I supply the darkness. The bourbon supplies the weightlessness. It's good bourbon too. Not the plastic bottle trash I used to drink back at my apartment. That, at least, is an improvement in my life. Something to hang your hat on. Not in here, though. There's nothing in here on which to hang a hat.

The good thing about bourbon, one of several, actually, is that it sets aside noise. Chaco rez is buzzing with noise, and it's about ready to break the people here, even if they don't know it yet. It's about ready to break me, and Caroline, and Grant, and even Chaco too. Grant used to tell me about this place he had in his bedroom back in Midland, between the dresser and his bed, where he would go to shut out the noise. Maybe this is my place like that. Grant doesn't tell me much of anything anymore, but after a few dribbled sips of bourbon, that doesn't sting quite as much.

Caroline is with the agents. She thinks they may be able to make sense of what we found in the book. They won't. I know it. They want nothing to do with the book. Caroline knows this too, which tells me she's more comfortable in upstate Washington with two guys that tried to kill us, however entranced they may have been, than she is with me right now. But after a few more dribbles and a big swish, that shuts up too.

With the noise turned down, the reality of our situation steps up. We've got a killer coyote on the loose, one that can take on the personage of any living person it comes across. It taints the ground it walks on, like lead seeping into the water, until the whole place is putrid and ready to blow. It wants to bring our world crashing down around us, and house odds are that it wants to do all the crashing at the Native Market. So we've got three days.

The Coyote Way might be able to trap it. Ben tells us it's a chantway. One of the spiritual ceremonies of the Navajo where Singers try to get the attention of the Navajo gods to bestow favors. Cure illness. Lend strength. It's the exact type of nonsense I spent a decade as a CHC doc trying to tiptoe around, being politically correct enough to acknowledge that yes, your spiritual beliefs have merit, but no, a heavy sweat will not cure your son or daughter of tuberculosis. Your grandfather will not be cured of his chronic emphysema by inhaling piñon smoke. Your husband's jaundice will not go away if he's chanted over for three days, no matter how expensive the Singer is. You need medicine for these things, or your people will die. I still believe that. Even after all I've seen. There's magic out there, but there's also medicine. And maybe they aren't so different.

And yet here I am. I pat my breast pocket, where the words of the book are transcribed. Each of us has a copy, in case the book gets fickle again and sucks up all the ink we only recently got it to bleed out. I've already memorized it, and I'll spare you the anticipation: the directions make no sense. The three of us and Chaco brainstormed all night over them without getting far. Maybe if I recite them out loud in the hollow of the trailer, the acoustics will make sense of them. Sort of like singing in the shower. Which is what Caroline does. I used to go over some of my trickier biopsy procedures in the shower. Same difference. Here goes. Number one:

"A birth bag," I say. Not sure what that is. Medically, it could be a lot of things, none of them appealing outside of a hospital setting. Don't blame me, I'm just telling you what the book says.

"A burned stick." Which shouldn't be too hard. In a sane world, you just go out, find a stick, and burn it. There you go. Or how about a match? That's a burned stick. Can it possibly be that easy?

"A broken pot." Same deal. Do I just break a pot? Caroline said that we have a Crock- Pot we sometimes use. She likes to cook enough for several days at a time when she can. It has her most recent concoction in it right now, a peccadillo that didn't go over very well. I can toss it. It'll be a shame to lose the ceramic piece, but if it means saving the world, I can part with it.

"A cane." There are plenty of those around here. We used to give them out for free at the CHC. We took up a donation in Albuquerque for them. Most of them were used walkers, though. Would that work?

"A whisk broom." We use a Hoover to keep the RV clean. Caroline said that's like a modern whisk broom. Maybe we toss the Hoover in?

"A broken stirring stick." We're at a loss here. I'm not quite sure what a stirring stick is. Grant suggested using our soup ladle.

I laugh out loud. If you think we can catch our coyote with a match, a crock pot, a walker, our vacuum, and a soup ladle, all wrapped up in whatever the hell a birth bag is, I've got a bridge in Brooklyn I'd like to sell you. Once again that damn book provides us more questions than answers. I dribble more bourbon into my mouth. Maybe I'll just sit in here until all the chaos blows over. Or until the world blows over into chaos. The latter is looking more likely these days. . .

A sharp series of knocks makes me literally jump up from my back in complete darkness. I forget where I am. All I know is that I'm sweating profusely. It must be a hundred degrees. I feel out wildly for anything, and my hands slap against the sides of what I slowly come to realize is the trailer. I stumble around in the darkness, slam my head against the back hatch, and knock over my bottle of bourbon. I scramble to pick it up then feel around the trailer handle for the lever that pops it open. The door snaps up into the ceiling in a jarring rattle, and I'm left peering out into the afternoon sun. My shirt is drenched in bourbon and sweat, and my hair sticks straight up like the tuft of some sort of tropical bird. What's left of the booze swirls around the bottle hanging from my left hand. I shade my eyes from the blinding sun. I can't even tell who's standing on the dirt in front of me.

"Can I help you?" I ask, trying to make it sound polite but challenging at the same time. The first thing that comes to mind is that another Itch found us.

"Everything all right, Dr. Bennet? It's three o'clock. We're supposed to be at the CHC in half an hour."

My eyes adjust, and I see the bulky outline of a big Navajo. A few single strands of his long hair hover about over his shoulders in the rising heat. He's dressed in a worn linen button-up and well-washed jeans. He wears creased leather cowboy boots and sports a shiny silver police badge on his hip, offset of a shinier silver belt buckle.

"Oh God. Chief Yokana. I'm sorry. I lost track of time." Truth be told, I lost track of the fact that we were supposed to meet to go to the CHC morgue in the first place. He knows it too. I can tell by the way he looks at me sidelong then peers behind me into the empty trailer where there's a wet outline of my head on the floor. He glances at the bottle of bourbon I have absolutely nowhere to hide. He sees me deflate. There are a million things he could say right now. Any number of accusations.

What he says is: "All right, then. Let's get goin'."

God bless the Navajo.

"Great," I say, a little too eagerly. "Let me just change my shirt."

. . .

WE DRIVE over in Yokana's SUV, a well-traveled Ford Explorer with NNPD plates but no other markings. It has a dusty clean to it—no trash, not even a stray coffee cup—but everywhere bits of the desert, even down to the cracked-earth smell of the AC. I get the feeling he could have a nicer car. He's the chief of police, after all, but I think he doesn't have one for the same reason he's traveling the rez to try and calm people down, and for the same reason he knocked on my trailer and picked me up today. Because he's more inter-ested in actually doing the job than just looking like he's doing the job.

As we roll down the double-lane road out of Crown-rock and onto the Navajo Service Route he just starts to talk. Not a lot, not consistently, but a few words here and there. Observations about what he's seen in the towns and outposts, none of them good. The one thing I can say I definitively learned working with the Navajo over the years is to shut up and listen if they're talking, so that's what I do.

"There's a backwater trading post ten or so miles north of Crownrock. It's where I was before I came to you. A man named Burner Forbath runs it with his wife. Has for decades. It works on the barter system still. If you want to set up a house account, you leave what you got as collateral, take what you need. All sorts of things get left and taken. He's had no trouble. Ever. Until his own son robbed him then ended up dead several miles west near White Rock. No visible cause of death. Nothing but coyote tracks around him. That was two days ago. Yesterday I got another call. I'll tell you about that when we get there. Just know that now we're up to five."

Yokana is quiet then. He shakes his head once then shifts his hardened gaze to the road. He doesn't need to embellish. That is implication enough. A two-fold betrayal: Navajo stealing from Navajo, and son stealing from father.

"Burner's boy was a good kid. I didn't believe him until I saw the boy's body myself, surrounded by the house bank he stole. You'll see for yourself, but our team found no cause of death, no markings. It's like the gods struck him down for what he did."

Sani turns north on 191 toward Chaco City. He seems to be working words around in his mouth, behind his closed lips. I know what he wants to say, that this makes no sense. That Burner's boy was struck mad. That the whole rez has been struck mad. That maybe this goes beyond the police work he's accustomed to, into another realm. If he said that, maybe I could shift this load I've been carrying, tell him he's right. That the bodies I'm about to see all were most likely struck by madness. That we've got a coyote skinwalker in our midst. That Burner Forbath's son didn't betray his own family and clan. The coyote did, using him.

But Sani Yokana didn't get to be where he is by swiping at shadows and ghosts. He charged real people with real crimes and put them behind real bars. Just like I used to practice real medicine on real people with real ailments.

"Maybe he didn't steal the house bank," I say. It's as close as I can come to saying what I feel without chancing Yokana pulling a U-turn and taking me right back to Crownrock with a *good day to you, sir*. He looks over at me.

"Burner has one key to the store safe. He gave it to the boy before he left for business in Crownrock that day. It was him."

"What I mean is, maybe Burner's son was ill. Mentally unwell." I look pointedly out the window at all the crows weaving above me, casting shadows like running clouds on the flats and across the heat-beaten road. Yokana follows my eyes, and together we watch a line of four crows flank the car then cut high and right. One tracks us with eerie calm before all are lost to view.

"If I remember correctly, the crows started to show up last time too," he says. "You know I sometimes wonder if they follow me? You believe that?" He smiles sadly and shakes his head.

The rest of the drive, Yokana outlines what he knows about the rest of the bodies. One of them is Bilagaana Bill. I already know his story, but I listen to Yokana tell me about him again. The one they found in the Escavada Wash is a woman from a little town called Los Cristos. An older loner, like Bill. It took three days for someone in her family to get to the CHC to identify her. The third they found the same day: a farm hand who worked seasonally in Nageezi for years. The ranch foreman identified him but couldn't say much other than that he always did his work well then left after harvest.

We pull into the CHC parking lot as the sun turns from the light brightness of high noon to the heavy, cutting rays of a New Mexico afternoon. I reflexively straighten the tie I put on when I changed my shirt, the first I've worn in months, and I'm struck by a nearly overwhelming nostalgia. I remember the heady, antiseptic smell of the place with such force that I can nearly taste it in my mouth. The sunlight reflects off the uniform windows of the squat, four-story building like each has a raging bonfire behind it, and most likely, many do. Not physical fires, but mental ones. Most of my time here was spent putting out fires with Caroline and nurses not nearly as good as Caroline.

We walk through the doors, and I see the front-desk receptionist, a Navajo woman named Lelah who was fairly old before I came around a decade ago. She looks up, mid-phone call, and smiles. Then she ends the call and stands up. She laughs when she sees my surprise. For the first five years I knew Lelah, she couldn't walk right. She was on the receiving end of the walker donations we started in Albuquerque. She walks evenly over to me and gives me a big hug and says, "All it took was every day." I don't know what she's talking about at first, until I see that she's holding out a tattered single sheet of paper with a series of physical therapy exercises on it. "Just like you said, Dr. Bennet," she adds as she hands me the sheet. I sense it's important to her that I take it. Like it signals the end of a long struggle.

I return her smile, and I laugh along with her, but inside I find I'm disappointed in myself. I've let her down by not walking in these doors a few times a week over the past five years. I cheated by handing her the instructions and leaving for half a decade and then walking in when her battle is done. I should have been here. I don't deserve her smile, but she pats me on the back and mutters over me in broken English and Navajo anyway until I have to excuse myself to follow Yokana.

He leads me past the elevator bay, where I'd usually wait to ride to the top floor then make my way down methodically from there, getting as far as I could, one patient at a time. Instead we walk to the stairs at the back of the main floor. They lead down to the morgue.

The formaldehyde tang washes over us slowly along with the increasing cold, all of it gradual, until we find ourselves standing under buzzing blue lights between cold lockers and stainless-steel tables. A medical examiner and his assistant work quietly on a naked body on a cold slab in the far back of the room. I recognize Tim Bentley, a mortician who comes up from Gallup twice a week on behalf of

IHS. He's a good guy, if a little weird. But what mortician isn't?

Bentley looks up at us as we approach. "Dr. Bennet," he says, "thanks for coming down." I wonder if he knows I've been gone for five years. Bentley never got out much. He ushers the assistant aside and makes way for us to approach the table. "We've been trying to make heads or tails of this one for almost a week now. He was the first. Take a look."

On the table is Bilagaana Bill. He's looked better, but I've definitely seen corpses look worse. I think whatever kept the grubs away is still lingering on him. The chaos. If it's anything like what we felt with the book, I'd want to stay away too. Yokana clears his throat.

"Got a tip from a group of hikers that said they saw something in the middle of the canyon near the west mesa. This is Bidzill Halkini, the one I told you about. Who went by Bill."

I hope it doesn't show that I've seen him before. That we were the ones that found him. That I was the one who called in the tip from a pay phone at the Chaco Canyon Visitor's Center, muffling the receiver a bit with my hand when I spoke.

"What's your cause of death?" I ask Bentley.

"On paper, organ failure. Same as the other four."

"On paper?"

The assistant glances at Bentley. He looks uncomfortable. So does Bentley, in his own way. He takes off his magnifying glasses and picks at some sleep in the corner of his eye. "There's some indication here of a. . . I'd almost call it a type of encephalopathy, although it doesn't follow modern examples of the disease. The blood flow in the brain was not normal."

"Do you have any postmortem scans?" I ask, slipping on

latex gloves. It comes back remarkably easily. Like I've fallen back into the routine of flicking on the coffee pot and stepping outside to get the morning paper. Yokana steps back and rests against the wall, watching.

"Mr. Yokana petitioned for two—one on Halkini, because he came in first, and then on Burner, because he was significantly younger than the first three victims." He moves over to Bill's file and rifles through it until he finds a photo printout of the man's brain. He hands it to me.

"Burner's looks much the same as Halkini's, in terms of blood flow."

As soon as I touch the glossy printout, I'm taken back to that moment in my apartment when Radiology patched through a brain scan of Ben Dejooli, effectively hammering the last nail in his coffin. I remember the way the crows exploded from the big tree outside of my apartment window after I read the scan. I'd been drinking bourbon then too. I half expect more crows now, their claws clacking against the flooring as they come hopping down the stairs. I get no such thing, only the low-grade buzz of fluorescent lights and Tim Bentley looking at me strangely.

Brains are not my specialty, outside of when they're anomalous with cancerous growth. This man's brain is not. I recognize no outstanding masses of any sort, nothing that would indicate a tumor or clot. But I've seen enough postmortem CT scans of brains to recognize what a normal one looks like.

Bilagaana Bill's scan does not look normal. Some areas of his brain look devoid of blood flow entirely. As if they've been cut off. Others are suffused with blood, bright white on the scan, like they've been overexposed. I bend over him and pull up his right eyelid. The tiny capillaries that web the eye are burst in places. Their red is softened to a muted purple by the milky film of death.

"When was this taken?"

"As soon as we got him in, five days ago."

I take a big breath. "On its face it looks like some sort of massive stroke."

"Except that—"

"Except that there are no clots or blockages of any sort," I say.

Bentley nods. "I thought the error might have been mechanical until I took his front plate off. The tissue samples corroborate."

I stare at the scans for another minute in silence, until Bentley says, "Thoughts, Dr. Bennet?"

"I'm not sure you want to know what I think, Dr. Bentley."

"Try me."

I weigh my thoughts. Test my words in my mind first. "I think his brain looks like it was changing, and his body couldn't take it. Let me guess, no indications of why his major organs gave out?"

Bentley shakes his head.

"He shut down," I say.

"Why?" Bentley's tone is academic. Distant.

"Maybe he didn't want the alternative." By which I mean whatever chaos was poisoning his brain. I wish I could just tell them, without Yokana taking me out in handcuffs.

"He does look like something got at his mouth," I offer, since it's all I can do.

"All of them do," Yokana says. "Paw prints around them too. Probably just a coyote worrying at the mouths. They do that sometimes."

"The rest of the decomposition process is occurring remarkably slowly," Bentley says.

More overhead buzzing. I look at Bentley only to find he's already looking at me. I tuck the scan back in the folder. "Can I see the other bodies?"

Bentley moves down the cold locker, snapping open clasps and sliding out corpses like a tailor pulling an assortment of fabrics. Soon the other four are stretched out before me. I'm looking for anything that might link them, besides the coyote bite. Something that might give me a clue as to the type of person the coyote wants. I feel like more of a cop than a doctor. But then again, maybe that's why Yokana brought me along. Because the best cop he knew for this type of stuff is dead.

After Bilagaana Bill is the woman they found in Escavada Wash. She's squat, fatter than Bill. There are no marks on her that might indicate how she died, but her face has the same creases from age and sun. The farmer they found near Nageezi looks similarly worn. Deep crow's feet around the eyes. Chapped lips and chapped hands. There's a slight crease around his forehead, and when Yokana sees me looking at it, he chimes in.

"That's from an ancient Stetson he always wore."

"These people are all old," I say.

"That was our first connection too. Until Burner's son came in."

I move down the line to Burner. He's darkened by the sun, but otherwise he looks like a normal young man. He's filled out at the shoulders, but his face still has a hint of that pudgy, teenaged veneer.

"How old was Burner's son?"

"Nineteen," Bentley says.

I walk as calmly as I'm able to the last slab down the

line. A thin girl with waist-length black hair lies here. She has muddy feet. She's quite pretty.

"And this girl. How old was she?"

"She's our most recent," Yokana says. "Sixteen. She comes from a family who owns a used-tire shop in a one-horse town off 57 called Animas. One of three daughters and two sons. She set fire to the building before she apparently walked five miles barefoot to the north bank of the Chaco River and laid down to die. No priors, no record of any kind. All anybody the NNPD questioned could say about her was that she was the quiet one of the family."

"Isn't it a bit strange that all of them seem to have been bitten?" I ask carefully, still looking at the girl. She has the gnaw marks on her face too, around the lower lip. Just like the rest of them. I look up at Bentley. "Maybe that ought to be looked into more carefully. There's a chance we need to tell people to look out for coyotes—"

Bentley winks at me.

Half of his mouth turns up into a grin, the other half down into a snarl. It's an awful, two-faced grimace that lasts maybe half of a second. I shake my head, take a deep breath, and when I look up again he's watching me calmly.

"Yes?" he asks.

I turn to Yokana. He seems to have seen nothing.

"Dr. Bentley has told me that they see this quite a bit," Yokana says, flipping through the chart in his hand as he speaks. "The coyotes get at the mouths of exposure victims pretty regularly."

I look at Bentley again. He's grinding his teeth softly.

"It's just what they do," Bentley says, staring at me, unblinking. "It's the softest meat." I take a step back.

"I can't help you," I say quickly. "I'm sorry. I wish I could.

Chief Yokana, I need to go. I've forgotten I need to pick Grant up from school."

I've forgotten no such thing. Grant won't let me walk him to school or pick him up. But I have to get out of here. The air is suddenly thick. I'm having trouble getting a breath. I look at the assistant, and he seems strangely doped. Oddly quiet. Has he spoken since I got here?

"Chief," I say. "We need to leave."

Bentley smiles and waves good-bye like a kid at a bus stop. I turn and just start walking up the stairs. It takes every fiber of my being not to run as fast as I can. I hear Yokana behind me with his slow, deliberate steps. I don't say a word until we're both out and in the baking sun, and only then can I finally breathe. I let the sun wash over me like a shower, craning my neck toward it.

"You OK, Dr. Bennet?" Yokana asks.

I watch the door. Nobody comes after us. Not Bentley, not anybody.

"I am now. Sorry. I haven't been around all that for a while." I wonder what I can possibly say to convince Yokana that every policeman on the rez needs to descend on the CHC morgue right now and shoot Bentley on sight. I almost start to say it, and Yokana is watching me, concerned, but after a few more moments in the Navajo sun I've calmed myself. No, that wouldn't do. The skinwalker will have thought of that, after all. It wanted to show me what it was doing, toy with me, and it said its piece. If I were to go back down those steps right now I'd probably find Tim Bentley dazed and confused, the skinwalker already gone.

"Did you see something down there?" Yokana asks, and not for the first time do I wonder if he knows more than he lets on.

"You brought me to hear what I think. Well, I think these

people were attacked by something. Something that broke their minds. They wandered out into the desert because they couldn't take it anymore."

Yokana cocks his head. "What kind of thing would do that?"

A coyote. I almost say it. But it won't come out. I shake my head in frustration. "And they're getting younger. The victims. From Bill on down to the girl."

If this was already obvious to him, Yokana doesn't let on. He only nods, his face falling another centimeter, lower and lower. Grayer and grayer. I wonder how much longer a man like him can stay standing if every day he gets lower and grayer. But I can't dwell on that now. Right now I'm wondering about who will come next. Who comes after the sixteen-year-old? A fifteen-year-old? Fourteen?

All I can think of is Grant.

17

THE WALKER

I'm sitting inside my clan hogan watching the daylight fade. The sun seems to be pulled through the smoke hole at the top as if someone is sucking it up with a straw. Gam used to call this type of light *dust light*, the last, sideways beams that catch the dust and the pollen floating in the air. There's no dust at my passing, though. I disturb nothing. I'm the only one here, and I'm not even really here, not like the fire pit is, or the swept earth, or the pollen-dusted beams. I've been the only one here for days. I come back in between calls, hoping to catch whoever keeps this place, but so far I've only seen crows. I think they can see me, or almost see me. They hop in through the eastward-facing door and cock their heads at me before turning around and hopping right out again. Maybe they don't like what they see.

I'm probably looking a little grim. I'm definitely feeling grim. We've got three days until the Native Market, where our coyote may be primed to pop off. The rez is slowly falling apart under the weight of the chaos it brings, and our only weapon against it reads like a shitty garage sale.

Something about all this is going over my head, and I can almost hear the *whoosh*. Something fundamental about the coyote, as a skinwalker. I'm missing something, and it's driving me nuts. If you think about it, this coyote and I have a lot in common. It's a mean bastard, but it has a job too, just like I do. It anchors the chaos side of the river. It absorbs the souls that are drawn there. It may look like the coyote has free rein here—it can change hosts with a touch, turn them into skinwalkers too, and moves with unnatural speed and strength—but the world it inhabits now still has rules. I take a swipe at the rocks ringing the fire pit, and my hand passes through. That's one rule. I can't interact with this world unless it's to take a soul to the veil. And as far as unnatural speed and strength, well, I bet if you were to ask some of the poor saps I have to chase down and drag to the veil, they'd say much the same about me. But I still have limits, so this thing must too. It's just a matter of finding them.

I wish Gam was here. I wish I could knock on some camper doors and rattle some tents at the Arroyo and figure this out NNPD style like in the old days. I wish I was a better Navajo and knew what a Coyoteway was in the first place. I wish Joey Flatwood had any idea. I wish I was with Caroline right now, playing cards on a TV table in my house while we talked all this over. I'd even be willing to take the chemo again. See what I mean about being a bad Navajo? My people aren't supposed to dwell. We don't look forward much, either. We take what is and work with it. But what *is* sucks, and all I find myself doing these days is looking back. Sorry, Gam, I know you'd be sucking your teeth at me, shaking your head, but can you really blame me? What's *back* is all I have.

I'm roused from my one-person pity party by a shuffling sound coming from outside. I walk out and take a lap around the hogan, tracing the sound back toward the Arroyo until I see two figures crest the rise, taking a well-worn path in my direction. The sunset falls right on them, and I see it's two men. Two old men. They're walking along the path in silence, backs bent with age, their eyes on the ground in front of them. They don't pick up their feet so much as slide them, right foot, left foot, with a sound like the slow sweeping of a broom, one in front, the other behind.

They pass the first three derelict hogans without a glance. As they make their slow way down the path it dawns on me that I know these men. They were at my chant. They're the sand painters. Two brothers, as old as the hills, who used to perform with Gam on the rare occasions she still sang. They're dressed in light jackets despite the summer heat, in that universal way of all old people, but theirs are over what looks like traditional garb: woven tunics and buckskin breeches worn as thin and white as paper at the knees. They wear beaded moccasins that look patched and patched again. I know they could walk right through me, but I step aside for them anyway. They pause briefly at the open entrance to the hogan, and the first reaches into his tunic. He takes a pinch of pollen in his hands and slaps the mantel. They gently help each other with the slight bending and crouching required to get inside, and once there they silently go about sweeping the place and shoring up the four corners of the framing by dusting pollen in each direction.

One builds a fire in the pit while the other smooths the dirt beside it like he's priming a canvas, and when the hogan is nice and hot, they take off their jackets. Then they take off their tunics. And then they take off their slippers and breeches. They're stripped down to saggy old-man underwear. I'm starting to wonder if maybe I ought to give these fellas their privacy, but that's where they stop. One nods at the other and then creaks his way downward until he's lying flat on the dirt between the fire and the canvas. His brother takes up several handfuls of piñon leaves and stuffs them in a paper grocery bag. I'm thinking maybe he's going to burn the whole thing, but instead he sets it carefully on the floor and kneels on it to save his bony knees from the hard-packed dirt of the floor. Now we've got one lying flat, the other kneeling over him, and the fire crackling and smoking. The kneeling man extends his right hand out over his brother, and he touches his dirt canvas with the knobby pointer finger of his left hand. Then he closes his eyes and begins to sing.

I don't recognize his song, but that's hardly surprising. Gam sang all the time, walking the foothills with me, cooking around the house, when she weaved and when she knitted. She sang Ana and me to sleep when I was younger, and it seemed like no two songs were exactly the same. The sand painter sings over his brother in a softy rhythmic chant that's surprisingly high and on key, considering I bet the guy is well into his eighties. His right hand still hovers above his brother. He draws in the dirt with his finger.

I peer over his shoulder and watch as he traces symbols. I recognize the hard lines and basic shapes that make up the symbols of power and the outlines of the Holy People, but I get the sense that he's improvising, moving his finger in time with his voice—deeper gouges when his song counts out beats, softer strokes as his words soften and his voice keens. He draws circles one way then traces them back in the opposite direction. I'm so lost in the finger painting that I don't realize he's opened his eyes and is staring now at his right hand. It's a complicated one-man dance that he's doing.

Singing, painting, and now moving his right hand slowly, evenly over his brother's body. His eyes never waver, and neither does his right hand. It cuts the air in a slow and steady slice. There aren't even any old-man shakes. That's when I figure out what's going on. This is a hand-trembling ceremony. This man is a hand-trembler, a Navajo medicine-man, although not quite like what Gam was. Tremblers can tell you if you're sick with something, then they send you to people like Gam, Singers who can perform chantways to get your spirit patched up and back in line with the Navajo Way.

After a time, the first brother abruptly stops, evidently satisfied with how still his right hand was the whole time. He gently wipes his tapestry clear, and then the two switch places. Both brothers are Tremblers, then. I can't help but smile. These two and Gam must have made quite the team back in the day. Gam didn't sing nearly as much near the end of her life, but I can only imagine what they must have been like in their prime. Gam was good. One of the best. I bet the brothers are too, if you believe that sort of thing. And if you were here, in the smoke and heat, and you saw the painting, the singing, and now the surgical stillness of the second brother's hand, I don't care how skeptical you are, some part of you might start to wonder.

The brothers now stand facing each other, which is odd. I don't remember this sizing-up as part of any hand-trembling ceremony I ever saw or heard about from Gam. As a matter of fact, they look like they're checking each other for blemishes, like they're pieces of meat at the butcher. They slowly circle each other. One turns his back on the other, and he scans it from top to bottom, even stretching out the underwear band for a glance down below. They check each other's sparse hair, like they're looking for ticks. They lift up one leg and then the other like old donkeys and check the soles of each other's feet. Last, they check each other's mouths, up and down. Then they both speak the first words I've heard them say all evening. It's in Navajo, but it's clear and I understand it: "No bead, no bone."

They nod to each other. They seem as pleased as they were to find their right hands steady over one another, and it occurs to me that this trembling ceremony wasn't to diagnose an illness of some sort but to pronounce a clean bill of health.

At the sound of the words, memories flood into my head, one after the other. I remember walking with Gam, both Ana and me, taking care to brush our feet over any track we saw, in case it was a snake's, and Gam laughed at us and said we just wiped out a lizard's slow *swish*-and-*clomp* track, not a snake's. Ana said something like, "Aren't they bad too?" But Gam shook her head. "The Gila gave us the trembling power," she said. "Its scales harden the Navajo warriors. It keeps us safe." And that afternoon, outside the front door, she stopped us and ran her still-nimble fingers through our hair playfully. "See?" she said. "No bead, no bone. The Gila has kept you safe from the witches."

No bead, no bone. The sign of a Navajo witch, of the skinwalker, is supposed to be a bead made from bone, embedded just under the skin. The sand painters wanted to make sure they were clean. They've been coming here time and again, judging from the pollen, to check each other for a bead.

And now other images hit me like bolts out of the blue. The first time I saw the coyote it was gnawing on its own cheek. It tackled the woman in green and lashed out at her mouth, and then she spat at her boyfriend in the red shoes. I remember the blood, the way it hit his mouth too. Then, while I was looking at her, he disappeared. I try to picture what happened next, and I go blank. I panic and take some deep breaths. The sand painters are packing up, and I watch them go in a daze, the very last of the light showing them the path that they seem to know by heart. Their slow, methodical gait calms me.

I remember now. There was a fight. A fight between Red Shoes and another man over an embrace with the waitress. Perhaps a kiss? Then the skinwalker jumped again, to the waitress, who then ran around the corner, where I lost her.

The coyote, gnawing at its mouth. The woman in green, bitten at the lip. Red Shoes, who took a full gob of blood to the face himself. The waitress he then kissed. A bone bead transferred to each. The hallmark of the skinwalker. Its source of power.

I call for Chaco. I call again and again like an annoying neighbor ringing the doorbell fifteen times. Eventually I hear the pop and feel the pressure drop, and he floats out of the sky like a piece of darker night.

"Walker, you better have a damn good reason to call me like this. Grant is in the trenches at that damn high school, and he's chosen right now to fall into puppy love. We got darkness closing in on all sides, man. I don't have the time to—"

"It's a bead, Chaco. A bead made from bone. That's what we're looking for. Everybody that became a skinwalker had it in their mouths. The five dead people that hit me one after the next, all soulless, they had it in their mouths, but it broke their minds. Maybe they carried it for too long, or maybe they fought against it. Either way they tried to take it away, lay down and die in a place where it might be forgotten, buried by the desert in the Chaco Canyon or Escavada Wash or wherever. But this thing has forged a connection to the coyote, and the coyote found it every time."

Chaco stills and half floats, half flops his way to the ground in front of me. "A bead. Another object of power." He's talking to himself more than to me, but I nod. "Of course," he says. "Your object of power is the bell. You're a Walker, this thing is a Walker. Why wouldn't this thing have one too?"

"The coyote carries it in its mouth. We find the coyote, we rip it out like a bad tooth, we destroy it."

Chaco flutters. "Then it's all over."

18

CAROLINE ADAMS

Owen is actually making Grant open up his mouth. He's got a penlight and everything, and he's telling him to move his tongue around. I'm torn between laughing and crying. This is what it's come to around here. The boat is getting weird.

"OK, no beads. You're looking good. Now you check me," he says. He holds the penlight out to Grant, but Grant just crosses his arms and shakes his head pityingly.

"You're not a skinwalker, Owen. I don't need to look in your mouth to know that," he says.

Owen shrugs. "Fine. Caroline, you can check me."

"How about we all just stop looking in each other's mouths, OK? None of us is the coyote. I would know," I say.

"Oh yeah, how?"

It's best not to get into how I have a detailed skinwalker checklist for both of them, wherein I would determine that Owen doing this type of fretting is actually *normal* for him. And Grant looking bored out of his mind is *normal* for him too. Instead I say, "I'd see it in your smoke."

"You don't know that. You've never seen it."

"I'd know." Although he's right, I haven't seen it. Still, I think there'd be some indication from the smoke that a body is possessed, being molded, being shifted by this thing into a vessel it can ride until it dies. Owen just got finished telling us his uplifting theory that the coyote needs a kid. A young person, at least. The bodies he saw were trending younger, and Owen thinks it's because it's harder for the coyote to take control of an old person, with set routines and embedded prejudices and experiences. Young people are malleable. Easier to warp because there's less to change.

"The point is that we all need to see that we're who we say we are, right now, right here, before we go to the Arroyo. It's a baseline panel. Do you know what a baseline panel is, Grant?"

Good old Owen, always finding a teachable moment. He's such a dad, which is remarkable considering Grant doesn't consider himself Owen's son. Predictably, Grant says nothing, just resigns himself to listening as Owen plods on.

"It's an establishment of control levels. For instance, a baseline lipid panel is something I recommend you get at twenty years old to establish cholesterol levels and enzyme activity for that moment in your life. Then we'll know in subsequent panels if there's cause for alarm."

"All right, can we go?" Grant asks. He looks at me with pleading eyes.

"What he's trying to say is that we need to know that at this moment we're bone-bead free," I say, snatching the penlight and doing a cursory check in Owen's mouth, more to get this show on the road than anything. "Because we're going into a dangerous area, and if something does happen and one of us starts acting weird from here out, we'll know at least we were all good here. And it's a good idea."

Owen gives me a proud smile that is surprisingly catching, considering we're on the edge of what you might call the rez war zone. It was my idea. Most of the really insane ones are. Chaco said Ben divined his bead theory from watching these two old hand-tremblers that sandpainted during his chantway years ago. I said it would have been great to ask them about the Coyote Way, seeing as they're old as the hills and might have some idea as to what the six odd ingredients are. If this creature attacks like a skinwalker and has some sort of affinity to the Coyote of Navajo lore, maybe we could use the lore it's wrapped itself in to catch it. I was just spitballing, you know? Just saying the first thing that came to mind. Like, it would also be great if I had a chai tea latte right now. Except instead of getting a delicious, warm drink the four of us now have to walk into Navajo skid row looking for two old guys.

"You're clear," I say, then I slap the penlight into his hand and pop open my mouth and say *ahhhh*. I hear Chaco squawk on the steps of the RV, where's he's waiting. After all these years I can tell when crow squawk sounds impatient.

"Chaco says it's not the coyote we need to worry about here. This crew is old-school. Way too much work to turn into a skinwalker. It's getting our asses kicked that we need to worry about."

"That's lovely. Thank you, Chaco. Quite helpful," Owen says.

Chaco squawks again. Grant translates, his voice droll. "He says if you know anyone else who's willing to translate old geezer Navajo, be his guest."

I do, actually. Joey Flatwood. But he's still not willing to break his banishment. Certainly not to show himself at the Arroyo again. He's stubborn like that. Just like Ben was, and still is. Chaco says Ben is going with us, but we obviously can't expect any help from his corner, not that it's his fault.

Chaco says that for the record Ben isn't all that hot on this idea. He suggested we bring Yokana in, but that's easy for him to say. He's not the one that would have to explain the existence of worlds beyond worlds to the Navajo chief of police. And the bottom line is, we have two days before the Native Market. We're running out of time. It's now or never.

We parked the boat in a well-tracked dirt shoulder just before the turnoff to the Arroyo proper. It's still a five-minute walk from here, and we could have gone closer, but the last thing we need to do is show up to this place in our suburban war-vehicle. The boat is nice. Not Liberace-On-Tour nice, but we've got about a hundred grand wrapped up in it (OK, Owen's got about a hundred grand wrapped up in it), and it would look obnoxious rolling up on old tents and tarp-covered lean-tos and cars on blocks. The idea is to look exactly as desperate as we are.

Owen clicks on a flashlight, and we set off in the silence down the rutted road to the Arroyo. The night is black in the rez in general, but it's blacker out on the fringes. Eventually we see lights in the distance, soft glows from inside cars and here and there tents lit up like wish lanterns. The clunky turning sound of a few small generators provides a hum of background noise over which snippets of conversation can be heard, blown our way by the soft night breeze. It's not late yet, just dark, and the Arroyo is still alive. You could even call it sort of pretty. This is the time to see the place if you have to, when the drop-off beyond looks like the velvety black entrance to some sort of mysterious cave and not the pit full of trash and rusted metal that it is. When the camp looks like a half moon of bobbing lanterns, you can almost believe it isn't full of people too poor to own a house or rent an apartment, right next to bootleggers and meth cooks and addicts. The rough parts are muted, covered in a blanket of velvet night and soft moonlight. I might actually like to take it all in, if it weren't for the fact that we were being followed.

I tug on Owen's cuff, and he turns to me.

"We've attracted some attention," I say. I can see the smoke of two or three people in the darkness to our right and left, like faint wisps of ground fog in strange colors. The people themselves blend in seamlessly with the dark horizon.

Owen and Grant slow, and Chaco stills. We wait. But neither the smoke nor the bodies it comes from move toward us, which you'd think would be heartening. Until you realize that all they want us to do is keep walking, farther from the main road. Farther from the boat. I can read it in the way their colors bubble and waft. But they're not roiling, either. They're not angry, or cruel. They're curious, and maybe a little bit opportunistic, but I think that's the game out here at the Arroyo.

"Let's keep walking if we're gonna keep walking," I say. "Act like you know what you're doing, Owen."

And he does. He straightens up and fixes the tuck of his shirt. He clears his throat and nods at the rest of us. I see the people around us pausing, reassessing. Maybe it's Owen, maybe it's the huge bird that sits on Grant's head. Either way, they follow at a distance, but more join. By the time we reach the inlet at the camp's edge, basically a big, rusted swinging gate bolted into the ground in the middle of nowhere, we've got six different smokes at the fringes that I can see, but so far they all hold back.

At the gate is a young man. He leans heavily against it, and his body makes the slight sways and constant adjustments of the veteran drunks we'd see at ABQ General. He smokes a cigarette that burns a soft red in the dark. He wears a stained Cleveland Indians jersey and sagging gym shorts with sandals covered in duct tape, and he watches us plainly as we approach. I hold Owen and Grant back a few paces from the guy. An element of everyone's smoke here is harsh, rough, but it's more of an undercurrent than what surfaces up top. Up top is still curiosity.

"You're definitely lost," he says. Then he takes a quick drag of his cigarette.

"No, we came here for help," Owen says, and although I can see that he's near to trembling on the inside, his voice is level and calm. Doctoral. I wonder, if I'd had the sight I have now back when I worked on the floor with him, how many times his outside would have belied his inside. When you work an oncology floor, you're almost always terrified. It's all about how you control it. I'm not at all surprised that Owen does it well.

"We're looking for two old men, sand painters. We were told they live here," he says.

The man is quiet, but inside he's surprised. First, three white people show up, then they ask about two old-timers who probably haven't been off the Arroyo in years. I think we've chosen the right approach, but then he shatters my confidence.

"Get the fuck out of here, *bilagaana*," he says. "Before you get hurt."

"We need help," Owen says again.

"Navajo medicine works best on Navajo. Go back to your pretty city."

"It's not for us, it's for the rez," Owen says.

"The *rez*? What do you care about the *rez*?" he asks. The six who lurk in the darkness start to move in as soon as he raises his voice. Owen senses that he's been too familiar. He takes a step back, another smart move. Now the smoker sees

Grant fully for the first time, with Chaco on his head, doubling his height.

"What the fuck is that?" he asks, and I see his color rise for a moment.

"It's my bird," Grant says, calm as a lake. Chaco rises to his full height.

The smoker is afraid, but not of Chaco, not exactly. He's afraid because in his past he had a friend who lived by the crow totem, but he died. A Circle member, although the smoker didn't know it. I see the words play over his head and his heart. They read, "Oka Chalk."

"That's a big fucking bird," the smoker says, speaking around his cigarette, taking in a long drag now.

"He's. . . not your normal type of crow," Grant says.

"Listen," says the smoker. "You take this circus and walk your asses back the way you came. Hear me? This ain't no place for you."

The six others are coming toward us, and now they're not so curious anymore. Now they've got one thing on their mind: getting us out. Maybe taking a bit of a road tax along the way. Chaco sees them too, and he snaps his head to the side, eyeing the closest. He shifts himself to fly. I speak first, loudly.

"Oka Chalk is the reason we're here. He was the start of all this. You remember him?"

Everyone freezes. The smoker comes a few steps closer. I sense Owen tense but keep a hand on him. "What do you know about Oka Chalk?" he asks, peering at me over the cherry of his cigarette, through half-hooded eyes. He smells like bad beer.

"He had a crow too, once. Different from the one there." I nod at Chaco. "But—"

"A bad omen," he finishes. "That stone crow of Chalk's, it was bad luck. He started his own totem pile with it. I bet it told him he was gonna die. Now the fuckin' things are everywhere —the sky, the roads. They're in the middle of the pit by the hundreds." He gestures vaguely with his cigarette behind him

I don't know what the man is talking about with totem piles and premonitions of death, but I know I have his attention. The problem is he's just getting more scared now, no more willing to take us beyond the gate. We need to play our cards quickly, or we're going to get the hook. As if Chaco can understand me, he lets out three shrill *caws* that are immediately echoed from the desert behind us and built upon by the crows in the trash pit. From the sound of the birds, their collective voices slamming against the dirt and the desert like they're all right next to our ears, there are more than a hundred in that pit. It sounds like an army, and it's worse for being nighttime. If you think about it, you never hear crows at night. You never really hear birds of any kind at night. There's a reason. It's not natural. And it's terrifying. Still, I sense a new respect for us in the smoker. If it's born from fear, so be it.

"Do you want us to get rid of the crows?" I ask.

The smoker eyes me. He's sizing us all up in a new light, especially Chaco and Grant.

"You know we can do it," I say. "We know why they're here. But we need to talk to the sand painters first. And we need to do it soon."

The six that surround us are still moving in, inching closer while the smoker thinks. At the last second, just as I see Chaco's beak flashing to strike, the smoker holds up a hand.

"Follow me," he says. "And stay on the path."

· · ·

WE WALK single file behind the smoker, and his sandals make loud clicks in the heavy silence that falls after the cacophony of the crows. Two of the six people that surrounded us follow in the rear. The rest fade away again, back to watch the road, I suppose. The first thing we pass is a big-wheeled Jeep. The tires look more expensive than the car, which is missing its back doors, and when the smoker passes the driver's-side door he taps the window three times. Someone is inside, and they honk three times. The honk is echoed across the camp. A warning that outsiders are coming in. Hide anything you don't want strangers seeing.

I'm not exactly sure what I expected to see at the Arroyo. Albuquerque has a pretty big drug problem and the vagrant problem that goes along with it, so I guess I was expecting something like Commons Park in ABQ, which isn't too far from my old apartment: a bunch of homeless kids mixed in with grizzled drifters, all of them milling around giving each other shady handshakes, rifling through piles of their belongings looking for some odd or end.

The Arroyo isn't like that. I don't know if it's the culture of the place, where they sort of police their own, or if it's the more private nature of the Navajo in general, but I don't see any trouble. I sense trouble behind shuttered camper windows or in zipped tents where lights are snuffed as we pass, but that's where it stays. What I do see is men drinking around a campfire, laughing. Quieting when we pass and watching us carefully, then laughing again (probably at our expense). I smell people cooking meat and beans and grease. I hear kids shouting and running, and I think of Ben and Joey dashing all over this place. Climbing and jumping and racing between campsites.

We round the corner and move from the more ramshackle tenements to places that look almost homey.

These are clean and swept. Some campers have welcome mats and potted desert flowers. Most of the cars look functional. The far side is where the reserved spots are. In the lights of the campers, I see people who look older, some very old. The smoker catches me peering, and I look straight ahead, embarrassed.

We walk the entire perimeter, to the opposite side of the entrance from the road, where the semicircle camp butts up against a low rock rise that isn't level enough to set a tent or a camper upon. The smoker stops us ten or so feet back from a pop-up camper that looks as though it popped up decades ago and stayed that way. In the low light that leaks from the windows I see pruned flowers and old-growth brush hemming it in on all sides. It looks like something that sprouted up from the desert itself, with the same sand coloring and the same stark lines.

"Wait," says the smoker. "Don't wander." He dusts ash off the front of his jersey and hitches up his shorts a little then walks up to the front door of the camper and knocks softly, stepping back to wait. After several minutes, a woman opens the door. She's dressed in a light- blue nightgown covered by a faded pink robe. He speaks with her quietly, but Chaco can hear.

Grant whispers to us the gist of what they're saying: "This is where both of the brothers live. She's related somehow. He's asking if they can talk to us. He's calling us outsiders but says we know the crows."

The woman takes a step down and peers out into the darkness at us. She shakes her head several times then speaks with the smoker. "She says no way. They're getting ready for bed." Grant's voice is low with disappointment. The smoker seems to understand. He's already turning away. The woman takes one last look at us, squinting into the dark. Her body turns to go inside, but her head lingers for another moment, as if she's confused. She stops and turns back fully to face us. Then she takes a step down.

"Doctor?" she says. All of us turn to Owen, who looks as surprised as anyone.

"Yes?" he replies.

"O," she says. "Doctor O."

"That's right. I'm Owen. Owen Bennet. Do I know you?"

The woman ignores his question and bustles down the last step and over to us. She holds out her hands to Owen, and he takes them. She's smiling, and her smoke is suddenly warm and reaching. She takes one hand and points at a small scar on her neck, where her thyroid is. Or was. I can see what happened there. Faint purple stretch marks circle the lower edge of her neck, where Owen most likely treated a goiter. It was probably large, but it's all but invisible now, save for the scar and what remains of the stretch marks. Owen laughs once.

"I remember you," he says faintly, his eyes wide. "Right when I first came here, the CHC volunteer crew arranged to pick you up for treatment near the turnoff. That was well over a decade ago, though. You still remember me?"

She doesn't understand, but she beams at his words anyway. "Maya," she says.

"That's right. You're Maya. My God, you look like a different person."

She smiles until her eyes nearly disappear. Then she looks at me and Grant. She takes Chaco strangely in stride, which I think is a good sign. She takes Owen's hand and brings him forward then motions for all of us. "Come," she says.

Owen follows her up and inside the main room of the camper, which is bisected into two equal sides, with two beds made neatly with similar woven blankets. The kitchen smells vaguely of a rich spice I can't place, but it's orderly as well, all the dishes freshly washed, still dripping on the rack. I'm wondering how the heck she thinks all of us are going to fit in here, especially since the smoker still isn't willing to leave us, for better or worse, but my fears are put to rest when she takes another few steps and exits down and out of the opposite door on the side of the camper facing the Arroyo.

Here there's a small fire in a raised fire pit about the size of a hubcap. Enough light to see close up, but not enough to mute the stars that seem scattered above the desert like an arc of thrown glitter. Two men look up at us, both seated in old loungers, the type you'd find in a frat house common room. They wear light jackets, and their legs are covered with woven throws. They're small men, diminished by age, but they sit still with a solid presence and seem absolutely unsurprised to see us here. Even Chaco. Maybe especially Chaco.

"Chaco remembers these two," Grant says quietly. "From his time before me. When he was a different bird, with Ben's grandmother."

Both men nod at Chaco first, and Chaco nods back. Each of us steps forward and introduces ourselves, and when it's done, all of us wait in silence. The men turn to each other and mutter something I don't think anyone could possibly hear, much less understand, but afterward the one on the left says, "Tsosi," and the one on the right says, "Tsasa."

That done, Maya starts fussing around looking for four seats in a square patch of land no more than twenty feet wide. I try to tell her not to worry, that we'll stand, but she's not having it. Eventually I end up in a slightly busted lawn chair, Owen and Grant on two glazed stumps of wood. The smoker seems content to stand out by the periphery of the light, toward the stars, where he lights up another cigarette and waits.

Everyone waits. I wait too, until I realize everyone is waiting for me. They want me to say something, to kick all this off, but to be honest with you I never really thought we'd get much past the turnoff. Also, I'm not sure what these people can understand, or what they can tell me, in English. So I'm sort of in a bit of a pickle, here. With no better ideas jumping to mind, I start by taking out the black book. As soon as they see it, the brothers frown, and Tsosi makes a sucking sound with his teeth that reminds me so much of Ben's grandmother that I have to take a breath to steady my head.

"Do you know what this is?" I ask. The brothers still frown. Maya looks back and forth between us and then shrugs, but I think it's because she can't understand what I'm asking. I look at Chaco, who squawks, and for one insane moment I think maybe they can understand bird squawk. I let it hang in the air for a second, but it does us no good. The sand painters don't understand bird—nobody does but Grant and Ben. I take a deep breath and rub at my face. This is going to be harder than I thought. Then the smoker chimes in from the dark. In Navajo. The brothers respond, and he interprets for us.

"They don't. Not exactly. But they don't like it," he says.

I glance at Chaco, who nods. We're all on the straight here.

"Neither do I. Not exactly," I say. "But it's important, because I think it can help us catch the skinwalker."

The word slips out before I can stop it, and it has an immediate effect. The smoke of both men, heavy and still and a rich chestnut in color, freezes. Maya's face is drawn, and the smoker hisses at us, then spits. "We don't talk witch-craft here. Not with the old generation. And definitely not now." The smoker looks carefully behind him at the trash pit, where the crows sleep again. He shivers, like we just sneezed in the cave of a sleeping bear and everyone's waiting to see if it'll wake up.

"But how will we ask them anything? It's what we came here for," Grant says.

"You talk about the crows. They'll get your meaning."

"But the crows aren't the problem. They're just here because they go where things are out of balance," Owen says, before the smoker cuts him off.

"Listen, *Dr. O*," he says, making it clear he doesn't have quite the shine for Owen's position that Maya does. "You and your friends gotta learn how to talk around what you mean, or you'll never get anywhere with the old-timers. It's not their way to be direct."

Owen sits back a little, and I can tell he's stung. That's something he should have known. Something I should have remembered too. But we've been gone too long. I hold up my hands in apology.

The brothers' smoke stirs again, tentatively.

"There's a list of things in this book that I was hoping you two could explain to us. Tell us what they mean. Tell us what to do."

That came off as desperate, all right. Which was my initial plan. But now that I realize how desperate it sounds I'm wondering if I should rethink my approach. The broth-ers' smoke is stilling again. Maya looks awkwardly at us from out of the corner of her eye. I can hear the smoker shaking his head, spitting again. I was too direct. That's not the way. But what is the way? I'm starting to panic. I scratch at my neck, and I can feel it puff up with irritation. Suddenly

I'm thinking about my puffy scratches and not about the book or what's inside of it, and now my train of thought is totally derailed and I'm thinking again about that stupid chai tea latte, which is *so* irresponsible at a time like this—downright *rude*—but I have nothing else to say. I feel like I'm breathing way too fast.

"Tell us about the Coyote Way," Grant says quietly. The tension snaps. The brothers seem to understand him, or at least those few words. Their smoke stirs then breaks and starts to flow over them again. They start talking to one another, nodding, not speaking to us, but letting us in on the conversation. The smoker interprets.

"The Coyoteway is a Way Chant. A healing ceremony. With a Singer and all that. Tsosi is saying how he went to one as a child, by Shiprock. His dad was the Singer. Tsasa was off chasing some girl, and he missed it. Their dad was pissed. They're laughing about it, because the Coyoteway is a super-long chant. Nine days long, if it's done right. That's a long time to chase after tail."

A healing ceremony doesn't sound like what we need. What we need is a plan to catch a coyote, not heal it. I don't think it can *be* healed. What it is, what it's made of, isn't something that can be cured. But even if a Coyoteway is the key, nine days is way too long. We have two until the market. The way Owen looks at me, I know he's thinking the same thing. If we started right now, we'd still be too late. It's a dead end.

I look at the book, and I'm feeling numb. The brothers' words wash over me, talking about their own stories, talking circles around our problem, and I stop paying attention. I see the strange objects written down in the book, glittering in ink that's impossibly black. I want to spit them all out at the feet of the brothers and see what sticks, but I know that would do us no good and only serve to still their smoke again. What would Ben do? I look desperately at Chaco, who titters at me, low and sad.

"Just talk," Ben would say. I can almost hear him say it too, and I wonder if he's here right now. I bet he is. He wouldn't miss this. I try to feel his presence, walking around us. I reach out desperately in my mind for the rich earthen red of his smoke. I knew it, once. I think of one of the first times I saw it, when I was in his house and he was strapped to the chemo, and I asked him what he wanted to do, to take his mind off the poison that was coursing through him.

"Just talk," he said. When I asked him what he wanted to talk about, he said, "Anything. You first."

We need to take another step back, here. What if we're not talking about a specific chant, but something bigger? Something like the *way* of the coyote?

"Tell us about the coyote," I say, interrupting, then cover my mouth. "Sorry, I uh. Was that too direct?"

The smoker actually smiles. "Sometimes the only way to get these two to shut up is to interrupt them. Otherwise you'll be here 'til you're as old as them."

He poses my question. The brothers take it in stride. Their conversation never misses a beat. In fact, they seem more animated, and Maya is even smiling now. I catch Owen's eye, and he grins at me. Grant seems transfixed by the old men and the loping sound of their voices. The smoker interprets.

"Coyote is a lot of things. A shifter. A trickster. He's good and bad. He can even be a god."

"How do you catch Coyote?" Owen asks. "If he's a trickster and a shifter and a god?"

The smoker speaks and then listens with us, his cigarette forgotten.

"Coyote may be a shifter and a god, but he's also a gambler, and sometimes a fool. He falls for tricks as often as he dishes them out, and he'll put it all on the line to get his prize."

Tsosi points to the sky as he speaks, and all of us follow his voice as it lifts up into the night above us.

"Coyote did that," the smoker says. "The Milky Way. Black God was putting the stars into the sky real careful like, one at a time, in all the right shapes, but Coyote was bored, impatient, so he threw the rest up to make the Milky Way. He's powerful, but reckless. To catch Coyote you just need to take away his warning signs. Without them he will run headlong into your trap."

"Warning signs?" I ask. I feel like we're getting closer, still circling around what we need to know, but the circles are tightening. The wood in the pit collapses to red ash, and Maya puts another log on. A desert wind kicks up, and it scatters tiny embers into the sky, where they glow for a heartbeat before they snuff out. Tsosi confers with Tsasa then clears his throat and begins to speak, and the smoker follows a few moments later.

"One day Coyote woke up at camp and decided to walk. He set out toward the east but started growling, you know? Like how dogs growl for no reason. So he turned back. Then he started south, but his nose began to twitch, like he smelled something bad, so he turned back again. He's wondering what all this means, right?"

The smoker's cigarette dangles in his mouth as he talks.

"He sets off west this time, but his ears start ringing, so he turns around again. All that's left is north, but as he starts off that way he gets all itchy. His skin twitches, and he can't take it, so he turns around again and goes back to camp."

The smoker pauses and lets the brothers roll on for a bit. Then he starts in, talking low so they'll keep going.

"So Coyote does this four times, right? And the whole time he's freaking out about all these weird feelings he's getting. He's trying to figure it all out when this guy emerges, right from the desert." The smoker cocks his head and listens then reassesses. "Well, not just a guy, but a thing too. Sort of both. And he says, 'I'm your birth bag, Coyote. I'm what you came from. And I say your home is that way.'"

Thankfully, it's dark enough and Maya and the smoker are so wrapped up in the story that the fact that the three of us are suddenly sitting like we've got steel rods for spines goes unnoticed. This is what we're looking for. I doubt there are a ton of stories about birth bags and coyotes in Navajo lore, and this night feels like it doesn't have any room for coincidences.

"So Coyote walks the way he was told, until he makes camp again. In the morning he sets out, runs into the same problems. The buzzing, the growling, the itching, the smells. He's stuck, until another thing comes up from the desert. This time it's a burned stick, but *not* a burned stick, you know? Something more, to Coyote. And the burned stick tells him where to go from there."

I imagine even Ben is still, now. If he ever was pacing around the fire, I bet he's not anymore. The smoker seems to struggle with his translation when he gets to the birth bag that isn't quite a birth bag, and the burned stick that isn't quite a burned stick, but I get it. I know all about things that aren't what they seem. All three of us carry objects that are more than they appear.

"Coyote does this four more times. Each morning he wakes up, he's lost again. He can't figure out what to do, where to go, but each morning he gets help from these things. On the third day it's a broken pot. On the fourth day it's a ratty old cane. On the fifth it's a little broom. The sixth day it's a broken stirring stick, like for a cook pot. They tell him where to go, and he eventually finds himself at his home, where he sacrifices again and again and again until he becomes a god himself."

Sacrifices again, and again, and again. I think of Owen telling me about the bodies pulled from the lockers one at a time so he could examine each. Of the way the mortician twitched. Bit at his own tongue. Could that really have been something like the Navajo Coyote, showing himself for a brief time? Gambling by laying out his cards face up on the table, showing us that his hand is almost full? The brothers suddenly laugh to each other, nodding in agreement. It's a warm *kyuk kyuk kyuk* that both men share. I look over at the smoker expectantly.

"They think it's funny that Coyote was warned again and again not to go the wrong way, but he didn't recognize it. Like most men. Without direction, we would be lost. Coyote came to see that the things he was feeling, the itching and the growling and all that, those were his warning signs. The things from the desert showed him that. Without those things, he'd be doomed."

"These things that warn Coyote," Owen begins then stops, obviously choosing his words carefully. I can tell this part frustrates him the most. His entire life, until he met me, he lived in a world where things were exactly what they looked like. Things worked exactly as they were supposed to. Treatments had outcomes. Things were documented, ordered, peer-reviewed. But not anymore. "Can we find these things here? Now? They seem so simple."

The smoker speaks with the brothers for a moment. They lob these beautiful words back and forth like a slow tennis match, where everyone playing doesn't have to move much because nobody cares too much about winning. Then he turns to us.

"They're simple, but they're not," he says. "They're things that Coyote took and made his own."

Tsasa leans forward and with his bare hands plucks a small strip of half-burned wood from the fire pit in front of us. The brothers watch it for a moment as it fades from angry red to dull then puffs a wisp of smoke into the air, the fire gone out. Tsasa starts speaking again, and the smoker interprets.

"Yesterday this would have been just a burned stick, right? Nothing more, nothing less. Eventually it would turn to ash and be forgotten. It's Coyote's stick just like every stick could be Coyote's."

Tsasa passes it to Maya then indicates for her to give it to us. It goes around the circle until Grant hands it to me.

"But today it's much more. Now it takes on your journey. Your strength in coming here. It has the Arroyo in it. It has all of us, this night, this sky where these stars look just like they do. Now it's much more. Now it's powerful. Now you have taken it back from Coyote."

Maybe it's just the night, or the fire, or the fact that I've got two ancient Navajo guys telling me an ancient story under the stars when half an hour ago I thought I was gonna lose my purse and maybe have my Chuck Taylors tossed over whatever passes for the equivalent of a telephone wire here at the Arroyo, but I feel it. The burned stick is heavier than it has any right to be. Its colors are richer. Its wood-smoke smell is stronger.

"Keep it," the smoker says. "They think you're gonna need it."

Both brothers watch us carefully now, their eyes reflective pools in the firelight. It occurs to me that when we asked how to catch a coyote, they immediately started in on the Navajo figure. They didn't go into, oh, say, how to hunt and kill an actual coyote, which might be the sane thing to discuss. Tsosi says something quietly, and the smoker speaks.

"If you find the rest of Coyote's warning signs, they invite you to the hogan over the hill. They say it's as good a place as any to set a trap."

The brothers seem half asleep when we say our good-byes, but they pat our hands and nod farewell. Maya clasps Owen's hands once more and says good-bye in a way that sounds more like *good luck*. On the walk back around the crescent, the Arroyo is much quieter, the lanterns fewer and farther between. There are no more laughing men or playing children. I get the sense that things should be different, maybe even had been different as recently as a few months ago, but people are circling the wagons even at the Arroyo. Afraid of what is happening outside.

"You gonna catch a coyote and get rid of my crows?" the smoker asks at the gate.

"We'll do what we can," I say.

He nods. "That one and his friends can stay, though," he says, pointing at Chaco. "I like that one." He takes a drag. "Old-timers talk in circles, but now that they're back there and we're up here, I'll go ahead and say it. Coyote may be a god—sometimes he is, sometimes he ain't. But for my money, he's definitely a witch. And a mean one at that."

Before any of us can answer, the smoker nods again, then he simply turns around and walks away.

19

GRANT ROMER

I'm walking to school with Mick. For the past couple of days he's been waiting for me at the edge of the Crownrock RV Park in the morning. He doesn't say much, just leans against the rusted park sign with his hands in the baggy pockets of his shorts then walks with me when I come down the path. I'm not sure how I feel about it, since the only reason he's doing it is 'cause I'm white. I mean, he can't know me yet as a person. I've been at Crownrock High for a week. But I suppose it's better than walking alone.

I know my mind should be on broken pots and stirring sticks and birth bags and all that crap, but instead it keeps coming back to the market and the Crownrock booth there that I gotta take apart and reattach after the dumbass morning crew drilled an unpainted crossbeam right through the middle of it on accident. And then there's Kai. And Hosteen, her brother, who now comes to every prep session I'm at and manages to get into an argument every time with Kai over something I still can't quite figure. Chaco thinks I'm nuts. He's flying high above us now, making a point not to talk to me, which is fine by me because I know what he'd say: "You're screwing around in this high-school-drama crap when the devil is at the gates." And I'd say what I've been saying: If Crownrock High is good enough for the coyote to case—and it definitely is, its tracks are everywhere, worse by the day—then it's good enough for me.

Mick isn't happy that I stuck with market prep. He doesn't understand why I'd want to do something for the Navajo, who never did a damn thing for him or his family and he thinks won't do a damn thing for me. Mick's family works in construction and got some contract on the rez that he says the Navajo are constantly messing with and rewriting and "dragging ass on."

"You sure you don't want to chill with me after school?" he asks. "I got some cool places to show you around here. Some cool shit." Mick hitches up his shorts and walks with a bit of a fake limp.

"Market's in two days, Mick. I wanna finish this thing, then you can show me whatever you want."

"You know Hos is gonna kick your ass if you make a move on Kai. You know that, right? He's been walking around for weeks now just looking for someone's ass to kick."

Of all the people in school, Hosteen is probably the one I should be trying to avoid. I've heard people talking at lunch about how he and his family go way back at the Arroyo and rumors of some bootlegging gambit his family runs. But of all the people in school, he's the one that shows the most signs of being wrapped up in whatever our coyote has planned.

"I dunno, man. I don't think it's me he's pissed at. It's something else. Like you said, he's been thugged up for weeks now. He's got something else in mind."

"I heard he's got something planned for the market,

something big," Mick says, and I wait quietly, in case he knows more than he's letting on, but his mouth is shut.

"You got any idea what it might be?" I ask.

"What the fuck do I care what these Injuns do? If you're worried about it, stay away from the market."

We walk the rest of the way in silence, but Mick gives me a fist bump when he turns off at the stairs for his first class on the second floor. Mick is weird like that. He talks like he's pissed off, then he's friendly like nothing happened. I've been trying to get a feel for what the rest of the school thinks of the guy, but all I've found out is that nobody talks about him. Same as me. I sort of came one day, everyone checked me out, then everyone moved on the way they've been moving all year. Everyone except for Kai, that is. Kai looks for me in the halls. I've seen it. She sort of cranes her neck around to look for me every day when she comes out of first period near my locker. She's the only one outside of Mick who really acknowledges that I exist here, but two is better than none.

The classes are fine. The classes are classes. Pretty easy, actually. I think Owen went a little crazy with his Professor Bennet's Education Emporium routine. From what I gather, I'm at least a grade, maybe two, ahead of the rest of the kids my age. I don't let it show. I try not to let anything about where I come from show. Not any cash, not any smarts, and definitely not the bell. I've got one shot here to make myself what I want to be, which is a kid who maybe could call this place home. Mick would say no chance, but I think Mick is kind of a loser.

The Crownrock booth has been moved outside into the back parking lot and roughly disassembled. It lies in five different pieces that will eventually join together to make a decent- sized, three-walled enclosure with a stage in the middle. The stage is for the dance crew. Crownrock has a dance crew that does your standard popular music routines but also traditional Navajo stuff. Sometimes a mix of the two. The three walls also exhibit student art, which is for sale. The art is OK. A few things are pretty good. But they tell me they sell out every year.

I fall in with the crew holding up the top part of one wall while another two guys take apart the bottom with power drills so we can get to the bare crossbar. A few people nod at me, sort of. At least they shuffle to make room for me. That's a victory, I guess. I find myself looking at people's mouths, trying to see what Ben saw on the street with the coyote and the bead, or what Owen saw with the guy in the morgue. It's tough, though. Everybody in high school chews gum all the time. And as for acting weird, well, hell. Take your pick. There's this guy in my history class who talks to himself all the time. Another kid in English lit blurts out cuss words at strange times, and nobody acts like it's weird at all.

I get pretty into the woodworking part. Pap would be proud. I picked up a good base from him, so I actually know a bit about this stuff. I break open the existing joint without cracking things then pull out the crossbar with the help of two or three other kids. We set it on a bunch of flat cardboard that we spread out so we don't get paint all over the parking lot, then get to painting. The other kids still don't talk to me, but I get the feeling that they're more comfortable every day talking *around* me. It sounds pathetic, but it's true. I think it helps just being here. I get to dippin' and slidin'.

I think I lose track of time a bit, because the next thing I know I'm done with the base coat and it's time to put in the designs, which are the type of traditional Navajo connected triangles that you see all over New Mexico, painted in the colors of Crownrock High, which I only just learned are the blue and red I've been getting all over my clothes for a week. Could be worse, I suppose. The Sargaso kids have to deal with adobe pink. That's rough.

I'm about to go search for the right buckets when two of them plunk down right next to me, and then Kai plunks down too. She's wearing paint-streaked jean shorts and an old art smock, which is really just a ratty men's dress shirt about ten sizes too big that she wears backward. She's got flecks of paint in her jet-black hair and a few little drops on her thighs. She sits cross-legged, leans back on her palms, and watches me for a second.

I think I must be staring, because eventually she looks down at her smock and then says, "What? I think it's a pretty good look for me."

"It works."

"What's your deal, Grant?" she asks. She's not smiling at me, not exactly, but her words sound like she's smiling. I think it's something the Navajo can do.

"My deal?"

"You've been here, what, a week? And instead of checking out the football team or the lacrosse club or just bugging out with the other white kids, you've been here every day, painting a market booth for stuff you have nothing to do with."

I shrug. "I dunno. Maybe because I want to have something to do with it. Plus, I'm not really the football or lacrosse type."

She nods. She's chewing gum too. I hope. Yeah, I know. It's just gum.

"Kind of hard to play in black jeans," she says.

"They ain't so black anymore." Two days ago I dumped a

blot of white primer on my jeans. It won't scrub out. They're sort of motley now.

"*Aren't.*" I correct myself, awkwardly late.

"Yeah, well then maybe you *ain't* gonna mind getting a little blue and red here and there," she says, and she pops open both cans, stirring each up with one side of the same stick. She hands me a washed brush. "Stick between the lines."

We paint in silence for a while. Or maybe I should say she paints in silence. I test about a million lines of dialogue in my head, and I'm about ready to sweat with how much I'm trying to stay between the lines when she says, "Since you basically painted the whole thing, are you gonna go to market to see it in action?"

To be honest, I'd been so focused on the setup and hopefully seeing Kai, exactly the way that's happening right now, that I haven't given much thought to actually going to the market or not.

"'Cause if you were," she says, turning back to the design, "there's this big party some of the alumni kids throw at Marcy Park—"

"Of course he's gonna go," says a voice from behind me. It's deadly even, and I know exactly who it is without looking. My shoulders want to sag, but I don't let them. "That's who the market's for," he says. "*Bilagáana* like him, right? Look at me when I'm talking to you."

I set down my brush carefully on a corner of cardboard and stand up. I turn around, and Hos is about a foot from me, his entourage of ogres with him. He's shorter than me, but not by much, and the way he's looking at me is like I'm about an inch tall anyway. He's wearing another cutoff T-shirt and loose jeans with boots. His shoulders sport a bunch of tattoos that look Navajo that I never noticed before. He's probably no more than two years older than me, but it looks like he and I are on opposite sides of the spectrum of life.

"Right, kid?"

I'm stunned. I think adrenaline has wiped my brain. I have no idea what he's talking about. "What?" I ask.

"The market, fucknuts. That's where your kind peruses our kind. Right? Like a zoo, sort of, except we dance for you and hold out pots and beads for you?"

"I dunno, man," I stammer. "I ain't never been to the market before." The other kids have stopped working, once again, and are gathering around the fringes. Hos is on a roll.

"Let me tell you, then. It basically goes like this." He takes the stick Kai stirred the paint with and wipes it on his hands. "A bunch of Indians from all around the country paint themselves up like this and hope white people notice them and give them money." He slams my chest with his open palm and leaves a blue-and-red palm print. I back up a pace but keep my feet. "And white people like you look for great deals on authentic Indian shit for their condos and then hope that the actual Indians will just go back to wherever they came from once the big show is over."

"Leave him alone, Hosteen," Kai says. She's still sitting down, facing forward, but all that hidden shine that she had is gone once again. "It's not his fault."

Hos looks at her and shakes his head. "I know that, Sister." He crouches down until his face is right behind her head, but she still won't look at him. "It's *our* fault. For not doing something about it. For letting them walk all over us. But all that's about to end. And it's not too late for you to join us. There's still time to make your clan proud."

He stands again and turns to me. He looks at his print on my shirt and smirks. "Looks better than it did before." He moves the paint stick closer to me. "Maybe we oughta mark you up a little more, huh?" His two ogre bodyguards move to the other side of me, and now Kai is looking up at me. She looks scared. And that's the first time in this whole fracas that *I* start to get scared. Hos takes another step and raises the stick to swipe it across my face, but then I hear a beating of wings. Big wings. It sounds like somebody is shaking out a sheet. And I know what's coming, so I duck. Chaco lets out a single explosive call, and all I see is a shadow with inch-long talons swipe at Hos from behind. I can actually hear one talon strike home on his forearm. It makes a *zip* sound as it cuts him from his elbow all the way up to his hand, then Chaco is away again.

I stand up and find Hos staring at his bleeding forearm. I can already see that it'll scab but won't scar. Chaco held back, but the paint stick is basically gone. Just a nub of it remains in his hand. Some of the kids start yelling, not sure what they just saw. They're pointing at the roof of the gym, where Chaco perches with the stick in his grasp. Even at this distance he looks big. Kai stands and shields her eyes to get a better view of him, then she starts to laugh. She points at Hos's big buddies. There's a clear line of bird shit running over both of them, shoulders and heads and all. It's as if I dipped my brush in a bucket of the stuff and flung it at 'em in a big arc. All three of them start fuming. They want to be mad at me, but they can't. I didn't do anything.

"Stupid fucking bird," Hos mutters. "Must have thought the stick was food or some shit."

"Maybe," I say.

He looks at me with fire in his eyes. "Maybe? The fuck does that mean, *maybe*?"

I shrug. "It means maybe."

He looks at me sidelong for a cold ten seconds or so then

turns to Kai. "Get up. Time to go. This booth is as done as it's gonna get."

I can see that Kai doesn't want to leave, but she gets up anyway and shoulders her bag. She looks at me briefly, and her eyes say *sorry*. She shoulders past Hos and his crew, and they close ranks behind her. I can't see her, but I can hear her walking away.

Hos takes one last look at Chaco, who takes this moment to let out three opportune *caws*. Hos looks to be weighing something carefully in his mind, then he shakes his head.

"See you at the big dance, *bilagaana*. Make sure you're there." Then he winks at me.

He walks off, his bleeding arm seemingly forgotten. The rest of his crew don't even spare me a glance as they follow him. Once they're gone, all of my adrenaline dumps, and I'm instantly exhausted. I feel like I'm gonna fall asleep onto the fresh paint, but I finish the design. When the crew leader, a big senior gal, says that's a wrap and that we'll reassemble everything in Santa Fe, I clap along with everyone else then grab my backpack and go. Nobody seems to notice except for Chaco. He flies right above me.

"You all right there, boss?" he asks me, the first words he's spoken to me all day.

"Yeah," I say. "Thanks for helping me out back there."

"No prob. You know, I think you're right, man. That one is trouble. He may be wrapped up in all this. Maybe our coyote."

"And all I did was piss him off."

Suddenly I feel like an idiot. Maybe Mick was right when he said I was crazy to help out with the market crew. Nobody seemed to give a damn if I was there or not. Even Kai thought it was weird. What was the point of all that?

What was I trying to do? Be an Indian? Did I think some paint and a few nails would turn me Navajo?

"It was all a waste of time, man," I say.

"You never know," Chaco replies. I can hear him coming in low. "Heads up," he says.

He backpedals above me and drops something from his claws. I snatch it out of the air and slow to a stop. It's the paint stick, half red, half blue. I can see little imprints where Kai's fingers smudged the paint. I can't stop staring at it. The paint is so bright it almost sparkles in the sun, and her fingerprints are cleanly pressed, like whorled ice crystals. Even the jagged end where it broke looks beautiful, like the splinters could tell a story. It feels heavy.

"What's that look like to you?" Chaco asks.

"A paint stick." But already I know it's not. It's more.

"See, to me that looks like a certain broken stirring stick we've been on the hunt for."

He's right. The story of my arrival at Crownrock is wrapped up in this stick. It might have been the coyote's once, before I came, but I took it back. Kai helped, and Chaco helped. Even Hos helped in his own way. I grin to think that our coyote himself might have handed me one of his warning signs.

Either way, that's two down, four to go.

20

THE WALKER

It's almost three in the morning, the night before the market, and I'm walking the soft streets of Santa Fe. They literally look soft. They're so old in places that the stones and bricks dip and crest like frozen ripples in a pond. A lot of Navajo kind of roll their eyes at Santa Fe. Part of it is because white people love it so much. Part of it is because for a while in the 1900s it was a place where the Navajo could actually live and work. Now it's a place where rich people eat and shop. I don't know a single Navajo who could afford a place in this city, so I get where they're coming from. But don't blame the city. It's old as hell. Since I died, I've gotten a lot of perspective. Forget what happened in the 1900s, try the 1500s. Or the 900s. People were here then too. You don't have that much history without also getting a little magic. You can feel it here, in the old streets, the old churches, the old hills dotted with old graves. This city is an old rock in the desert. It's been hot and cold and hot again, and it doesn't seem to care what anybody thinks. I like it. So sue me.

Usually Santa Fe is a pretty quiet city too, despite all the tourists, but not tonight. Not even at 3:00 a.m., and it certainly won't be tomorrow. Whatever creeping unease taints the rez has spread here. I know the coyote has been here too. His breath seems to hang dead in the night air. Distrust is everywhere, even between the volunteers and cops that sit at the intersections. These guys should be shootin' the shit, sneaking off to get arepas and maybe even a beer if they aren't in uniform. Every year the NNPD sends a couple lucky bastards to represent here. I was chosen one year when Chief Yokana felt particularly sorry for me about everything around Ana. It's a cakewalk. A paid vacation. But not today. Today everybody is yelling at everybody. Micromanaging things like cordons and cones that nobody really needs. Waving cars off and getting pissy whenever the booth people ask for something.

I'm trying to mark these things more than just in passing. I'm trying to look for patterns, maybe find a way to track the coyote, to be where he wants to be before he brings down the house, because I think he's gonna bring down the house. We've got a way to catch him now, if we can beat the clock, thanks to the sand painters, and thanks to Caroline, but we've got to act fast.

You should have seen her by the campfire. She was unreal in the night light of the Arroyo. I couldn't quite believe what I was seeing. Caroline, right there where Joey and I used to raise hell. Caroline, walking into the very place the NNPD tells even the Navajo to steer clear of if they can help it. I never thought I'd live to see the day an Arroyo campfire would play off the warmth of her eyes. Turns out I didn't live to see it. But what I got was the next best thing. At one point, I swear she looked for me. I was there, listening, next to the smoker (which, at the rate that guy rips cigs, I bet I'll be seeing again pretty soon), but her eyes passed right through me just as sure as my hands pass right through booth after booth after booth under the heavy moonlight.

I feel the telltale pressure drop of a Chaco arrival, like an itch in my ear. There's the pop, and then I feel the wind of his wings and the heavy weight of him as he settles on my shoulders. I relax without knowing I was ever tense. Sometimes when your fingers pass through too many things, it starts to key you up, I guess. The solid weight of Chaco feels good. Like a fat file folder of finished work. Not that I'd ever tell the ungrateful bastard.

"We got two," he says.

"No kidding?"

"Yeah, the stirring stick. It came from the school. It came around because of Grant."

I smile. That kid surprises at every turn. Here I was thinking maybe he'd give up and join a metal band. Instead he insists on enrolling at a Navajo high school and, for better or for worse, seems like he's hacking it. That can't be easy. They picked on me in high school because I was small, but even a small Navajo is still a Navajo. In the circles I ran with in high school the social scene went from the popular-jock-badass Navajo kids at the top to the skinny white boys like Grant at the bottom. What he's doing takes guts.

"I also think maybe he's right about the market," Chaco says. "Something big is gonna happen here, tomorrow night during the dances, most likely. Keep an eye on a kid everybody calls Hos." Chaco settles into the crook of my neck and gets small. He hasn't done that in years.

"That's a lead, Chaco. Why do you sound like you ate some bad Chinese?"

"I didn't believe him. I should have, but I didn't."

"Don't start moping now, right when we gotta get to work." I kind of gloat. I can't help it. Usually it's me whining and crying imaginary tears at one of my pity parties. I never get to sit at the other end of the table. He says nothing, only gets smaller.

"Look, man. The kid is fourteen. I'm sure he wasn't exactly being a good friend to you, either. His brain just got soaked in puberty. He'll even out eventually."

Chaco titters on my shoulder, which is his way of laughing. Then he gets bigger. "You'd think I'd know that after a couple thousand years. But I forget every time. Every Keeper is new for me, and I. . ."

"You care," I say. "It's a good thing. But if you're right about the dances, then we gotta bust our asses. They start in like twelve hours."

"Can we make a move on this Hosteen kid? If he's really a skinwalker, could the Circle jump him right now and take the bead?"

I shake my head. "The coyote is too tricky for that. If we make a move and it senses us coming, it could jump from Hosteen, maybe change up its plan totally, and then we've got what cops call an unknown. Unknowns are dangerous. Especially with this thing."

We walk down Canyon Road toward St. Francis Cathedral, which is this big church made out of stone that takes on a copper color at night. The cathedral marks the west boundary of Santa Fe Plaza, which is normally a big open square where people hang out and eat or drink around the obelisk statue at the center. A circle stage has been constructed around the center statue. It's where the dances will be performed. Beyond the viewing area, the entire square is crosshatched with rows of booths like mini city blocks on a grid. The booths spill out into adjacent streets in every direction. I see twenty or thirty people still setting up. The real procrastinators.

Then again, you could say the same about me right now. I should be hunting down artifacts of my own, I should be running around like a chicken with its head cut off, but instead I have this strange calm. Like I used to get in the car with Ninepoint when we'd quickly sketch out our approach to bringing in whomever we were after. I got some ideas that I want to run by Chaco first. I want to sketch out my approach like I used to.

"Man oh man," Chaco says, surveying the scene. "This is gonna be a beehive."

"The booths seem to go on forever this year. There's a great park at the edge of all this mess. You got a second to check it out?"

Chaco nods, and we set out, walking through the honeycombed streets without turning a single head.

The walk from the plaza to Marcy Park is a pleasant one. I take the uphill approach, through the old neighborhoods, every one of them the same type of covenant-controlled adobe and wood pillared construction. You get the sense that you've walked back in time, especially when you come across the houses that were built well before the covenant came around. The original adobe, patched and repatched, and still strong.

"I've been thinking about this bone bead," I say. "I don't think we're gonna be able to beat the coyote unless we destroy it. It moves too fast. It jumps from person to person. It's made of chaos, so there's no way we can reason with it. And if we do manage to trap it, it's gonna be mad as hell."

Chaco cocks his head. "I think you're right. But we gotta tread carefully. No doubt this bone bead is a super powerful object. Think of it as a chaos bell."

"Then you're saying we shouldn't destroy it?"

Chaco does this *tiktiktik* thing with his throat that I've

learned is the same as when humans say, "Well, hold on just a second, now. . ."

"From what you said you saw in that cavern with the black pearl, I got a hunch that the pearl uses chaos souls to form the bead. The coyote has a place at the center of that pearl, and at the center of the coyote is the bead. So if I'm right, and we can fix all this by destroying the bead, the souls will just go back to making another bead for the coyote, only the coyote will be back where it's supposed to be. No harm, no foul."

"And if you're wrong?"

"Hellfire and brimstone. Take your biggest pile of shit and throw it right at the biggest fan you've got. Then throw in a bunch of crow feathers for giggles."

"I'm serious, bird."

"So am I. But it's no worse than what will happen if the coyote roams free. Either way, the river is out of whack, man. For all I know, beyond the veil is already a huge cluster. This bastard has been on a joyride from hell, not doing his *job* for *five years*."

Chaco hates when people don't do their jobs. That's what happens when you diligently do yours for a couple millennia.

We crest the hill and come up on Marcy Park from on high. It looks like a concert is being set up here. Tents and merchandise booths flank a big stage at the far end of a wide grass field. A handful of technicians are turtling around, checking stage equipment and lighting.

The two of us are quiet for a moment, taking in that strange stillness that can fall over a place in the twilight hours before it gets jammed with people.

"What happens when the bead is destroyed?" I ask

quietly. "I mean, I imagine that it's more than just a little crack of breaking bone."

"I'd imagine so, yeah."

"You don't know, do you?"

"I'm in new territory here, brother. Right along with you. I do know that no anchor object like that has ever been broken in living memory."

I suspect Chaco knows more than he's telling me. I can sense it in the way he's looking away from me, focusing on the park below. But that's OK, because I have some thoughts of my own about what happens when one of these things breaks, and I want to keep them to myself for a bit too.

"We're still a ways away from breaking the thing, Walker," Chaco says evenly. "We need to catch it first. We've got two of the coyote's artifacts. We're four short."

"Three," I say.

Chaco looks at me, his bird brow raised.

"We're three short. I think I know where one of them is. The broken pot. But it's not in any place any of the five of us can reach it."

"So what do we do?"

"I got an idea. The four of you keep at it. It's about time I visited my old buddy Joey."

21

CAROLINE ADAMS

I t's just before dawn on Saturday, the kickoff for the market. We've got twelve hours before the dances begin. Usually my 3:00 a.m. insomnia centers on obsessing over what passes for my love life. This time I've been up all night thinking about a whisk broom.

I'm not going to lie to you, I had to look online even to see what a whisk broom is. Turns out it's a little hand-held straw broom. Something old farm women dressed in babushkas would use to dust out their cook fires. I had an absurd urge just to buy one, right then. Enter my credit card information, pay for same-day shipping. Voilà. An individually packaged whisk broom, brought to my door. But I get the feeling that's not what the sand painters meant when they said the object is about the journey. A journey from a warehouse in Albuquerque to an RV park mail room doesn't have an ounce of spiritual weight to it, no matter how expedited.

None of us has slept. There's no time for sleep anymore. Not right now. Grant is already at Crownrock High with the setup crew, packing up for their trip to Santa Fe on a school bus. He was as chipper as he usually is, which is to say not at all, but at least his eyes were open. I have that gritty feeling that I used to get doing night shift at ABQ General. The one where it feels like the sandman comes by to knock you into sweet oblivion, except you have to tell him that no, in fact, you won't be sleeping tonight because you have to do rounds on a thirty-six-bed floor, but the sandman doesn't take that too well—he's the jealous type—so instead of sprinkling his dust on your forehead he chucks the whole bag right at your face. It fuzzes up your teeth and gets behind your eyes, and I know it won't be going away any time soon, so I put a pot of coffee on our little stove and get down to more thinking.

I'm halfway through my second cup when it occurs to me that Owen and I haven't had sex in a month. Don't ask me why this hits me out of the blue. It certainly has nothing to do with whisk brooms, but just like that I'm very disappointed in myself. I look out of the back window of the boat, where Owen is standing and watching the sunrise. He's been walking back and forth, checking odds and ends on the hitch and around the outside of the RV without actually doing anything. That's how he thinks. I can see it on him: he's completely invested in this, every ounce of his smoke is wrapped up in it, and I can't believe I haven't noticed the change in him before now.

In a way, he looks the same as he always did on the floor. He's driven, totally focused on the problem at hand, and you'd think that would be a good thing, but I also know that when he was that way on the floor—blind to everything else but the patients he was tasked with getting healthy again— it was a willful blindness. He told me so. He told me that work was the only thing that could take his mind off me.

I search the smoke sifting off him in the early-morning

light in slow, thick waves, and I can see it. I can see that longing, but it's tamped down. Packed under. He's doing it again. He's swapped one distraction for another. He's doing everything he can not to think about me, about us, about loving me the way that he does, and it's working. But it's also blocking him, plugging up his soul. The colors I see on him now aren't the true colors I know. His blue isn't as blue. Sure, there's a lot of it—he's throwing himself into this search with everything he's got—but it isn't as strong. And it makes me feel like garbage.

I set my coffee down and walk outside. He sees me coming and musters a heartbreaking smile. His hair, normally meticulously combed and evenly parted, is tufted here and there where it looks like he's been running his hands through it again and again. He's frustrated and stumped.

"I know I'm missing something with that damn broken cane." He lets his hands drop to his sides. "It's right there, on the tip of my brain, but I can't. . ."

I don't even say anything. I just take one hand and pull him gently toward the boat. He looks confused at first, then I see him understand, and a few things cross his smoke. At first he's incredibly hungry for me, in every way. I don't do this type of stuff. I'm not one of those girls that does this, grabs a guy by the hand and whispers something into his ear and takes him away to the bedroom on a whim. I'm a planner. Even when it comes to sex. I think of it in terms of time frames and schedules and recommended amounts. I know it's not romantic in the movie-star sense, but then again, I find weird things romantic. Opposite things. Things like the fact that there's no physical way Ben and I could ever be together, but sometimes I can still feel him reach for me. Things like I'm very probably ruined emotionally by what I've seen and done, but Owen still stays with me, by my side, and he loves me so fiercely he's afraid to let it show because he thinks it'll scare me. And it does. And I sort of like it.

The second thing I see in Owen's smoke is hesitation, and he pulls back gently.

"Caroline," he says, "I don't want this. I can't keep doing this."

He's not lying, not exactly, but his color tells me more of what he's thinking than his brain can right now. He does want this, and he can keep doing this, but it's taken him a long time to get right with living with half of my heart, and when we do things like this and I lose myself and he does too, there are a few seconds of eternity where I'm his completely. It's a beautiful lie that our bodies speak to each other.

And it's a lie we both need right now. I just need to let him know this without hurting more of him than I already do every day.

"I don't know why I can't move on from him, Owen. I'm split in half, and I don't know how to fix it. I wish I could tell you how awful I feel. I wish you could see it on me like I see it on you. You've been walking around with half of a companion. Half of a friend too. And I have no right to ask you to see it my way, but if you could, just think about what it's like to *be* half there. To live life with part of yourself missing. You help me. You shoulder some of that loss for me. Your heart is so huge, it makes up for what I'm missing. Not all of it, but enough to make it OK for a while. So I know it may not be right, or healthy, or whatever, but I'm just gonna say it: I need this. From you."

It works. I can see it immediately. Owen likes to know he's needed. Just like me. Just like everybody. He lets me take his hand again and follows me inside. We lock the little door and pull down the little blinds and clear off our little bed. We undress, and he hangs his shirt in the closet to keep it off the ground and lays his socks over his shoes, right to right, left to left. He folds his slacks at the crease and lays them over the pull-out dressing table. His little routine always makes me smile. I have one too: shorts folded under shirt, folded under bra, all set on my tiny nightstand, and panties off and in the hamper. No socks or shoes for me. I haven't worn shoes since May. Just flip flops. We do this in comfortable silence, like we have ever since that first time years ago, when it was a hilariously awkward dance around this box of a bedroom— but one that I had planned down to the minute while Grant was off getting groceries. All went according to plan, of course. I think you could actually hear the bubble of sexual tension pop that time. It was long overdue.

Owen gets in bed and makes a place for me under his arm, and I get in bed and fit there, and that's how it starts. We know each other now. I could sketch the dimple in his shoulder from the bullet he took for me, entry and exit. I know it by heart. I've felt it with my hand and with my arm and with my mouth. I also know he can fit the entire back of my head in the long palm of his hand. We know where we fit with each other, and that is exactly what we both need right now, when we don't know where we fit with everything else. We forget all that. All the to-dos, the artifacts, the ticking time bomb at the market, it's all blown from our minds for about twenty minutes on a scorching summer morning in the Navajo desert.

Afterward, Owen's smoke sifts peacefully down and around him, pooling in that teacup spot at the base of his neck, and it matches the blue of his eyes again. He's staring at the ceiling but seeing through it. It's like he's been abraded of something, scrubbed clean, which is why he says: "It's not the cane."

"What is it, then?"

"It's the exercises. Lelah, the secretary at CHC, she gave me the PT sheet I gave her with the donated walker, years ago. She didn't need the exercises anymore. Her pain was gone."

I sit up on one elbow. Now I'm really confused.

"It's been staring me in the face for days now. That was my journey, right there. That program was the first walk I took with the Navajo, with the CHC. The coyote tried to take it from me. I took it back."

Owen gets up and goes over to his nightstand, opens it up, and starts pulling things out. He shakes his head, moves over to the built-in table, lifts a stack of wiring instructions for the trailer, then lifts my magazines and rifles through all the pages. He shakes his head again. I can see him thinking for a minute before he goes over to his little closet and flips through it to find the slacks he wore that day. He frisks his pockets. Nothing. He turns around with his hands on his naked hips.

"It's in Chief Yokana's car," Owen says heavily. "I left it in his damn car."

He picks up his watch and clicks it over his wrist. He checks the time and frowns. I know what he's thinking. We're in the final hours now. I slide out of bed, walk over to my little pile of clothes, and get dressed. He does the same, careful to put the correct socks on the correct feet. I smile again, even with the seconds on the clock hammering home.

"Let's go find him, then," I say. He looks up at me and nods, and I feel like something that was coming loose between us is tied tightly again. We reach underneath our pillows for our totem pouches, and as soon as I grab mine it's like I'm stunned. It feels heavier, richer, like it's made of velvet and it's carrying thousands of diamonds instead of an ancient lump of turquoise fashioned into a crow. Owen has already pocketed his and is moving to the door, but he pauses when he sees me.

"Something wrong?"

I open up the pouch and pour it out on the bed, expecting something more than the crow, expecting that stream of diamonds to come pouring out, but it's just my totem, tumbling onto the bed. Solid as ever. I see the irregular notches in its wings, the sharp point of its searching beak. Its head, slightly turned, mid-flight, as always. And I realize it isn't the crow totem that shocked me this time. It's the pouch I'm still holding in my hand.

"What's up?" Owen asks, moving over to me now. He relaxes when he sees my totem, safe and whole.

I hold the pouch out to him. "Take it and tell me I'm not crazy. Touch it."

He takes it, and his eyes widen. He pulls his own pouch out of his pocket and squints at both, weighing them up and down in his hand.

"Is this the same one I gave you?" he asks. "It definitely feels different from mine. It's like it's in high def or something."

"It's the same old pouch."

"But I picked up both of them in that truck stop in Alamosa. They were a pair." He tosses mine back over to me. I catch it, and I'm struck again by how soft and full it feels. Like it's woven silk, when I know it's just old leather. Then I get it. It's not just old leather. It never was. It's more.

"You gave it to me," I say. "It's because you gave it to me. Only I never realized it until now."

"That I gave it to you?"

"No, what it meant. It's about the journey, right? That's what the sand painters said. When we got those crows and you said you wanted to come with me, it was because you wanted me then. Just me. But when you gave me the bag, and you got the same, it was because you wanted to do all of this *with* me. You weren't just there for me, you were there alongside me. Both of us were born into this new life together."

I see it dawn on him. "The birth bag," he says.

I blow out a breath, and a little bit of the weight that is pressing on me is lifted. "Thank God. I thought that one was gonna be really gross."

22

THE WALKER

Joey lives in an old conversion van just like his grandfather did at the Arroyo. Matter of fact, it's his gramp's van. After Joey drove off the rez that day when the tribal council turned their backs on him, and I did too, he kept going north, almost like he wanted to drive himself off the map altogether. I often picture him as he must have been then. Blinded by sadness and pain but refusing to give up until he made things right for my family. He was on a cannonball run, fleeing some demons, chasing others down. He must have been a hell of a sight.

For some reason he hit the brakes in Montana, just south of the Canadian border. He was running from the agents then, and the cops, so a border run was risky. He needed a place to lay low and figure things out, so he rolled his van into Hamm, a speck of a town fifty miles west of I-25 in the middle of the plains. He pulled up under an abandoned carport that was once attached to a tiny house, but the house collapsed who the hell knows how long ago, certainly well before he and I were racing around the rez together.

He parked the van, and it promptly died. And that's where it still sits to this day, over a decade later. Joey doesn't like to let anyone in the Circle know about it, but that's where he still lives most of the time. He might call it home, if he called any place home. But he doesn't call any place home anymore, and that's the problem.

Hamm, Montana, is one of those little towns you don't even catch a whiff of when you're cruising by. There are small towns—the kind where you might stop to gas up or grab a coffee to keep you going—and then there are *really* small towns. The kind that have four or five businesses on half a block, and that's Main Street. The kind that have one crossroad and no real trees and every single building is a flat, single-story square. And if you step back a few paces, you can take in the whole of the town in one look, underneath an enormous open sky that seems twice as big for how small everything else is. There are only ever a handful of people there, and they come and go all the time. A guy living out of his van, even a guy who looks a little rough and haunted like Joey, can do whatever the hell he pleases so long as he doesn't bother anybody, and Joey never does, because all Joey does is work on phasing.

Joey was the type of guy who did anything to get out of work back in the day. He and I were always looking for corners to cut, ways to slip away and do our own thing, which usually involved drinking beers or smoking cigarettes or throwing things at other things to see what happened. If you'd told me all those years ago that Joey would devote all of his time to studying and practice, I'd have laughed you out of the rez. It just wasn't him. Then again, he probably thought the same thing when he heard I became a cop. Sometimes shit doesn't go the way you think. People change.

His work with the crow totem damn near killed him. It

would have killed him at first, the way he just dived into the thin space and held the phase as long as he could, but he took so many drugs that his body stopped rebelling like it should. He overrode his instincts with chemicals. Soon he was able to spend hours in the thin space, then days. He started meditating in the thin space. I watched him as he sat in one place, cross-legged, crow in hand, until I thought he'd blow away into the cold, sepia dust that the thin place seems made of. But he never blew away.

Joey learned to do what the agents did, which was essentially to live in the thin place. Of course, the agents were driven by our coyote at the time. They had a connection with him through the book that I think was the only reason they were kept alive. Joey had drugs. Still, he was able to inhabit the place for long stretches of time, test what it had to offer. He came out of his meditations and trances with a connection to the world beyond that I haven't seen in anybody else, except maybe Caroline. That, and a raging pill habit.

I've watched Joey a long time. For a while I thought the pills would get him. That I'd get the tug and show up at his van and find him conked out against the door in a puddle of his own vomit. One time, about two years after I died, I checked in on him and saw him down one pill after another for about three hours, then he snorted one for good measure, and I just lost it. I screamed my lungs out at him. Forget that he and I are on separate planes and that nobody on earth could hear me. I yelled and I yelled at him about everything. Got it all off my chest, saying stuff like how Caroline and Owen needed him, and even pulling out the big trump cards like how Ana would be disappointed in him and how his own grandfather would turn his back on him if he saw him right now. About fifteen minutes into my tirade, he said, "I'm done."

That's when I figured out that he could sense me.

He dumped all his pills, locked himself inside his van with a jug of water and a tin of jerky, and got clean over a hellacious forty-eight hours in which I spent every free second I had next to him. I can't touch him, of course, or hold a conversation with him. Nothing like that. But all the time Joey spent in the thin place changed him just like it changes everybody, and it made him more aware of me. He knew I was with him in the van over those two days. At the end of it he emerged sweaty and stinking into this lucidity that still allowed him to walk the thin place but kept him from killing himself with pills, and he thanked me.

So Joey knows when I'm there. Which is good, because I owe him something, and it's time I gave it to him.

When Gam was murdered, she essentially had three things to her name: her Singer's bag, the bell, and her crow totem, which she kept in a little bone box. The bell was never mine to have, and it found its next owner all on its own. As for the Singer's bag, well, singing was Gam's talent. I never had the will or the brains to get the chants and the ceremonies right, plus, each Singer's bag is personalized, filled with things that have a powerful connection to the individual Singer. With her gone, it became just a bag of things. Ninepoint stole her crow totem, and then the agents stole it from him, but I got it back and gave it to Caroline at the same time I gave Owen the gambler's totem. That leaves the bone box.

The bone box is a holder of things. Important things. Much like a pot. And it just so happened to break when Ninepoint ransacked it. It has the story of that night wrapped up into it, and that night means so much. I keep thinking about how the coyote was there, at my front door, when I came back. In a way, when I left the rez, the coyote moved in and took that box. I know in my heart that the bone box is our broken pot, and it's time I took it back. The problem is, I can't get to it.

When I walk into the lean-to I see the van door is closed and locked and the windows are rolled up, but it's basically hotboxed: the windows are white with smoke, and there's a big hole cut in the top where Joey rigged up an exit pipe. Good thing there's nobody around here for acres in either direction, because I bet it reeks of piñon smoke, and probably a few other things too, of the more hallucinogenic sort. He's essentially created a makeshift hogan out of his grandpa's old conversion van. The sliding door is even facing east, now that I notice it. I gotta admit, I'm impressed. I walk inside.

Joey's head, which had been resting peacefully on the back of the inside wall, straightens as soon as I take a second step inside the van, which is roomier than you'd think.

"Hi, Joey," I say. "Nice setup you have here."

He doesn't answer, of course. Like I said, our connection isn't like that, but he does look everywhere with his eyes for a bit before taking a deep breath of whatever mixture he's thrown in this little coffee can he has smoldering on a piece of corrugated metal siding in the middle of the floor.

"Walker," he whispers. "*Ya at eeh.*"

I shake my head. "Will you cut it with the Walker crap? I'm Ben. Just Ben."

No answer, of course. Which is going to present a problem, because while I know that the bone box is our broken pot, I also know Joey has to deliver it to Owen and Caroline, which is hard for two reasons. First, the bone box is still at the rez. Second, Joey won't go back to the rez. He's still abiding by his banishment. Part of him still thinks he was thrown from the Navajo Way, even after all that came to light. Even though we know he had nothing to do with Ana's disappearance.

The artifacts are about the journey, and Joey needs to make the journey back to his home. His real home. That's how the bone box becomes the broken pot. But it's not like I can tell him that. He can't hear me. I've tried so many times to get anyone to hear me. It's never gonna happen. There are rules.

Joey looks troubled. His eyeballs dart around under his lids like he's having a bad dream, but I can't shake him out of it. Joey was always sensitive, even before he hazed himself in the thin place, so it would make sense that he's feeling the crush of the coyote here too. If the balance of the river is off, the balance of the living world is off as well. Soon enough, even Hamm, Montana, will feel it.

When Ana was having bad dreams, I'd tell her stories. You can't go to bed again right after a nightmare. You'll fall right back into it if you do, so you have to switch things up. Get a glass of water, go pee, or in the case of Ana and me, tell each other stories. But I can't just tell stories here, can I? Joey can't hear me. Unless, of course, he doesn't need to hear me. Not my words, anyway. He's pretty far under right now. You never know what kinds of things can cross over during a sweat. I have firsthand experience. I saw Ana during one.

So I sit back in the smoke and tell him stories. Just like I used to with Ana. Just like Joey and I used to as well, back around the campfires we'd make in my backyard.

"Remember that one time we made a big fire out back of my place, in the pit there by the rocks, and we tried to jump it? Remember how dumb we were?" I say, and I laugh out loud. That was a huge fire. The neighbors who had the other half of our duplex were not too happy with us, but then again, they never were.

"And then Ana came out and saw us and said she was gonna jump it too, and she ran for it, but you caught her up just in time and swung her up on your shoulders instead? Remember that?"

I remember. That's a big memory. A special one that I almost don't want to think about too much because I'm afraid I'll change it by how badly I want to be back there again. Like I'll make up things that weren't there because I want more from it. But it's now or never.

"We were all whooping around that fire, you, me, and Ana on your shoulders. Then we convinced Ana to go sneak us some of Dad's beer. Of course she would have done anything for you, bro. So she ran off, but she didn't know what she was doing, remember? She came back with Gam's knitting. How the hell do you get *knitting* out of *beer*? That crazy girl."

She came back so proudly with Gam's knitting that we didn't have the heart to tell her it wasn't remotely what we asked for. We cracked up, and she cracked up along with us, which always used to worry me because she had a weak heart, even then. We all just laughed until we were lying on the grass and the fire was soaring above us.

"So you say, 'Listen, man. I'm not getting your Gam pissed off at me. She's a big deal. We gotta sneak this shit back.' And you were right, but turns out Gam was watching TV right outside her room, so we try to send in Ana again, but now she's having none of it when we tell her to put it back."

Joey's eyes are still closed, but they aren't flitting as much anymore. And is that a smile on his lips? Maybe a ghost of a smile?

"It was up to us, remember? So we had Ana go in and do a little song and dance in front of Gam to distract her and then you and I snuck into her room. You almost lost it when you saw how Gam was watching Ana, like *what the hell is this child doing now*."

Is that a nod? No, no nod. Just his chin falling gently to rest on his chest. The makeshift sweat brazier he rigged up here is slowly dying out. Which is good. I look out of the foggy window of his van, and I see that the sun is past high noon already. Montana time is New Mexico time. And we're running out of both.

"We did it, though. We snuck in, on our bellies, thinking we were Hoskininni sneaking around in the valley or some shit like that. Trying to ambush the white man. But you thought her knitting went up on her shelf, remember? Up high. So you put it up there at first, and I kept whispering to you that it's supposed to go in the basket by her bed, but you were up there and you weren't listening because you were staring at that box. Remember that box, Joey?"

Somehow I think that Joey remembers that box. Maybe he's even having some sort of vision of that box. Maybe in his vision it's half box, half pot.

"I didn't know what that was, man. Not then. I forgot about it five minutes later. But I bet you didn't. You always had a head for this type of shit. All of it. The world I live in now. The thing I am. I can't tell you how many times I thought you'd be better at this than I am. I think a lot of people would be better than I am. But at the end of the day, I'm on this side of things, and you're on that side of things, and hell if I know if any of this is even getting through to you. It shouldn't be. Because there are rules, and the rules say it shouldn't be."

I can see the sun moving down the line. I can feel the

gathering pressure of the coyote. Suddenly all this seems like grasping at straws. We're chasing after legends when there's a killer at the doorstep. But then Joey laughs. I snap up and watch him carefully. He's laughing and nodding. The way he did when he had Ana on his back and we were dancing.

"I need you to get that box, Joey," I say. He quiets, and his face slackens again. I don't know if he's listening or if his mind is on some other faraway fantasy, but it's getting late.

"It's on the rez, man. The NNPD took it to bag and tag it as evidence in a case they never closed, just shuffled off once I disappeared, and Ninepoint disappeared, and the agents disappeared. It's in the evidence room."

I get up and move over to Joey so I'm right by his ear.

"Joey, you gotta get that box, and you gotta take it to the hogan today. Before five. I know you're afraid of the rez. You don't want to go back there, but you gotta think about Ana. About me. About your home there. What you did for my family. . . nobody I know is a better Navajo than you. Please, man. Do this for all of us."

He's very still now. I want to say more, want to plead more, maybe scream in his ear just in case louder is better, but I get a tug. The job never waits. I open up the map and step through and do what I need to do, which is escort a very polite Swedish guy through the veil. He puts up no fuss. Doesn't even seem scared. Of the two of us, I bet I'm the one that looks scared. I'm checking the position of the sun, making mental calculations in my head as our time ticks away from us.

When I get back to Joey's van and step inside again, the air is clear, the coffee can is clean, and Joey is gone.

23

GRANT ROMER

This whole Native Market thing is nuts. I've never seen so many people in one place before. We left for Santa Fe early, took the school bus all the way up with a rickety trailer attached that held the parts of our booth, but when we get here the place is already crowded. People are milling about on the back streets, and all the cafes are jammed. They put us in a section of booths a little ways off the main plaza, where the local schools are all set up, and we get to work.

Chaco hops from terrace to terrace, watching me, watching the crowds. He finally agreed that it's OK that I'm even here. With Owen and Caroline tracking down the rest of the artifacts then heading to the hogan, it makes sense that somebody actually shows up where we all think the coyote is going to do work.

Once the booth is up and ready, I retreat into the crowd. None of the art is mine, of course, and I don't really feel up to explaining the indigenous programs of the high school I've been at for a little over a week to potential donors, so it makes sense, but more than that I sort of get the feeling that people want to see Navajo kids at the Navajo high school booth. The bottom line is this is a fundraiser. They're showing art, yeah, but also trying to drum up money and community buy-in, and I'm not the type of kid that tourists think of when they think of a high school on the rez.

You'd think this might piss me off. It doesn't. I knew what I was getting into when I suggested we head out this way in the first place way back when we got chased out of Pueblo by the guy with the itch. It's guys like Mick who can't seem to get over it, which is why I let out a bit of a groan when I see him milling through the crowd around ten in the morning, heading toward our booth. He sees me, and his eyes light up. He worms his way to where I stand under the shade of a wooden awning, my back against stucco that's already getting hot. It's a bluebird New Mexico day, and the sun shines so bright already you'd think it was plunked right there on the hills just to the west.

"What's up?" he says, not quite looking at me. He turns his back to the wall too and wipes his hands nervously up and down his shorts.

"I thought you said this place sucks," I say.

He's bobbing his head, watching the crowd intently. "Somethin' to do. You see any weird shit yet?"

"Naw, man. Looks to me like everybody is having a decent time."

That isn't exactly true. I've seen some fights over prices, I've seen a lot of shoving, and I've heard a lot of grumbling, but that's the coyote effect. I can see his greasy steps here already. Mostly walking around the big statue at the center of the plaza, almost like he was doing some sort of pilgrimage or something. There's even some tracks by our booth. But all I've seen so far are the tracks, never the thing making them. This is a prime place to pass that bead around, but I'm not about to get into all this with Mick. The guy gets on my nerves. I don't like how he assumes I'm his friend.

"C'mon, man," Mick says, pushing off the wall. "They're already pre-gaming at the house party off Marcy Park. I got some stuff in my trunk. Come check it out."

I look at my watch. "It's eleven in the morning, man."

"It's the kickoff party. Tradition and all that."

"You go ahead. I gotta make sure they got what they need here until the afternoon crew comes."

Mick shakes his head, jams his hands in his pockets. "Whatever," he says, then he slinks off. He doesn't go far, though. Already a crowd has started to gather around the obelisk statue where the plaza stage is. I can just see the edge of it from where our booth stands. Kai finishes talking to some old couple who claim to be alumni and comes my way to catch a look. I've been carefully trying to bump into her all morning, but she was always busy, either with her friends or chatting to someone who stopped by the booth. Now she swoops in where Mick left. A pretty damn good trade, I'd say, although she does look uneasy.

"You all right?" I ask. I give her my best Clint Eastwood squint and hope she doesn't see how much the sun is making my forehead sweat. Someone is talking into the microphone. The sound is mashed with the crowd noise, so I can't quite make it out. I hear scattered applause.

"You seen my brother?" she asks.

"To be honest, I've kind of been on the lookout to avoid him. But no."

She swallows hard. "Don't take it personally. It's not you he has a problem with. It's *all* of you." She gestures around me, at the scene just behind me of rows and rows of white people wearing sunhats and running shoes, scurrying toward the stage.

"Should that make me feel better?" I ask.

"I guess not." She's still looking for Hos. She's distracted, biting down gently on the dark pink of her lower lip.

"C'mon," she says. "Let's go check it out. We'll stay back from all the mess of people."

She could have asked if I wanted to go straight into the black pearl of chaos itself just then, and I probably woulda said the same thing: "All right."

She actually takes my hand and weaves her way through the crowd, around the booths. Our grip sweats, but she doesn't let go. I *was* looking for Hos because I think he may have a bead in his mouth, but now I'm looking for him because if he sees his little sister holding my hand, I think he'll kick my ass, coyote or not. We skirt the plaza, moving along the outer square until we reach the big cathedral, and she hops up on a low brick wall. She drops my hand and uses both of hers to shade her eyes. She pans the crowd slowly, breathing fast.

On stage, four Navajo women dressed in long blue gowns and leather moccasins are holding up what look like thatched shields in the shadow of the statue. One drummer at the edge of the stage starts banging out a quick-time rhythm. The women bob on the balls of their feet then start to gently hop forward and back in four distinct lines as the drummer chants in a rolling rhythm.

"It's the Basket Dance," Kai says. She's still nervous about something, but I hear a note of pride in her voice. "That's Navajo. We're kicking off the dance competition."

The women are mesmerizing. They do everything twice. Move up, move back. Circle right, circle left. Lift up the baskets, lower them down. It's like they're writing a poem in dance then erasing it again. They walk off stage just as they came on, but the air around them is somehow cleaner.

Kai feels it too, the brief calm that follows the dance as the Navajo walk off and another tribe sets up in the wings. People are feeling the way this place should be, if it weren't for the trail of the coyote. I look over at Kai and find her smiling at me.

"Looks like Hosteen and his buddies decided not to come," she says. "And right about now the afternoon crew is taking over the booth. How about you and I head over to the Marcy Park party? I bet it's ramping up."

Chaco sits above us on a worn stone eave of the church, his head just visible if you were to look up from the square. He ticks his ears downward, the way other crows might listen for worms in the ground. I know what he's trying to figure out. There's relief in Kai's voice—whatever she thought Hos was going to do, maybe he isn't going to do it after all. Maybe that was his window, when his people were on stage, and he missed it. But Chaco doesn't buy it, and I don't either.

"We ain't out of the woods yet, chief," Chaco says to me. "No matter how pretty Kai smiles."

Already whatever brief calm the Basket Dance settled upon the crowd is unraveling. The coyote still prowls these parts. Waiting. I can feel it.

Kai takes my nod as agreement, so she grabs my hand and hops down from the wall. She looks back at me and smiles. The spark is back, but I feel like the air is heavier than ever. Still, it is one hell of a smile she's got. I can't do anything but let her lead me wherever she wants to go.

24

OWEN BENNET

We've got an hour until we're supposed to be at the hogan. Grant is in the thick of coyote country in Santa Fe, and Caroline and I are about to break into the NNPD chief of police's car.

The first place we tried was the NNPD main office in Chaco City. We asked for Yokana at the desk and were told he wasn't there. Caroline pressed, in her unique way. Soon enough she had the secretaries up front laughing and chatting away like they were all best friends. We learned Yokana was actually dealing with something at CHC, so off we went. And here we are, staring at his old Ford Explorer, parked in the same spot in the CHC parking lot as it was when we both first visited.

I don't think I need to tell you that I have no experience breaking and entering. It's not really my cup of tea. Once, back when I was a resident working myself blind and prone to all sorts of brain farts, I was trying to warm up my old box of a Subaru for the drive to work in the dead of February, and I locked the keys in the car while it was running. I fiddled around with a clothes hanger for an hour as if I knew what I was doing, praying the neighbors weren't watching, before I gave up and called a locksmith. Still, I know the basic idea, and I did manage to swipe a wire hanger from the coat rack at the CHC without anyone noticing, so here we go.

I take two deep breaths, step out from behind a docked service truck, and walk slowly and evenly to the SUV. Caroline follows behind. She keeps a lookout while I try to worm the hook end in and through the upper window like a blind man trying to thread a sewing needle. I've got my tongue out and everything, wincing at every scrape, until Caroline says, "It's open."

I slowly pull my hanger out then simply open the passenger-side door. Of course it's open. Why would the chief of police lock his car? What lunatic would try to break in to the chief of police's car?

I pop my head in. I left the tattered paper in the cup holder sometime during the car ride, but it's gone now. The car is as clean as it ever was. Same brushed cloth seats, same mud-mats devoid of mud, same baking smell of trapped desert heat. Nothing else. I pop open the glove compartment. It has the owner's manual, a first aid kit, a wind-up flashlight, and his registration in a plastic sleeve. That's it. I'm thinking that perhaps he threw it in the back, or it was blown back there if he was cruising the service roads with the windows down, but as I'm moving to open the back right door, Caroline whispers again.

"He's coming."

"Really? Shit. How long?"

"Whoops, he sees us."

I turn around in time to find Sani Yokana and another policeman I don't recognize watching us from across the lot. Thank God I closed the passenger door. There's a chance he thinks we're just hanging around his car for some reason I can't imagine, but as he starts walking again I see in his face that chance is pretty slim. He knows what we were doing. It's obvious in the way he takes off his sunglasses. Thankfully, for us, I also see he has bigger problems. Between him and the other officer stands Tim Bentley, the mortician, looking very out of sorts. His hair and clothes are disheveled. He seems to be missing a shoe. His face is scruffy. They're not escorting him, not exactly, but they're very clearly keeping him between them as they approach us.

"Something I can help you with, Dr. Bennet?" Yokana asks, glancing at me then at Caroline. The lines in his face seem a hair more dug out even than when I saw him last. A notepad sags in his breast pocket, his shirt is tucked in, and his jeans are still clean, but they look two- or three-day clean, not one-day clean. He's wearing his gun this time too. It's hooked to his belt next to the badge and the buckle.

"Dr. Bennet?" Bentley is squinting at me, slack jawed. "When did you get to town?"

Yokana and I exchange a knowing glance. Yokana's face darkens further.

"Can you take me away from here, Owen?" Bentley asks. He scratches violently at the side of his face and then rubs his head like he's clearing it of sand. "I don't feel right, you know?"

"We're gonna get you out of here, Dr. Bentley," the other officer says, gently holding on to his shoulder.

"Where do you want to go, Tim?" I ask.

He shrugs hugely, lets out a big *harrumpf*. He tries to scratch at his face again, but the officer prevents him. He doesn't seem to notice or care.

"Anywhere. I just need to walk. I've got these thoughts.

These terrible pictures in my head. They itch. My brain itches."

Caroline steps in. "Does he have anything in his mouth?" she asks point blank.

Yokana shakes his head. "He was causing a scene in the morgue. His assistant said he tried to drink formaldehyde and swallow some tools, saying he had to clean his brain. We checked his mouth to make sure he wasn't hiding anything else."

"I'm gonna sit him in the car, chief," the officer says. "Before he gets really out of hand."

Yokana nods, and the officer leads Bentley away to his squad car two spots down. Bentley drags his feet, and he seems unsteady. He keeps looking at the desert to our right and reaching for it.

"We've seen a lot of cases like this recently," Yokana says, watching him along with us. "People seem disoriented. My first thought was severe dehydration, but the few we've checked out are fine. Physically, at least."

Yokana turns back to us. "He didn't remember our first visit at all."

"I think he had. . . some type of fever then." I'm trying to think of the best way to phrase this so that I sound like a doctor and not a lunatic. Bentley doesn't have the bead in his mouth any longer, but the hangover seems to linger, and it looks awful.

"The fever broke, but he's going to be very disoriented for a time. Depending on how long he was ill."

"A fever, huh."

"Something like that, yes."

I'm an awful liar, but Yokana doesn't call me on it. Instead he reaches in his pocket and hands me a tattered sheet of white paper. My gift from Lelah. Her journey from hobbled to healthy is wrapped up within it, and my journey is too.

"I was gonna throw this away, but when I grabbed it I sort of just held on to it. Not sure I can say why. Seemed like something I should get back to you. I suspect that's what you were looking for in my car?"

Caroline clears her throat. "Sorry about that. We needed the paper. You're right. It's more important than it looks. Also, is there any chance you might have stumbled across a broom that feels equally important? A little broom?"

"A broom?"

"Yeah, a little broom." She holds her hands out a foot apart. "About yea big?"

"No, can't say I have," he says, his tone uninterpretable. Maybe droll, maybe sarcastic, but definitely honest. His phone rings in his pocket, and he picks it up, looks at it, then shakes his head.

"If you'll both excuse me, I was due in Santa Fe hours ago. We doubled our force there, but my men still feel like things are more unruly than usual. Looks like a lot of people are feeling off today."

We step aside as he gets in his car and starts it up after several rolls of the engine. He slowly shifts into reverse. He's exhausted, but he's got his job to do, and Sani Yokana is the type of guy to work himself into the ground if that's what's required of him. He rolls down his window and plops his elbow out.

"Can I ask what you expected to find in his mouth, Ms. Adams?"

Caroline looks to me. I shrug. *What the hell.* I think Yokana has always been more aware than what he lets on, and what he lets on is that he's aware of quite a lot.

"A bead," Caroline says.

He taps his teeth. I wait for him to press us, but he doesn't. Instead he says, "The funniest thing happened to me earlier today. I was going through some files in the basement back at NNPD, and I swore I saw Joseph Flatwood in the evidence room."

Caroline shuffles her feet. I can't think of anything to say either that won't dig us any deeper than we already are. Thankfully, Yokana doesn't seem to mind.

"I did a bit of a double take. I looked up again, and nobody was there. Walked around the whole evidence room thinking I'd lost my mind. Nobody. Funny thing is, I was happy to see him. And sad when I realized he wasn't there. Maybe I got a touch of that fever myself."

"You don't," I say. "I'd know."

He takes a deep breath. "No, I 'spect not. Not yet, at least. I'll see you folks around."

With that he backs up and makes his way out of the parking lot, the sand and grit crackling beneath his tires. He gives us a slow, single wave then pulls out onto the street.

I take the tattered sheet of paper and tuck it carefully in my bag along with the burned stick and the stirring stick. Caroline has the birth bag, her crow still inside. It sounds like Ben and Joey may have come through with the broken pot. The sun is hitting us sideways now. Our time is almost up.

"We need to get to the hogan," I say.

"We're missing the broom, though."

"We've got no leads on that one, nothing at all. Maybe it isn't ours to get. At the very least, if we're all together, maybe we can come up with something."

Caroline looks unconvinced. I'm right there along with her. But we're out of time. Five is better than none, but five isn't six, and I get the feeling when it comes to these things, there are no half measures.

"Come on," I say. "If Yokana can keep going, and Joey, and Ben, and Grant over there in the middle of it all, we can too."

Caroline holds out her hand, and I grasp it, then together we grab our crows and snap into the thin place, on our way to a line of hogans in the desert.

25

GRANT ROMER

Marcy Park is about a fifteen-minute walk from the Plaza, but it feels a world away. By the time we get there the afternoon shadows are long, and the park—which seems lower than the rest of the city, as if it's dug out of the rock—is dark while the hills are still bright. There's a crowd here too, but it's younger, spread out in pockets around a big stage set against the far side. A band is playing country rock. Where Kai and I stand at the lip of the park, we catch snatches of music. The wind has picked up, and it's blowing most of the sound away from us, along with clouds of smoke that puff up from the pockets of people.

As Kai leads me down and through the park, past the crowds and the music into a low-lying neighborhood, Chaco is talking nonstop. His shadow flits across the green, right to left, left to right.

"They're all gathering at the hogan, man. Maybe you oughta think about laying low while they call for the coyote. Nobody knows what's gonna happen."

His voice is louder than usual in my head. I think he

knows I'm only half listening. And almost completely help-less, hand in hand with this girl.

"The coyote is here somewhere," I say. "I know it, and you know it. We need to get a bead on it before the dances are over."

"Is that a pun? At a time like this?"

"When the others call it, don't you think it would be good to know exactly what, or who, it is they're calling?" I'm spitballing, because I know and Chaco knows that there isn't anything on this plane or the next that would keep me from this party with Kai, but I still think it's a valid point. Nobody likes to just open the door to their home without checking through the peephole first.

She takes me through an older, simpler neighborhood than the one immediately surrounding the park. Here the cars are more like the stuff I see in the RV park, and the houses are smaller and closer. Blaring dance music comes from one of them, a long, flat ranch house at the end of the block. I smell a loaded grill and can see its smoke coming up from the backyard. A cul-de-sac circles up to the front, and it's already a parking lot full of cars. Souped-up trucks and beater sedans, mostly. I recognize a lot of them from the Crownrock parking lot. A few kids hang out front sipping from plastic cups and talking loudly. Kai leads me inside, but she drops my hand.

This is my first party. Unless you count my birthday parties, which basically consisted of a bird and two people twenty years older than me sitting around a grocery-store birthday cake on a table bolted to the floor of an RV. We made the best of it, and all of them ended up being more fun than they sound, but still. That's not a party. This is a party.

People are everywhere, almost all of them Navajo, but a

few white kids and some Mexicans too. The air smells like BBQ and beer and cigarettes and weed. The music is stupidly loud for five in the afternoon. I lose track of Kai in the crush of people, and suddenly I'm alone. A few kids look my way, but most ignore me, until I'm pulled aside by Mick. He's smiling and weaving, his eyes already glassy. He's grinding his teeth a bit too. Owen sat me down years ago and told me all about the stuff he saw at the CHC, and a lot of the bad cases were people without teeth on account of drugs. Mick's got a sloshing cup of beer in his hand, but I wonder what else he has in his system.

"'Bout time you showed up," he says. My guess is he's spent more time here than he has at the market. He leans toward me and sort of bounces off the bell under my shirt. I have to catch him, but then he seems to come to. He nods. "Sorry, man. I think I got started a little early. Hey, listen." He leans in again. "Hos and his crew, they're here. I wanted to catch you before you did anything stupid like show up with Kai. Whoops."

I hear sound coming from the back of the house. It sounds more urgent, angrier than the rest of the party noise. I hear Chaco from somewhere outside, his voice faint. "It's the Hos kid," he says. "Grant, be carefu—"

And then he's there in front of me, with his whole crew. And they're dressed to kill. Literally. They've painted their faces like Navajo warriors. Black smeared around the eyes, and red down the face. Some have dots of white peppering the base colors. The loud room tapers to quiet. Kai is pushing back on Hos but getting nowhere. She whispers urgent Navajo at him that he doesn't seem to hear, pointing down at a lumpy duffel bag, one of several that his crew is carrying.

He's trying to head out the door. He's not expecting to

see me. This isn't like one of those moments when the new kid confronts his bully and turns him around or makes him see the light. For that to happen Hos would actually have to care about me, have me on his radar, and he doesn't. He never has. When he grabs my shirt in a bunch in his fist, he's looking at me, but he's not seeing Grant. He's seeing a white kid at a Navajo party for a Navajo school in a part of the country that was once full of Indians and is now full of white people.

"What are you doing here?" he says simply. I turn to look to Mick for help, but Mick is slinking away again. It's just me. "Your place is up at the market, walking booth to booth."

"I ain't got a place," I say then wish I could bite back the *ain't*. But it's already out there. "I figured maybe this was everyone's place right now."

I'm not sure what I think that's gonna do. Change his mind? He's painted up for war and smells like whisky, and he's carrying what I really hope isn't a duffel bag full of guns. He jerks me right into his face. His eye is twitching, rapid fire.

"Wrong, *bilagaana*. It *ain't* everybody's place. It's *our* place. We're taking it back."

He pushes me against the wall and watches me for another span of seconds. I realize that this is my moment. This is when I try to stop him. You think about this stuff sometimes, when you're bored and staring out the window of the boat as the miles roll by. You think about all the crazy shooting and ultra-violence that happens everywhere you go, especially nowadays, when this stuff seems to happen more than usual, and you wonder if, say, you were there that night when some asshole decided to shoot up something or raise some hell somewhere, and he came at you first. Say he's stalking the cubicles or walking the pews or something with destruction in his eyes, and everybody just wants to live, so they shove themselves deeper down into whatever foxhole they've dug, but you've got a chance. You could smash the guy in the face, or better yet call him out before he gets violent. At least ask him to open up the duffel bags and explain himself. Face what he's doing before he gets crazy.

Sitting safe and sound on the boat, watching the miles roll by, you think, "Of course I'd call him out. No brainer." But then it actually happens, and you know what I do?

Nothing. And neither does anybody else.

I watch as he shoulders his duffel and gives one last look my way. I can see he's already forgotten me. His mind is on whatever lies ahead. Then he shuffles off. His crew follows him. There are five of them, all guys painted like him, all grim looking. And then they're gone. Kai yells something in Navajo after him, stopping at the front door. It does no good. Kai watches after them for a second, and the room watches after Kai, and then the music comes back. Maybe it was always playing, but the ringing in my ears that started when Hos grabbed me cancelled it out until I got my brains together again. I can hear Chaco, faint but freaked out.

"You all right, my man? Hos and his gang are moving in the back alleys and neighborhoods toward the plaza. The dances are almost over, but he still has time to pull something."

"It's up to Owen and Caroline to pull him back now." I'm a little numb at how much of a wuss I was. How much of a wuss I am. Mick is looking at me with this gleam in his eye, and it says to me, "Your only hope for the next four years is to stick with me," and what gets me down most is that he's probably right. He's a bit of a goof and a little weird, but Hos didn't grab him on his way out. Nobody told Mick to get back to shopping the booths where he belongs. It occurs to me that I've given Mick a bum rap. The guy is quiet and down low, but he keeps his head above water. Nobody messes with him, even though nobody really brings him in either, but maybe that's the best I can hope for.

Kai turns around from the doorway with a strange gleam in her eye. I wouldn't call it the Kai shine, not the one I saw in her when she sat next to me and told me to stop slapping and start sliding. This is twice as dangerous, and when she turns it on me, I go twice as numb.

"Well that's that," she says. "He never listened to me anyway. Never once." She forces a smile, and I see that her eyes glisten with damp. She walks past me and grabs my hand again. I was facing the door all ready to go out, all ready to leave with Chaco, maybe call Sani Yokana or one of the officers for help, but then Kai spins me around and I'm back in the party. I'm following her past the living room, into the kitchen, where a bunch of kids are sitting around a table with full cups, and they're spinning a bottle.

"People actually do this?" I ask Kai, and my voice seems distant. "I thought this was just something on TV or whatever."

Kai says nothing, just plops me down in a seat and takes the one next to me. I recognize some of the kids from class. They're all my age, and they're laughing and smiling. I don't think they saw Hos leave. They've been out back drinking the whole time. Mick finds his way to the table soon after and shoulders in as well. He looks pretty far gone now. Chaco is trying to say something to me about getting out of here. He says he has eyes on Hos and his crew, but he'll lose them soon.

"What are we gonna do?" I ask out loud. I mean it for Chaco. And it's not really a question. But Kai answers.

"You spin the bottle. If it lands on a guy, he's gotta drink. If it lands on a girl. . ." Her smile is dangerous. Her words trail off. "Just a little kiss. You go first."

I spin the empty rum bottle. It has smooth edges and seems to spin forever, around and around and around, until it lands on Mick. I'm sure I look disappointed, because Mick snuffs out a breath and says, "Sorry, friend." But his eyes are narrow and angry. I think he's gonna chug his drink, but all he does is take one dainty sip. Then he says, "My turn," and spins. The bottle turns and turns, and Mick stares at it without blinking until it lands on Kai. He says nothing, but I get the weirdest feeling he was expecting this.

Kai's a good sport. Either that or she wants it over with. Either way she pops up, goes over to him, and leans down for a peck, but he grabs her and kisses her deeply. At first she tries to pull back, but then she leans in to him, almost falling on top of him, until she climbs off and away and stares at him for a second. I think maybe she's gonna slap him. The circle is hooting, and some of the girls are calling Mick an asshole, but Kai doesn't do anything to him. She walks quietly back to my side of the table with this strange grin on her face.

"My turn," she whispers. She's standing behind me, but she reaches over me, pressing her chest to my back, and spins the bottle right in front of me. I look at Mick, and he seems lost. He's staring at his hands, at the table, at the spinning bottle. He looks at the circle of people as if seeing them for the first time. Then he looks at me.

"Grant?" he says, as if surprised to see me sitting across the table from him. "My head. . ." He sags in his chair and presses his palms to his forehead. His gaze runs a thousand yards.

Chaco slams against the back window. The whole party jumps in fright, and Chaco slams again. The glass splinters, and kids scream and run from the kitchen, everyone but Mick and me and Kai. The bell starts to push at me, to push me away from here, from this place, but it seems to realize things at the same time I do. Which is too late.

The bottle stops dead to rights on me. Kai grabs my head and wrenches it around and pries my mouth open with her tongue. Her lips seal against mine.

Everything hits me. A million flashes of a million jagged edges of a million shattered memories where everything is falling apart. People, things, emotions, all of it splintered and scattered at random. The bell is burning like a white coal pressed to my chest. My heart feels stuck in an endless loop of the terrible space between beats, flopping out of rhythm inside of me like it's lost and will never get right again, and still I'm hammered with these memories that aren't mine, over and over and over and ov—

26

CAROLINE ADAMS

The line of hogans is mostly falling apart, and their cracked mud tops go: bleached white, bleached white, bleached white, then black as night. We take a well-worn path that snakes down and around the bumps and rolls of the desert, and as we approach I see that the black we mistook for the roof of the last one is actually about a hundred silent crows. A hundred black beaks pointing, and two hundred black eyes following our movements. When they shuffle a bit to keep us in view, it makes a sound like flipping through a huge phone book. It gives me goose bumps.

"Here for the show, huh?" Owen asks them, stopping before the low entrance. No answer. Just blinking. As creepy as they are, I'm not entirely against them being here. We've been in more than a few scrapes where a curtain of black crows has come in handy. Although if it comes to that, somebody is usually dead or dying, so I hope they stay right where they are in the peanut gallery.

Inside, the sand painters are waiting. They sit together in one corner, shirtless, their scrawny brown chests hairless.

They wear leather breeches and sit cross-legged on a bed of pinion leaves. They watch us in silence until we both eventually sit too. We have no Chaco/Grant combo to translate this time, and no smoker to be our voice. I expected the smoker, but when we walked through the Arroyo to get here, it was quiet and closed, like a town battened down for an incoming storm. We didn't see anybody, and nobody approached us.

One of the brothers—I don't know if it's Tsosi or Tsasa now that they're out of their recliners—points at the fire pit in the center, where berries, wood, leaves, and pine needles are clumped in two neat piles, one large and one small. He takes a pack of wooden matches from a pouch at his waist and tosses them to Owen, who bobbles the catch but snatches them up from the ground.

"Me?"

The sand painter nods.

"Small," he says, pointing at the little pile. Owen crawls over on his hands and knees and strikes a few matches until he gets the needles to burn. The rest takes care of itself. The pile is already burning fast and putting out a great deal of smoke. The brothers watch the smoke waft until it envelops all four corners of the hogan, then they close their eyes and breathe deeply. Owen and I do the same and immediately start coughing. The smell isn't bad, necessarily, it's just strong. Like a gin martini. But as the fire fades, the smoke eases. We sit still until the hogan is almost completely clear again. I get the feeling that was a prep round, maybe a burst of purification to ready the place for the big pile.

"Broken pot," says the other brother. Owen and I look at each other. That was Joey's task, and Joey isn't here.

"Looks like we didn't get very far," Owen whispers to me, his face grave.

I rub my smoke-irritated eyes and think about how I'm gonna explain that it looks like we're missing step one in this business, when I hear the telltale *whoosh, pop* of a Circle member arriving. When I blink my eyes I see a shadow outside of the entrance. A leather vest falls to the desert floor outside, followed by a shower of pollen, and then in comes Joey. His eyes are wide as he looks at Owen and me, but it's really the sand painters that he seeks. When he finds them he bows his head, as if awaiting sentencing from them.

The two men watch him coldly for a moment, and in the silence Joey chances a sad little glance at them. When he does, they can't hold their scowls any longer and both burst out laughing, their smiles genuine. Joey looks up again and after a moment starts to grin. The brothers gesture him over to them, and they scooch apart then slap the space between them with their hands. Joey sidles in between and smiles at us sheepishly, which is something I've never seen him do before. It gives me a quick glance at the type of guy he might have been when he was young and it was just him and Ben here, running around the Arroyo like it was their personal playground.

Joey Flatwood has been welcomed home.

"Broken pot," the sand painter says again, and this time Joey reaches in his own pouch and pulls from it a small box that looks like it's been carved from bone and hardened with glaze. I recognize it immediately from the night I said good-bye to Ben's grandmother. It was on the ground next to her. It's cracked at the back, where its two leather hinges have been snapped, and Joey takes the top entirely off.

The sand painters nod. Crisis one is averted. I think about confessing that we don't have the broom, but it looks like things are on a roll here, and basically I don't want to have to see the looks on everyone's faces when I tell them our recipe is missing something and our cake isn't gonna rise. So I don't. Besides, the guy sitting right next to me once told me to hold on if you can, because you never know what one more second might bring.

"Burned stick," says one brother. Owen reaches in his satchel and pulls out the first artifact we found, given to us, actually, by the sand painters themselves. One brother mimics putting things in the bone box. Joey holds it out to us, and Owen drops the stick in. The burned part juts out over the side.

"Broken stirring stick," says the other brother, struggling with the words. Owen places the second stick in the box, and the brother readjusts it so that they cross each other and stick out evenly.

"Old cane" is next. Owen plucks the tattered page from his bag and looks at it for a moment, smiling. The brothers mime sliding it under the sticks in the box, and he does.

"Birth bag." I pull out my totem pouch and frown. And here I pause. I know it's crazy, but I don't want to part from the old thing. I know it's to save the rez, and maybe the world, but it still sort of sucks. This thing has been under my pillow for years. It's rubbed silky smooth on one side where it sits against my skin when I wear it. I look over at Owen, and I'm surprised to realize that I have tears in my eyes again, and not from the smoke.

Owen gives me a soft smile and leans over to me. "I'll find you a new pouch."

"You too. We do this together. Same pouches."

"Same pouches."

I sniff and nod. Then I open it and let my crow totem tumble to the floor of the hogan. The brothers pass me a strip of cloth, and I wrap my crow then tuck it in my pocket. I place the pouch on top of the sticks in the box.

I know what's coming next.

"Whisk broom."

And here we've hit our wall. I take a deep breath, look the brothers in the eye, and shake my head. They don't frown or *tsk tsk*. They don't do anything, really. Their faces are impassive as they speak to Joey between them. After a minute Joey gets up and lights the big pile, and I think we may have dodged a bullet. Maybe the artifacts were more like guidelines after all.

"Are we good?" I ask. But Joey shakes his head.

"We wait," he says.

"For what?" Owen asks.

"For the whisk broom."

What's that supposed to mean? Wait for the whisk broom? What's it gonna do—come waltzing into the hogan like one of those talking candy bars in the movie theater ads?

"What's the fire for, then?" Owen asks. I can tell he's as disappointed as I am. In the fact that we can't move forward without the broom, but mostly in himself. We've let everybody down.

"That's how much time we have to wait," Joey says. "When the fire dies, the window closes."

Owen looks like he wants to say more, but suddenly he twitches and paws at his own totem pouch. I feel it too, at the same time. The crows are deadly cold. So cold that I can feel it through the cloth wrapping of mine. We pull them out of our pockets at the same time and set them down on the dirt. The cloth around mine is already frosting, despite the heat.

"Something is wrong," Joey says. I look up to find him holding his bead-wrapped crow before he, too, sets it down, working the chill from his fingers. "The bell is calling for help."

The three of us—Joey, Owen, and I—stare mutely at each other until the sand painters break the silence.

"They say I am needed here, and Caroline is needed here," Joey says. He looks at Owen and shrugs. "I don't know why, Owen. But that leaves you to go to the bell."

Owen looks down, nodding to himself. Grant is foremost in his mind. He's more than willing, but his smoke still takes a hit at the fact that he's not "needed." When I touch the small of his back, he perks up a little. Not much, but a little.

"All right," he says. "I'll go."

"The market," Joey says as Owen flutters his fingers over his crow on the dirt floor.

"Be careful," I say.

He turns to me. Kisses me on the forehead. "You too," he says. Then he grabs his totem and pops out of sight.

The sand painters take all this in as evenly as if they were watching the sun setting behind their camper. Joey takes a deep breath of smoke from the new fire, and I watch as it streams out of the top of the hogan. The pile is bigger, but it's burning fast.

We wait.

27

OWEN BENNET

I step from the tense quiet of the hogan into a madhouse of people at the Santa Fe Plaza. I hold my phase for now, reasoning that it'll be easier to spot the bell in the crush of people if I'm in the thin place. And it truly is a crush. The blurred effect of the thin place seems to double the mayhem. All around me people are shoving and yelling. Walking over each other to get away from the main stage for some reason. There, someone holds the microphone. A young man with a painted face. A security guard appears to be unconscious on the ground next to him, and two others are being held back by a group of other young men painted similarly. So this is Hos. This is our coyote. I'm not sure what he's saying—sounds are muted by the whipping wind of the thin place—but judging by how badly everyone wants to get away from him, I know it's not good.

He lifts up a duffel bag and drops the mic. A sea of panicked people passes right through me, but none of them is Grant. I chance a quick scan of the plaza, looking for the glow of the bell, but I don't see it anywhere. Back on stage, the coyote and his pack are fishing through the duffel and each pulling out what look like duct-taped aerosol cans. They fan out around the stage. Policemen on the perimeter are struggling to get to them, but they look like fish fighting a waterfall. Every step forward is two steps back.

Hos holds up his bomb and screams, "My people are not entertainment!" so loudly that even I can hear it. Then he chucks his bomb at the obelisk statue in the center of the stage. His gang follows his lead. There's a split second when I see six floating packages sailing toward the center, and I realize we blew it. We missed our chance. We couldn't bait the trap in time. I wonder what fire feels like in the thin place. Will I live through this? Does it matter?

I can't hear the bombs explode, but I can see them. They send out great gouts of color, all of it tinged a glittering black to my eyes. Then I tense for the blast, but it never comes. The crowd has pushed their way through me, and my way is clear now, save a few people injured in the stampede. I blink into reality.

"This symbolizes the blood of our people, shed for the benefit of yours, year after year after year!" yells Hos, just before he's tackled by police along with the rest of his gang. Behind him, the plaza statue is glistening, absolutely soaked in red paint.

Paint? That's it? That's what the coyote had planned? It almost makes me want to laugh. They've got Hos rolled over, they're cuffing him, and all the while he's still screaming about Native American rights. I let out a deep breath. Maybe we misjudged this whole affair after all. Then a piercing scream rings through the crowd. Everyone hears it, even the cops. Even Hos stops his tirade. All of us look west. There, high in the sky, I see Chaco. Immediately I know something isn't right. He's diving down fifty or so feet then pulling up. Diving down again then pulling up. He looks harried, like when a bunch of smaller birds chase away one large bird, but this is worse. Panicked. He calls again, and it sounds like he's in pain.

I look at the square. Hos is back to his tirade. The crowd is calming down at the edges. This isn't the right place. The coyote tricked us.

I position Chaco in my mind, do some quick thin-place calculations, then snatch my totem and blink out.

28
_____

THE WALKER

I sit at Caroline's side, and both of us watch as the fire
burns down. I want to hold her, reassure her that
everything will be all right, but the fact is, I don't think
it will. The simple cloth that covers her totem is frosted
completely over. Soon the fire will be down to embers. But
neither of us needs those things to know how south all this
has gone. She can feel it as well as I can. Grant is in serious
trouble, and now Owen is too.

One brother says, "Sweep," but Caroline shakes her
head. "Sweep," he says again, pointing to the little ash pile
from the first fire and then to the box. He wants the whisk
broom to sweep the ash into the box, but Caroline can't, and
she starts to cry.

"We don't have the broom, old man!" I yell, and maybe I
see a flicker from Joey's eyes, but otherwise it falls on deaf
ears, as always.

"Sweep," the brother says again, gently this time. Caroline reaches for the ash with her hands, but the second
brother is up on his knees quickly and stills her arm. He's

firm but not unkind. He has sad eyes. His grip tells us that each artifact is integral.

"Please," he says, his voice breaking. "Sweep."

That's when Caroline gets it. But it doesn't lift her spirits any.

She takes the black book from her breast pocket and looks at it. She bends it this way and that, fluttering the pages. They flop heavily. For Caroline the book was always weighty. To her, it represents a link. A chance. A possibility to reach me. Her heart is tangled up with memories of me in the blank pages of that thing.

She holds it by the spine and carefully sweeps the small pile of ashes into the box that Joey still holds. Then Joey caps it. The brothers mime that the book goes on top, to hold the box top in place and press down on the package. And then the whole thing goes into the fire.

Joey holds out the box, but Caroline still holds the book.

"I'm sorry, Ben," she whispers. I know she can't see me, but I also think she knows I'm here. She's really speaking to me.

"You have nothing to be sorry about," I say, even though my words will not reach her.

"I was hoping I might be able to finish our story some day," she says. "All these blank pages. Why couldn't one be for us?"

Tears are rolling down her face now, dripping off her cheeks and onto the book. I reach out to try and wipe them again, but this time I stop myself before I pass through her. If I passed through her right now, it might break me apart.

"You've had half of my heart ever since I first met you," she says. "If we'd had time, I think I'd have given you the whole thing, but we didn't, and over the years what I had left has gone to Owen, piece by piece. Even I didn't realize it until it happened. But it happened, and I can't live like this anymore. Half measures don't work when it comes to hearts."

Her head droops low, she speaks into her lap, but her words are for me.

"Ever since you died, all I've wanted is closure. I didn't even have to have you back, if I could just figure out how to say good-bye to you properly. But I know now, I don't need closure. If it means that I have to forget you, forget who I was when I was with you and forget the person you helped me to become, I don't want it. And that piece of my heart you have, it's always going to have a bit of you in it, but I want to give it to Owen. I need to give it to Owen."

"I know," I say. "I know you do."

I didn't think I had any tears left. I thought they all dried up when I rang the bell. Boy was I wrong.

Caroline takes a shuddering breath. "I can't ask you to give back to me what I gave to you. It's up to me to reach out and take hold of it again myself, so that's what I'm doing."

She gently sets the book on the box and nods to Joey, who moves over to the fire and places the whole package in the searing coals. It's alight in moments. Now both Caroline and I are slumped over ourselves, as if the strings that bonded us, that moved us together and mixed us up and were hopelessly tangled when I died, have finally been cut.

As the coyote's warning signs catch fire, I feel a sea change. The hole at the top of the hogan seems to be pulling more than just smoke up and out. It's subtle but definite: the wind from outside is pulled in, then a bit of desert sand. The hogan darkens as if a stream of the rising night itself is being pulled in from the eastern door.

One of the brothers says, "Now we wait."

I feel like a wrung-out towel, but I know that this is my

time to get to work. I'm the one that has to catch this thing in between planes. Keep it from jumping from person to person and away from us again. I don't know how I can do anything but collapse with Caroline's words still bouncing around my head, but I have to do my part too.

I stand, but as I do, I feel the tug. I'm getting a call.

"You've got to be kidding me," I say. "Now? Really?"

It's insistent, much more insistent than it usually is, and it makes my stomach flip. I swirl open the map looking for the fray, for the guttering soul string that calls to me, and I find it almost immediately. It's very close. Someone is dying, and they're dying in Marcy Park.

29

OWEN BENNET

My half step in the thin place takes me to a park, where I'm thrown into mayhem of a different sort. A band plays on a stand in the distance with a large crowd all pressed together, but the wind makes their music sound whiny and off key. The stage lights are rattling in the gusts, and one falls from the overhead rigging, spinning wildly and throwing a chaotic beam across the darkening green before it shatters behind the band in an electric flare that shorts out all the music. Now all I can hear is the wind and a screaming crow.

Chaco is behind the stage, off to the right, above a bunch of houses. I sprint toward where he dips and hovers, still struggling. The wind seems to be pushing back at me, and the sound is as loud as if I was back in the thin place, but this wind is real. It throws dirt and grass and grit in my eyes and mouth, but I carve through.

I break free of the park and into a small neighborhood, and now I can hear Chaco's wings beating just under the cut of the wind. He's in the sky over a house at the end of the block, but he's moving my way, because Grant is moving my way. I almost collapse with relief.

"Grant! Are you OK? Where's the bell?"

Grant stops dead in his tracks and looks at me. Chaco lets loose another painful cry, twice as loud.

"Grant?"

He runs toward me with this insane smile on his face, but there's nothing happy about it. It's the type of smile I used to see back on my psych rotations in medical school. It's the smile of the mentally broken. The unhinged.

He's in front of me in the blink of an eye, and then he's grabbing my throat with one hand. My air shuts off full stop. His grip feels like a knot in my windpipe.

Chaco dives again and pulls up, and now I see why. This is not Grant. This is the coyote. He's turned Grant into a skinwalker, and Chaco doesn't know whether to attack him or help him. I try to speak but can't. My words feel like they back up from my mouth all the way to my brain. My head is about to burst, but then he drops me.

I suck in a crackling breath on my hands and knees. But the air isn't coming fast enough. My vision dims, tunneling to a pinpoint, but then I feel the soft head of Chaco brushing against my arm. I've never actually touched Chaco before, not in five years, but here he is, standing beside me, and I focus on that touch until my vision clears. When I look up again, I see that the whole party is outside on the front porch watching. But then Grant's insane smile is right in my face again.

"Let him go," I say. It comes out in a growl. The coyote wears Grant's grin, stretches it wider than it should be, and he shakes his head like an ornery child. I push myself standing, and the coyote follows me, inches away. The crowd of kids behind him is half cheering, half terrified, and totally unaware of what is happening. He backs up their way, and I stagger after him. He sticks out his tongue, and I see it. The bone bead. It's the size of a pea. How could such a small thing cause so much destruction?

"Spit it out!" I say. I lurch after him, but he dodges me at the last second, lurching this way and that like we're playing tag. He zips his tongue back in and clamps the bead behind a mad grin that bares his full set of teeth. I lunge for him and grab him by the shoulders.

"Give me my *son* back, you bastard!"

The coyote backhands me across the face so hard that I end up spitting out a molar. Now the crowd silences. One girl starts to scream. I see Kai, the girl Grant is so fond of, sitting down outside on the grass, her head between her knees. She's moaning, "No, no, no, no, get out of my head!"

The coyote pulls me straight again. "Your son is mine," he says. "Until he dies."

"I'm not going anywhere," I say, my words bubbling with blood. "Take me! Take me, but leave him!"

The coyote shakes his head very slowly, his eyes wide. It's hard to imagine that Grant ever had those eyes.

"No," the coyote whispers. "I want the Keeper."

"Then you're gonna have to kill me first."

The coyote looks behind me, and his eyes light up. He takes in a big, overjoyed breath.

"I don't have to kill you," he says, pointing behind me with all five trembling fingers. "Because he will."

I spin around to find a small figure standing alone in the middle of the block. He's talking to himself. Hitting his head, muttering loudly then quietly. It's Grant's friend Mick. And Mick has a gun in his hand.

"I told you," Mick says. "I told you they'd never like you. I told you I told you I told you to come see what I had. To come check it out." He raises his gun. He's pointing it at Grant, but he's aiming through me. With his other hand he's hitting and scratching at his head, just like Tim Bentley was. He's trying to shake free the cobwebs that chaos left there. "Nobody wants to see what I got. Nobody. Well, fine. If you don't want to come see, I'll just *show it to you anyway!*"

Mick shoots three times, and all of the bullets punch into me. The first thing I think is how different it feels from when I was hit in the shoulder years ago, back at the hospital. That time the shot passed clean through. This is so much worse. These hit the meat of me. They scramble all the beautiful things that are packed inside of me, the things I studied all my life to learn. I picture them now. My stomach, miles and miles of delicate instrumentation for converting food to energy, pulverized to mush. My liver, that miracle machine, which I've mistreated from time to time. I'm sorry you had to go like this, punctured and riddled with filthy lead, your delicate connections to my bloodstream destroyed. My lungs, with their millions of tiny balloons keeping me afloat, popped forever. It hurts terribly. It hurts worse than I'd ever imagined anything could hurt. It hurts for the blink of an eye.

And then I die.

30

THE WALKER

W hen I step out of the soul map, I don't understand what I'm seeing.

First, I see Grant. He's standing tall with his arms out like he's taking in the adulation of a crowd, but all I hear is screaming. He's smiling, so at first I think he's happy, that maybe we got the coyote, maybe it's finally all over, but then the true nature of his smile creeps over me. When he turns to look right at me, I know it's true. I'm face to face with the creature of chaos that has fashioned himself after Coyote, and he's taken over Grant.

"Welcome, Walker," he hisses. It's Grant's boyish voice, but it's *off* somehow. Like it's slightly out of tune for a human range. It makes me sick to hear it.

Then I see Owen on the ground, and a lot of blood. I feel like my mind is lagging way behind my eyes, because I can't put together that the holes in Owen's body made all that blood. I feel like I'm looking at a tricky math problem, letters as numbers, numbers as letters, none of it making any sense.

"What did you do?" I ask.

"He killed me," Owen says. Then his soul sits up from his body and looks down around him. "What a waste."

Owen's soul stands and walks over to me. "Hello, Ben. Long time no see."

I back up. "No, no. What the fuck are you doing? Get back in there, Owen."

"I can't."

"Get back in your body. Now."

"Ben," he says, reaching out to me. And he touches me. He touches my shoulder. That can only happen when people die. That's my window to interact. But I never wanted this from Owen. Ever. I throw it off.

"Don't you fucking *touch me*, Owen. You get back in your body *right now*!"

"Ben, it's over."

But I'm not having that. I don't care if the coyote is in Grant's body or not. I'm taking that thing down. Grant's bones can heal. I launch myself at the coyote. But once again, I fly right through. And the coyote laughs like a maniac.

"You'll never cross over, Walker. Ever. But I will. Again and again. Now that I have the bell, this world is mine to remake."

He rips the bell from Grant's neck and holds it high. "Do it, Mick!" he yells.

That's when I see the boy. He's been warped by the coyote, and he has a gun. Owen tries to stand in front of Grant's body again, the poor bastard. As if he had any physical body left to take the bullets. And finally it dawns on me what the coyote wanted all along: the bell, just like everybody else. With the bead and the bell he'd be unstoppable.

His chaos would smother the rez and then the world. And we brought it right to him.

Mick raises the gun again, but then my world lurches, just a touch. It feels like an invisible train just blew by, and my clothes and hair are sucked back a bit. The coyote doesn't seem to notice anything.

"Owen, get over here," I whisper.

The coyote closes his eyes, waiting to die. Waiting to ring the bell. Double his power. And Owen still won't move, so I run over and grab him.

"Hold on."

"What?"

I felt a warning sign. And the coyote missed it. The crew at the hogan did their job. When you wear the robes of Coyote, you play by the history of Coyote. I see the veil in the distance. Closing fast. It's here to take Owen away from me. From Caroline. Forever. But not yet. It's gotta catch us first.

"Just hold on tight."

If what I felt before was a breath of the train's passing, what I feel now is the full damn train. The coyote opens his eyes at the last second, but he still doesn't understand. He's confused. Mick fires his gun, but the coyote is yanked backward by another lurch, this time across both of our worlds. The bullet misses, careening off the pavement. The coyote growls, slaps his hands over his mouth, but he can't keep the bone bead from the pull of the hogan now. It leaps from Grant's mouth, a little white dot, like a floating snowflake, and Grant collapses next to Owen's body. That's all I see before I'm pulled away along with the bead like a fish yanked out of water.

We blow though the soul map, and I see a coyote form

itself around the bead, muzzle first. Both of us are dragged by the nape toward the hogan, helpless to fight the pull. The coyote growls, but I grit my teeth in silence, my arms straining, because I'm carrying Owen's soul right along with me.

31

THE WALKER

A ll three of us hit the dirt of the hogan with enough force to kill us, if any of us were alive in the first place. We bounce and stagger, and my vision spins. All three of us seem confined here by the ceremony, but the only thing that makes an actual impression on the living world is the bead that the coyote still holds in its mouth. It's real on every plane, just like the bell. It rips into the dirt when the coyote's chin hits, digging a little trench on the ground, but the coyote holds on. The brothers notice it, Joey notices it, and so does Caroline. They watch it with strange calm.

When I find my focus again, one of the sand painters is saying something quickly, and I hear Joey's voice quietly translating.

"Nobody move."

Apparently I'm the last to wake up at the party, because when I sit up I see Owen's soul quietly getting to his feet. The coyote is already prowling the edge of the hogan, testing the walls, bead in mouth, his oil-dipped eyes furious. The fire is still burning bright. The bone box is in the middle of it, glowing red, the warning signs vaporized. The sand painters start singing in tandem, their voices rising and falling easily. I recognize the song too. It has nothing to do with Coyote. It's not even a Chant. It's what Gam sang to Ana and me at night. The song about the coming sunrise.

"You've been duped," Owen says.

The coyote growls.

"You should have stayed on your side of the veil," I say. "And done your job."

Owen moves around behind him, and the coyote lunges at him, but it's just a feint. I take the opposite tack, coming at him from the front. I stop when I'm standing right behind Caroline.

"I told you to spit it out," Owen says. "I told you."

The coyote laughs. It's a grating, high-pitched yipping, and it makes me cringe, then he jumps at Owen. Owen falls back, but the coyote changes direction at the last second, bounces over Owen's head, and heads straight for Caroline.

Time seems to slow without me having a thing to do with it. The coyote leaps, his mouth open, the bead bared, aiming to jam it into Caroline and take her as well, and he looks like he's grinning. He sees his way out. But I know something the coyote doesn't know. I know Caroline. And I know that no matter how crazy this may be, somewhere, somehow, through all those sleepless nights, Caroline thought of this. Thought of how it might come down to this, and how the coyote might come for her, and she's been watching the bead carefully.

At the last second, Caroline shifts her head to the right. The coyote's bead misses her mouth by a centimeter. His spirit body passes right through her, but not through me. I catch him by the neck and hold on for dear life. The coyote bucks and twists in my arms, yipping and growling. Owen jumps on the coyote's hind legs to keep them from raking at me, and together we wrestle him still, but it's a tense, primal type of stillness that won't last if we give it an inch.

"Now you have a choice, Walker," the coyote says. I shove its face against my chest to keep it from talking. I shove it hard, because I know what it's talking about. I think I knew the choice I'd be faced with back when I danced around the subject with Chaco while we walked the streets of Santa Fe.

I can feel the veil coming. I look at Owen and know that he feels it too. The curtain call is here. Throughout everything, agents of chaos, runaway souls, skinwalkers, and coyotes, one thing has always remained constant: the veil comes for everyone eventually.

Even Owen.

A moment of strained silence, then the veil's shadow falls over the hogan.

"It's here," Owen says, looking out of the eastern door, still holding tight to the coyote with me.

You'd think I'd be the one with the stone jaw here. I've seen the veil millions of times. I've had long-winded, one-sided conversations with the damn thing over the years. But suddenly I'm the one blubbering.

"Wait. Owen. We can think of something here." I ease my grip, and the coyote bucks and twists, and I almost lose him. Owen and I slam together to still it. "Just hold on a second, man."

Owen shakes his head. "I've got to go out there, Ben. I've got to meet it like a man."

He looks me in the eye until I nod.

"Together, then. This thing crosses back over too. Carefully."

Owen takes a deep breath, and then he looks at Caroline. She's watching the bead. The only thing she can see, but I sense that she understands. Her face is falling. Her whole being is falling. She's like a sandcastle being slowly picked apart by waves. But it's Owen's look that hits me hardest. He's saying good-bye to her in the only way that he knows how. With his entire heart wrapped up in one last, longing gaze.

We walk out of the hogan together, with the coyote between us, and there's the veil. It's as tall and as still and as red as I've ever seen it. And it's creeping toward Owen.

"Jesus," Owen says numbly. "It's a lot bigger than I thought it would be."

Owen might be intimidated, but I sure as hell ain't.

"Listen, you old rag. I know you don't like me crossing over, but we got something here that shouldn't be here, and you know it. See?"

The coyote bucks again, and we have to wrestle him still. It's like hauling in a hundred- pound catfish. The veil pauses its relentless approach.

"Yeah, you see it. Now, the only way we can get this thing back where it belongs is if Owen and I take it together. So are you gonna let me cross over or not?"

The veil hesitates. It's always been a stickler for the rules. But it knows better than any of us that since the coyote has been gone, things have gone to seed on the other side. It flutters slightly. That's a yes in my book.

"C'mon, Owen," I say.

"You're coming with me?"

"Let's get a move on. Before Big Red here changes its mind."

So it is that Owen Bennet and I cross over into the land of the dead, wrestling the coyote the whole way, together.

32

OWEN BENNET

I t's not bad, if that's what you're wondering. Death doesn't feel bad. Except for the solid weight of the coyote between Ben and I, like a python trapped in a bag, I don't feel anything, really. I just feel dead. But then I see the river.

The river of souls is beautiful. It reminds me of flying over LA at night, but instead of a million different roads and a million different people going a million different directions, it's one road. Billions of people. Two directions. Left, or right.

"Man oh man, has this place gone to shit," Ben says.

I lose my focus. I feel this crazy pull toward the water. To float to the right. That's all I want to do. I want to do it as badly as I've wanted anything, as badly as I wanted Caroline, even. And I drop the coyote.

Immediately the coyote starts bucking, throwing itself left and right, and Ben can't hang on. He throws him down on the sand and sets up in front of the veil like a goalkeeper. The coyote rights himself and shakes his fur free of sand. He slowly raises his head and snaps his teeth a few times, showing us a few flashes of the bead, then he starts to prowl the perimeter of the veil, looking for a chance to jump back through.

"Owen, a little help," Ben says.

"It's just that this river. . ."

"I know, man. I know. But not yet. We gotta deal with this thing first."

I shake my head. The pull of the river lessens if I look away, turn back toward the veil, toward whatever was beyond it. I try to focus on Caroline. Not on how she looks but on how she feels. The color of her. It's the color of the skin of a bubble, and I want to be with it again. I finally understand what she sees on people all the time. What she calls "smoke."

I step up next to Ben, both of us eyeing the coyote as it walks back and forth in front of us, its eye on the veil.

"The bead and the bell," Ben says. "That would have been a pretty sweet deal for you. Eh?"

The coyote snuffs and kicks up a divot of sand.

"You'd have the soul map, so you could go anywhere. You'd have your pick of the dead, the ordered and the chaotic both, it wouldn't matter. All of them would have been yours. And you could take any of them at any time." Ben whistles. "That would have been one powerful setup."

The coyote growls. I'm not sure what Ben's going for here, but he taps my leg gently in a way that says *get ready*.

"Turns out you blew it, though. We took your warning signs from you. Took back the world you were trying to steal from us. And then you never saw us coming."

The coyote snaps at us, and I see a flash of white bone in his mouth.

"As a matter of fact, I doubt you can even make a run at

the veil anymore. You got nothing left in the tank, old man," Ben says.

The coyote stops prowling. Ben taps on my leg again, down low, by my knee. Then the coyote jumps.

We take him down together. I hit low, Ben hits high. Together we stun him, throw him to the sand, his tongue lolling. I see the bead.

"Grab it!" Ben screams. "Grab the bead!"

I jam my hand in the coyote's mouth. He bites down, but I feel nothing. No pain, no pressure, nothing. That, more than anything, drives home that I'm gone. I've left the living world behind me. But I snag the bone bead.

"You should have spit it out when I told you to," I say, then I rip it from the coyote's mouth. The coyote howls, leaps at me as he sees the bead leave him. Then he starts changing. He goes from coyote to person in a blink. It's Bilagaana Bill, then its Burner's boy, then it's the young girl. All the while it's screaming, its voice changing as its body changes. It flickers faster, through hundreds, then thousands of people. For a split second I see myself there, and Ben, and Caroline. I try to remember that Coyote is a trickster, so this creature of chaos might be showing me things to try and throw off my nerve, but it doesn't help much. Not when you see yourself screaming.

Ben isn't fooled. Ben holds on when I scramble back. Ben picks up this chaotic blur of a thing and wrestles it to the river.

"Time to go home," he says. "Your souls are calling for you."

He tosses the coyote up and kicks it out, like he was busting down a door. The coyote flies out and over the river, and the river reaches for it. The river is overflowing with souls that strain toward it, souls stacked upon souls stacked upon souls, and no matter how much the coyote kicks, there is no escaping them. They grasp and coil and stick to the coyote like tar, then they start to pull it down.

The coyote stops fighting. Its flickering muzzle forms a translucent grin. "Now for your choice, Walker," it says. Then it's swept under the river. I see its form like a shark under water, jetting down the left side of the river, toward its home in the pearl.

That isn't my way. My way is to the right, and as I face my way, the pull of the river is twice as strong. It's like a glass of cold water in the desert. You never realize how much you want water until water is gone from you forever.

I stagger forward, but Ben comes around and presses a gentle hand against my chest. "Owen, we need to talk."

It hurts quite a lot now, turning from the river. It's like fighting sleep after staying awake for days, but I figure after all we've been through, I at least owe Ben a chat. He turns me around so I'm facing the veil again. The pull is less, but not by much.

"You have the bead?" he asks.

The bead. I'd forgotten about the bead. I suppose I do still have it. I hold out my hand and open my palm. "Take it," I say, but Ben recoils. He steps back and then shudders, and in the way that this place strips emotions bare, I realize that he wants to take it more than anything he's ever wanted in his life. It takes every ounce of him to do what he's doing right now, to keep from touching it.

"What?" I ask. "What is it? Take the bead, Ben. We've won."

"It's not worth it," Ben says.

"Of course it is. Just take it."

"No! It's not worth it if we lose you. If they lose you. If *she* loses you."

"What are you talking about?" My head turns toward the river. The pull is insistent now. Ben slaps me in the face, and when I look back at him I see he's trembling with the effort it takes to stay away from the bead.

"We need to break that thing," Ben says.

"So break it." My voice sounds clouded. Dreamy.

"Here's the thing. When we do, a big hole is going to be ripped between worlds. Look at me, Owen. A big one. One that someone could walk through without anything stopping them."

I feel as though I come around again for a minute. "Anyone could walk through?"

"Anyone," Ben says. "No matter what. Free pass. But it's one for one. That's the way things work here. Balance rules."

I get it now. I'm happy for him, really. I thought I'd be angry, but it makes so much sense now.

"You did it, Ben," I say. "This is your chance. Cross over, man. For God's sake, do it. You have no idea how much she loves you."

"Don't say that," Ben says.

Enough of this. I didn't get killed to sit here and bandy the obvious with Ben. I set the bone bead on a rock at the edge of the river and a grab a bigger rock. I'll make his choice for him. Before he can say anything I slam one rock into the other, and the veil is blown open with a staggering *crack*, like all the thunder in the world saved up for one massive explosion. It sloshes the river like a child would a bucket of water and kicks the sand into a dust-devil frenzy until we're thrown to the ground.

When both of us can stand again, and the sand of the riverbank is settled enough to see, we find the veil is parted. Not in the way that it parted to take me across, either. It's as if a hole has been blown completely through it. No rules need apply for this one time, in order to right the balance of years and years of the coyote prowling and taking what wasn't his to take. As if in emphasis, the five souls he stole seem to crawl from the rock where we shattered the bead. Bill, Burner, and all the rest. They pay us no mind but go directly to the river, which is where I should be.

"Go, Ben," I say.

"Don't say that!" Ben screams.

"Then just cross!"

"I can't," Ben says, sobbing. He drops to the sand. "I can't."

"Why?"

"Because I belong here, and you belong there."

"Are you kidding me? *Belong there?* They don't need me. I spent a year of my life wiring a goddamn trailer hitch. I've got a fourteen-year-old boy who doesn't care if I'm alive or dead. And as for Caroline, she's spent five straight years just trying to *talk* to you. She'd *kill* to have just *one moment* of what I'm doing right now. So cross over. Take the bell from Grant. Take the burden from both of them. You could be everything to them, the Walker and a father and a husband."

"That's not how it works. I know that now." Ben's hands are limply brushing the sand, his knees digging divots. "I don't know what else to say except that when you thought you were spinning your wheels, you were winning her heart. Both of them. You were building a family, and you didn't even realize it."

Ben comes to some sort of decision, and he stands up. He looks at me in a way not entirely different from the way he looked before, when he grappled with the coyote.

"What are you doing, Ben? Think for a second."

"Oh, I've thought," he says. "I get a lot of time to think.

Sometimes I feel like it's all I ever do. And I've made my decision."

I back up, look toward the river. I can feel its warmth calling to me, but Ben's voice pulls me back.

"I think a lot about my grandmother these days, about the stories she told me." He swings slowly to the right, pacing in the still-fresh tracks of the coyote. I realize he's herding me. "My favorite, always, is about the Slayer Twins. Have you heard of them?"

"Ben, this thing isn't going to stay open forever."

He ignores me. "All the young Navajo kids love the Slayer Twins. Monster Slayer and Born For Water are their names. We used to pretend we were fighting with them, running around with sticks, slapping at yucca and dirt like they were the monsters the twins were sent to fight."

I start to walk toward the river without realizing it. I'm almost at the bank when Ben steps in front of me and shoves me back. He's not gentle either.

"They're the twin sons of Changing Woman. She's the Big Deal for us. Basically the Earth itself. And the twins, they had this huge job to do. They had to rid the earth of monsters like the thing we just dragged to the river. So that people could live their lives."

He's backing me up now, so I just rush at him. He grabs me, and we grapple for a minute while the souls behind us swirl and hop. Ben gets me in a headlock pretty quickly. I never claimed to be a good fighter. I'm facing the river again, and its pull is enough to start me writhing and kicking, but Ben flips me around so that I face the veil again. He presses my face to his chest.

"The Slayer Twins cleared the earth so we people could live there, but I always wondered *what then*? I asked Gam, when I was a kid, what happens if the monsters come back."

Ben's dragging me toward the break in the veil. I hit him in the arm, in the shoulder, in the face. He doesn't flinch.

"You wanna know what she said?"

I spin Ben around again so his back is at the veil. He's right there. He could go through. I get this wild idea to just push with my legs and fling him backward, but as soon as I tense he reads me and flips me facing forward. Facing the veil myself. The scene just beyond the veil is the hospital for half a heartbeat. The room where Ben died. That's where he would step back to. He'd walk out of ABQ General whole again. But now that I face it fully the scene shifts. Now I see my body lying in the street, and Grant's body stirring slightly next to me, both of us resting in my blood. Ben sees what I see.

"Gam said, well, if monsters come back, then somebody will have to stand up in their own way. Fight them back again. I used to think that was me. The problem is, I can't fight in the land of the living anymore. My time there is over. But you can. You and Grant and Caroline and the rest of the Circle."

"Ben, don't do this," I croak. "She won't be able to take it if I tell her you had a chance to go to her and you didn't take it."

"She's already made her choice. I was there. And she's right."

Ben lowers his head to me, loosens his grip, and presses his forehead to mine.

"It's not your time to die, Owen. Watch your son grow tall and strong. Be there to wipe away her tears. And whatever you do, don't ever let go of her."

Ben tosses me forward just like he tossed the coyote. The veil is all around me, like an ocean of red, and then it's behind me, and all worlds go black.

33

GRANT ROMER

I come to face down on the hot concrete street, and my cheek is lying in a pool of cooling blood. I have no idea what happened to me, only that it was very, very bad. I do the first thing that I do every morning when I get up. I feel for the bell around my neck. But it's not there.

I sit up, and a string of blood comes up with me, drips down my face. My hands are painted in it, my clothes are saturated. And my head is killing me. It feels foggy and scratched up. I have shadows of strange memories, and I don't think all of them are mine. I feel like I needed to do something terrible, but I forgot what it was.

I see the bell and let out what I feel must be my first breath in hours. It's lying by my shoes, like it was dropped there. The necklace is broken, and both bell and necklace are smeared in blood. Then I see Owen. He's facing away from me, his nice shirt soaked.

"Hey, Owen? Get up, man. Something bad happened here."

Owen doesn't move, but that's OK, because I know he

will. He's just pulling it together, like me. I shake him a little bit.

"Get up, Owen. We gotta find the coyote. C'mon."

Owen still isn't moving, and at the very back of my brain I know why, but I'm keeping it there, in the back. I refuse to let it come to the front. I shake my head hard, and it's jarring. The shadows of the terrible thoughts threaten to make noise until I sit very still again.

"Owen?"

The truth of what I see is creeping to the front of my brain an inch at a time. I'm remembering Pap. He was lying on the ground like this, and there wasn't even any of the blood then that there is now. And I know how that ended.

"Owen. Please." I pull him over, and he flops on his back. His front is a mess. His nice shirt. It's a mess. It's way too big of a mess for anything to ever be right in my life ever again. That's when it hits me that all this blood is *his* blood. I don't know whose blood I thought it was before, but it's *his* now.

"No, no, no." I scoop a little bit of it up and hold it in my hand. I don't know what I'm doing with it, so I set it on Owen, like I could maybe put it back in him or something, even though I know that's not how these things work, but this just *can't be*. Owen being dead is also *not how things work*. There is not a scenario in which the world can exist without Owen in it.

I sort of choke then, with the weight of it all. I don't cry, I just start coughing, and I close my eyes because I don't want to see any of this anymore, and I lay my head down on Owen's ruined stomach, and I just want to go to sleep.

With my eyes closed, the sounds of everything wash over me. Kids are screaming. I hear sirens in the distance, and over everything is the roar of the wind. The only completely silent thing is Owen. Then I hear footsteps. I look up and see Mick standing above me. He's looking down at me, and he has a gun hanging limply in his hand, but he looks completely lost. There's a big gust of wind and the light brush of black feathers over my face as Chaco lands between us. He snaps at Mick, but Mick doesn't even seem to notice him.

"My dad is dead," I say. I don't know what else to say. I don't even know who I'm talking to. Chaco lowers his head and folds his wings in and turns around to tuck himself between Owen and me. Mick shakes his head, and I hear a big clunk as he drops the gun before he shuffles over to the curb and collapses there.

I don't know how long Chaco and I lay like this, resting on Owen. Certainly until I fall asleep, because I know I must be dreaming when I start to hear a small beat in Owen's chest. It's like his heart is telling me a secret, it's so quiet, and then I think it goes away again, and it was nothing after all. But the bell heard the secret too, because it gets a little bit warmer in my hand. I try to listen, and even Chaco presses himself closer. He hears it too.

Another beat. Another whisper. Louder now. I can hear it. And I know what it's saying. It's saying *not yet*.

Not yet. Not yet. Thump-thump. Thump-thump. Stronger and stronger and stronger. *Not yet. Not yet. Not yet.*

Chaco rises, then I sit up, and when we look at Owen, we find he's looking back at us. He rolls on his side to grab my hand, and there are three soft *tink, tink, tink* sounds as the bullets that were inside of him fall to the ground.

"Not yet," he says, smiling at me. "Not just yet."

34

THE WALKER

The Serenity Room at Green Mesa is back to normal. Well, normal for a psychiatric hospital, anyway. I guess I was giving myself too much credit when I said it was me that was spooking all these people. It was the combo of the coyote running loose everywhere and then me walking in on top of that. This time, with the coyote back where he belongs, I only get a few mutters when I pass. That's it.

Mom is in her usual spot, by the big bay window, and she's watching the Jemez Mountains again. Only this time, when I sit down next to her, I see that she's actually seeing them. The sunset is an explosion of soft pink, and the clouds look like strings of cotton candy. She's watching the crows fly under them, away from here. They're scattering again. That, as much as anything, tells me our job is done for now.

"You look good, Mom," I say. She says nothing, but she does smile. I know it has nothing to do with me talking to her. That's the rub with a job like mine. When you do it right, nobody notices you. If things are going the way they should, you're invisible.

"She's moving on," I say. "Caroline is. Which is good, because until she told me, I didn't realize how tightly I was holding on to her. To the past. To my life. I've been dead for six years. You'd think I would have realized it by now. But it took her showing me. It took her letting go to get me to ease my grip too."

Mom reaches back and brushes her fingers through her silky hair, still watching the sky. Her eyes are moving from cloud to cloud.

"She's good at helping people realize things that are staring them in the face. Like the rez. How it needed help. It still needs help, but at least its problems are normal problems now. They're gonna stick around, all three of them. She told Owen that if he was gonna keep screwing around with that trailer hitch, he ought to at least put it to work. He's turning it into a mobile doc's office. He and Caroline are gonna work the rez."

It makes me absurdly happy to know that they're staying on Chaco rez. That when I need to find them, I won't have to search the map. No more uprooting. Grant's staying at Crownrock High. Even after all that happened. He said he was done running. Caroline is helping with that too. The coyote messed with a lot of people's minds, and she's got a knack for fixing them. Grant's and Kai's. Even Mick's. Although that kid was troubled for a long time, maybe even before the coyote came through. The cops found an arsenal in the back of his car and journals with all sorts of terrible plans. He was ripe for the coyote to begin with. Still, Caroline got permission to visit him at UNM's acute care psych ward, where he's under lock and key. She says she at least wants to undo whatever the coyote did, and I know she can. The rest is up to the docs.

Things at Chaco are settling down again. Life is moving forward.

"I think I was afraid that for me, there was no such thing as forward. All I had was what lay behind me. Like when Ben died and I became the Walker, that was it for Ben. I thought the two were totally separate things. So I held on to Caroline for dear life, thinking that if I let go, not only would I lose her, but I'd lose Ben too, forever. I looked high and low for a way to get back to her, for a chance to be Ben again. But that's the thing. Ben's still here. Ben never left. And the Walker is still here too. It's all one thing. It's all me."

Mom's gaze is broken when another patient sits down in the chair next to her. A woman her age. One that used to sit with her all the time, until Mom started to go downhill.

"Evening, Sitsi," she says. "It's almost dinnertime. Any interest?"

"I think so," Mom says, and hearing her voice brings tears to my eyes. "I think that would be nice."

The two women help each other up, and together they walk right through me, on their way out.

I don't mind. Not anymore. It makes me smile, actually. It makes me feel good. This is my job. This is my journey, and it's moving forward now. Caroline, Owen, Grant, they all walk it with me. We're all still in it together. For now. And even though they can't see me, I know they can feel that I'm there, walking next to them.

It's what I do. I am the Walker, after all.

AUTHOR'S NOTE

Coyote is one of the most fascinating and contradictory beings in Navajo lore. Karl W. Luckert, a mythology scholar on the subject, calls him, among other things, a "fool-gambler-imitator-trickster-witch-hero-savior-god."

Signs of Warning, the tale told in Chapter 18 of this novel, was taken from the Curly To Aheedlinii version of *Navajo Coyote Tales*, translated from the original Navajo by Father Berard Haile, OFM (and interpreted by the smoker in the narrative). The six objects that present themselves to Coyote (birth bag, burned stick, broken pot, cane, whisk broom, and broken stirring stick) are all accurate at their origin.

Signs of Warning is but one of many tales about Coyote, and anyone looking to learn more will benefit from both Haile's compilation and Karl W. Luckert's essay on the theoretical and historical framework of Coyote that is presented as the introduction.

ABOUT THE AUTHOR

B. B. Griffith writes best-selling fantasy and thriller books. He lives in Denver, CO, where he is often seen sitting on his porch staring off into the distance or wandering to and from local watering holes with his family.

See more at his digital HQ: https://bbgriffith.com

If you like his books, you can sign up for his mailing list here: http://eepurl.com/SObZj. It is an entirely spam-free experience.

ALSO BY B. B. GRIFFITH

The Vanished Series

Follow the Crow (Vanished, #1)

Beyond the Veil (Vanished, #2)

The Coyote Way (Vanished, #3)

Gordon Pope Thrillers

The Sleepwalkers (Gordon Pope, #1)

Mind Games (Gordon Pope, #2)

Shadow Land (Gordon Pope, #3)

The Tournament Series

Blue Fall (The Tournament, #1)

Grey Winter (The Tournament, #2)

Black Spring (The Tournament, #3)

Summer Crush (The Tournament, #4)

Luck Magic Series

Las Vegas Luck Magic (Luck Magic, #1)

Standalone

Witch of the Water: A Novella

CPSIA information can be obtained
at www.ICGtesting.com
Printed in the USA
LVHW080814160422
716377LV00029B/1170

9 780996 372640